A VINE

IN THE BLOOD

A Vine
in the Blood

Leighton Gage

112

Published by
Soho Press, Inc.
853 Broadway
New York, NY 10003

Library of Congress Cataloging-in-Publication Data

Gage, Leighton.
A vine in the blood / Gage Leighton.
p. cm.
ISBN 978-1-61695-004-0
eISBN 978-1-61695-005-7
1. Silva, Mario (Fictitious character)—Fiction.
2. Police—Brazil—Fiction. 3. Soccer players—Fiction. 4. World Cup
(Soccer)—Fiction. 5. Kidnapping—Fiction. 6. Brazil—Fiction. I. Title.
PS3607.A3575V56 2011
813'.6—dc22
2011027272

Printed in the United States of America

10 9 8 7 6 5 4 3 2 1

For my daughters, Stephanie, Danielle, Melina and Alana.
And for their sister, Nicole.

Thy mother is like a vine in thy blood
ᴇᴢᴇᴋɪᴇʟ 19:10 (King James Version)

A VINE

IN THE BLOOD

Chapter One

LESS THAN AN HOUR after Juraci Santos was unceremoniously dumped into the back seat of her kidnappers' getaway car, Luca Vaz crept through her front gate and poisoned her bougainvilleas.

The way he figured it, he didn't have a choice. And it wasn't his fault. It was the fault of that lying lowlife, Mateo Lima.

"You're sure about the color of these bougainvilleas?" Juraci had asked when he was planting them.

"I'm sure, Senhora," he'd assured her. "Blood red, like you told me."

"Guaranteed?"

"Guaranteed, Senhora."

"All right, Luca. But you'd better be right. Because, if they flower in any other color . . ."

She left the threat unspecified. But a threat it was—and he knew it.

Three weeks later, the roof fell in: Luca learned that those new plants of hers were about to flower in a color his wife, Amanda, had described as *the palest purple I've ever seen on a bougainvillea.* If Juraci Santos, a woman known to be as vindictive as she was distrustful, discovered the truth, he'd be in big trouble.

Luca's advance notice of the situation stemmed from the fact that he'd swiped one of the cuttings and planted it to the right of his front door. Unlike the bougainvilleas along Juraci's wall, it had been standing in strong sunshine for the last three weeks and Amanda, with her sharp eyes, had spotted the first little bud. She'd taken him by the arm, led him over to the plant and pointed.

"Isn't this bougainvillea supposed to be red?"

"It's not red?" he asked with a sense of foreboding.

He wouldn't have known if she hadn't told him. Luca wasn't just color blind; he suffered from the most severe and rarest form of the malady: achromatopsia. He saw the world in black, white and shades of gray.

Six people in the world, and only six, knew about his condition. Unfortunately, one of them was Amanda's no-good brother, Mateo, who owned a flower and shrub business, and whom Luca blamed for his current troubles.

The truth of the matter was that Mateo Lima was a nasty son of a bitch, and there weren't many people in Carapicuiba, or the surrounding communities either, who were willing to buy flowers and shrubs from the likes of *him*.

Nor were there many people willing to hire a guy who was color blind to care for their flowers.

So there they were, Luca and Mateo, stuck with each other.

The survival of Mateo's flower and shrub nursery depended upon Luca's work as a gardener. And Luca's continued employment depended on Mateo keeping his mouth shut about Luca's condition, which Mateo, the blackmailing bastard, had made clear he'd do only if he became Luca's exclusive supplier.

It was remotely possible, of course, that Mateo had made an honest mistake about those supposedly blood-red bougainvilleas. But Luca didn't think so. The most likely possibility was that Mateo was trying to pull a fast one because he had no blood-red bougainvilleas in stock.

The other possibility was that Mateo had been having a joke at Luca's expense. He found color blindness funny.

Either way, Mateo had underestimated the consequences for both of them. If Juraci saw those bougainvilleas flowering in pale purple, she'd have a fit. And then she'd shoot her mouth off to all of her neighbors. Luca would wind up losing his customers, Mateo would be stuck with his flowers and shrubs, and both of them would soon be scratching to make a living. That was why the bougainvilleas had to go before they brought flowers into the world.

Killing bougainvilleas, as any gardener will tell you, is a tough proposition. The normal technique is to dig them out by the roots. Luca would have to be subtler than that. He'd have to make it appear they'd fallen victims to some mysterious blight.

After giving the problem some thought, he decided on his instrument of death: herbicide coupled with industrial-strength bleach. He mixed up the concoction in a four-liter jug, set his alarm clock for quarter to five in the morning, and by five-thirty on the day of the kidnapping he was creeping through Juraci's gate. He missed encountering her abductors by about fifty-five minutes, a fact that undoubtedly saved his life.

He, like the kidnappers, had chosen his time with care. One of her maids had mentioned that Juraci was a night owl, and that she seldom retired before two or three in the morning. But Luca always smelled freshly-brewed coffee when he arrived, which was usually around 7:00, sometimes as early as 6:45. That led him to believe that the maids were up and about by 6:30 at the latest.

His plan was a simple one, and he was convinced he'd be able to pull it off without a hitch. The only imponderable was that yappy little poodle of Juraci's, the one she called Twiggy. He prayed the dog would keep her mouth shut, because if the little bitch didn't, she might wake up the big bitch, her mistress, and then Luca's fat would be in the fire.

He'd brought a flashlight, but, as it turned out, he didn't need it. The moonlight was bright enough to work by. With gloved and practiced fingers, Luca dug down to expose the roots of each plant, severed them with his grafting knife, poured in a healthy dose of the poisonous liquid and packed the earth back into place. With any kind of luck at all, the heat of the sun would cause the sap to rise, thereby drawing the poison upward into the twigs and leaves.

At quarter past six, after a celebratory cigarette, Luca began his normal workday. He went, first, to the shed at the foot of the garden. From there, he took a plastic trash bag and started working his way up the slope toward the house. Juraci's slovenly guests were in the habit of leaving paper cups, paper plates, and gnawed-upon bones scattered about the lawn after every barbecue—and she gave a lot of barbecues. It was one of his tasks to gather them up.

6:30 passed, then 6:40 without a single sign of life from the house; no yappy little Twiggy running around the garden pissing on the plants; no smell of coffee.

At 6:45, curiosity and a craving for a *café com leite* getting the better of him, Luca decided to investigate. Up to that point, he hadn't been alarmed. But when he rounded the corner and caught sight of the kitchen, he stopped dead in his tracks.

The door had been smashed—not just forced open, but completely destroyed. Pieces of solid, varnished wood were everywhere, a few of them still hanging from the hinges.

Burglars, he thought. And then: *Already gone . . . or maybe not.* He started moving again, more cautiously this time. A rat in the kitchen reacted to the sound of his footsteps by scuttling out of the door to take refuge under a nearby hedge. Luca had no fear of rats. He'd killed dozens in his time. He quickened his pace. From somewhere beyond the dim

"They used a free, Web-based account and logged in through an unsecured wireless link."

"Whatever the fuck that means." Sampaio's language tended to get saltier when he was under pressure. "Have you booked your flight?"

Silva nodded and looked at his watch. "It leaves in fifty-five minutes."

"Get a move on then." Sampaio took another bite of nail. "We'll continue this conversation when I get there."

Silva raised an eyebrow. "You're coming to São Paulo?"

"Are you hard of hearing, Chief Inspector?"

The Director loved to throw his weight around. Unfortunately for his subordinates, he generally threw it in the wrong direction. Allowing him to go to São Paulo would hinder, not help, the investigation. Silva acted immediately to defuse the threat.

"I'm sure Minister Pontes will be pleased with your personal involvement," he said.

Antonio Pontes, the Minister of Justice, was the government's Witch Hunter-in-Chief.

For a while, Sampaio didn't reply.

Silva knew what he was up to. He was turning it over in his head: *Go to São Paulo and assume all responsibility, or stay in Brasilia and blame Mario Silva and his team in case of failure?*

For Sampaio, a political appointee and a political animal, it really wasn't much of a choice. He did exactly what Silva expected him to do.

"Damn," he said, "I forgot about the corruption hearings. I'll have to stay here. I could be called upon to testify."

There was not the least chance of Sampaio being called upon to testify. The congressional corruption hearings were dead in the water. The politicians charged with conducting them were stonewalling, some to protect their buddies, some to protect themselves.

But Silva nodded, as if what the Director said made perfect sense.

"Mind you," Sampaio added, "You'll be calling me with updates at least twice a day."

"Of course," Silva said.

He had no intention of doing any such thing.

Chapter Three

THE FEDERAL POLICE'S SÃO PAULO field office operated under the direction of *Delegado* Hector Costa.

Some people said he owed his position to his uncle's influence.

They were wrong.

Silva had done everything he could to convince his nephew to embrace a less dangerous profession—and failed. When Hector had been accepted to the Federal Police, Silva had steadfastly refused to promote his advancement in the hope he'd quit. The result was to make Hector more stubborn, more determined to succeed. He'd worked hard, and in the end, it had made him an even better cop.

While the Director and the Chief Inspector were having their conversation in Brasilia, the Delegado was already on his way to the crime scene. São Paulo's morning rush hour was still in progress, but traffic was flowing toward the city's center while Hector was moving away from it. Less than forty minutes after leaving his office, he'd already entered Juraci Santos's closed condominium in the suburb of Granja Viana.

He parked next to an ambulance, complimented the agent minding the crime-scene tape and entered Juraci Santos's home through the front door. Someone had propped it open with a block of wood.

There were nearly as many crime scene technicians inside the house as there'd been reporters outside. Some were taking photographs, some mixing luminol, some dusting for prints.

And, in charge of it all, was Lefkowitz, the chief crime scene technichian.

"Brought a few friends, I see," Hector said, looking around him.

"I brought everybody I've got," Lefkowitz said. "Nobody wants to nail those bastards more than me. I've got a bet with a cousin of mine in the States. He actually thinks the Americans are going to get into the quarter-finals."

"They just might. They almost did last time."

"The Americans? In the quarter-finals? You've got to be kidding. They don't care about football. Not our kind, anyway."

Hector wasn't there to talk about football. He got down to business.

"They took down my car's number plate when I came through the gate. You've probably already thought of this, but. . . ."

"Did we get a copy of the gate records? Yes, we did. And there's one car we've yet to identify. It arrived at 2:00 AM, left at 5:00."

Hector rubbed his hands. "A lead," he said. "Thank you, Lefkowitz."

"The Lefkowitz giveth, and the Lefkowitz taketh away," Lefkowitz said. "We ran the plate through DETRAN. It doesn't exist."

DETRAN was the regulatory body that controlled car registrations in the State of São Paulo.

Hector chose to be optimistic.

"It might be from out of state," he said.

"The other states are being checked as we speak. Another possibility is that the guard got the number wrong, so we're also trying partials."

"Other than the gate I came through—"

"Additional gates? None."

"Damn! Somebody talk to the neighbors?"

"Franco did." Letitia Franco, Lettie to her family, was Lefkowitz's assistant. The crime scene techs in São Paulo seemed to have a thing about calling each other by their last names. "The neighbor over there"—Lefkowitz hooked a thumb over his shoulder—"and the one across the street, didn't hear, or see, a thing. That one"—he pointed in the direction of the nearest house—"heard some commotion. You'd best have a chat with him."

"Name?"

"Sá. Rodolfo Sá."

"What kind of commotion? Screams? Shouts?"

"No screams. No shouts. Just a loud noise. Something else: I think they sedated the victim. We found an empty syringe in her bedroom."

"Containing?"

"A few drops of a pale yellow fluid. We're analyzing it."

"How big is this condominium?"

"You're thinking house-to-house search?"

"Uh huh."

"Forget it. It's huge. It stretches over two municipalities. You'd need a hundred men, and it would take a month."

"Have you gone through her papers?"

"We have."

"And?"

"Juraci had a private investigator following the Artist's girlfriend around."

"Interesting. Got a name?"

"Prado. Caio Prado. I got an address, too. Rua Augusta, 296, second floor."

"You find any of his reports?"

"Receipts, mostly. Only one report."

"Interesting?"

"Boring. But the investigation was ongoing."

"Who's the girlfriend?"

"Cintia Tadesco."

"The model?"

"Actress, she calls herself these days."

"I saw her in one of the nighttime soaps. She can't act worth a damn."

"Who cares? Watch her with the sound off. That's what I do."

"She is, I agree, a knockout. A splendid example of womanhood. Drawn to the Artist, no doubt, by his great physical beauty and awesome intellectual capacity."

"Sarcasm, Hector, does not become you."

"So I've been told. Any indication as to what prompted Juraci to hire Prado?"

"No."

"Anything else of interest in her papers?"

"A receipt for house keys. Four sets. Made last week by a locksmith named Samuel Arns. He's got a shop in the strip mall you had to pass in order to get here. We went through this house with a fine-tooth comb and found only three sets. One set was in a drawer in her office. One was in her purse, which the kidnappers left behind. And one was in the purse of one of the maids."

"And that's significant because?"

"A theory I have, which I'll get to in a minute. Let me see. What else did we find? Oh, yeah, the footprint."

"Footprint?"

"Juraci must have heard them coming. She locked herself in her bedroom. But the door was flimsy. He smashed it with his foot. In doing so, he was kind enough to leave us an impression of his sole and heel."

"He?"

"No woman has feet that big, not even my wife. Once he was inside, Juraci panicked and lost control of her bladder. We found urine on the rug and on the sheets. We figure he tossed her onto the bed, threw himself on top of her to hold her down, and injected her with whatever was in the syringe."

"*Tossed* her? Is the victim a lightweight?"

"Juraci? Hardly. There are pictures of her all over the house. She weighs ninety kilos if she weighs a gram."

"Big guy, then."

"Big feet at least. And strong. We recovered a few fibers from the sheets. Looks like he was wearing a wool sweater."

"Any sign of blood?"

"Not in the bedroom. The kitchen is full of it. That's where they killed the maids."

"The bodies are still here?"

"Still here. I've got an ambulance on call to bring them to the IML, but I figured you'd want to see them first."

"You figured right."

The IML, *Instituto Médico Legal*, was where São Paulo's criminal autopsies took place.

"Who will be doing them when they get there?" Hector asked.

"Gilda."

Gilda Caropreso was an assistant medical examiner—and Hector's fiancée.

"Did she do the *in situ* as well?"

"No."

"Who then?"

"That new guy, Whatshisname."

"Plinio Setubal. Did he estimate time of death?"

"He did. The same for both. Between four and five this morning."

"Both. So there are two of them?"

"Brilliant deduction. You a detective?"

Hector ignored the sarcasm. "Shot?"

"Shot. Small bore pistol. A .22 would be my guess. No exit wounds. Come on, I'll show you."

* * *

IN THE kitchen, a wooden door leading to the garden had been battered in. Some fragments still hung from the hinges; the remainder, in pieces, was scattered across the white tile floor.

Through a door to his left, open and intact, Hector could see two beds, a wardrobe cupboard and a poster of a rock star. The maids' quarters, apparently.

Near the sink, the dead women lay side by side, their blood mingled in a common pool.

"One bullet for each," Lefkowitz said. "Point blank."

"Yes," Hector said. "I noticed."

Hot gases, escaping from the murder weapon's muzzle, had singed the hair around their wounds. Singeing occurred only when bullets were discharged at very close range.

"Execution style," Lefkowitz said. "No passion here, nothing spontaneous, very deliberate. Poor things must have been scared to death. Look at that."

Lefkowitz pointed. The women had been holding hands when they were shot. Their dead fingers were still entwined.

Hector felt a twinge of sympathy. No matter how hard he tried to maintain his objectivity, retain his distance, there were often little details about murder that touched his heart.

"Sisters," Lefkowitz said, "from Salvador. Their purses and identity cards were in their room. The one on the left was Clara. She'd just turned nineteen."

The floor around Clara's body was sprinkled with shards of broken glass. Some were tinged with blood.

"What's that?"

"It used to be a drinking glass. There are others in that cabinet over there. Intact ones, I mean."

"She wouldn't have bled like that if—"

"—her heart wasn't pumping when she sustained the cuts. And a shot like that would have stopped her heart immediately. So, yes, she was cut before she was shot. See how this part of the pool is more red than brown? There was water in the glass. The blood that flowed into the water got diluted. It wasn't able to fully coagulate."

"Is that a dog?"

Hector pointed to a bundle of fur near one of the bodies.

"What's left of one," Lefkowitz said. "A toy poodle, a female. They broke her back."

"Broke her back?"

"Stepped on her. Snapped her spine like a twig."

"What kind of people do that to a dog?"

"What kind of people shoot young women in the head? In a moment, I'm going to sum it all up. Just one more thing: look at Clara's face."

Hector had to drop to one knee to see what Lefkowitz was talking about. He did it from a meter away, to avoid kneeling in the blood.

"Bruises," he said.

"Pre-mortem, according to Doctor Whatshisname. And none on Clarice. Ready for a reading?"

"Please."

"Okay. Here's what I think happened: Clara got up in the early hours of the morning to drink some water. She took a glass out of the cabinet, went to the sink and filled it. The kidnappers came in and startled her. She dropped the glass, and it broke. She screamed, or tried to fight them off, or tried to run, and they hit her. She went down, landing on her back, cutting herself."

"And her sister . . ."

"Heard the noise, jumped out of bed and came into the kitchen. Or maybe tried to hide, and the kidnappers found her. The fact that her face isn't bruised suggests they were able to intimidate her without hitting her. Maybe just looking at what they'd done to Clara was enough. They made Clara get up. They made both of them kneel. And then they shot them in the back of their heads."

Hector had been visualizing the progression of events and was experiencing a wave of nausea. He paused a beat before asking his next question.

"Which one first?"

"Clara," Lefkowitz said, without hesitation.

"How can you—"

"Blood spatter analysis."

"So Clarice knew it was coming?"

"Must have. But not for long."

"For her sake, I hope you're right. But why shoot them at all? Why not just tie them up?"

"You want a guess?"

"Tell me."

"To forestall identification."

"You think they came in here without masks? That would have been stupid."

"We already know they're vicious. What's to say they're not stupid? But there's another possibility."

"Which is?"

"Maybe they had masks, but hadn't put them on. Maybe they'd planned to do that *after* they were inside. But then, surprise, surprise, there's Clara standing in the darkened kitchen."

Hector shook his head. "I don't buy it," he said. "She would have heard them; she would have tried to run."

"Ah, but how about if she *didn't* hear them?"

"How could she not? They smashed that door over there. That's how they got in, right?"

"That's what we're *supposed* to think. *I* think they smashed it on the way out."

"What?"

Lefkowitz held up a hand for patience. "Bear with me. Remember that commotion I mentioned? The one the neighbor heard? It was a loud *bang*, and it woke him up. Seconds later, he saw a car driving away. Between the bang, and the driving away, the killers wouldn't have had time to do anything other than run up the ramp to the street. And, if they'd been lugging an unconscious woman, there wouldn't even have been time for that. I figure they put her into the car first."

"You're saying the very last thing they did was smash the door? And then took off on a run? What would be the sense of that?"

"To make us think they didn't have a key."

"But *you* think they did."

Lefkowitz nodded. "No other explanation computes. Clara had just filled a glass with water; she'd no sooner dropped it than they were on her. She probably started to scream, and that's when they hit her. She went down on the shards of glass. None of that could have happened if they'd really done what they want us to think they did, which was to get into the house by battering their way through the door."

"So you think this is an inside job?"

"That's what I think. If it happened the way *they* want us to think it happened, wouldn't Clara have taken off like a rabbit? Wouldn't we have found her body somewhere else?"

Hector was unconvinced.

"Not necessarily," he said. "They could have gone after her and brought her back here. Any other signs of forced entry?"

"None." Lefkowitz was emphatic. "All the other doors were locked. So were the windows. The glass in all of them was intact."

"Maybe they picked the lock."

"Not *that* lock. It's virtually pickproof."

Hector put a finger to his lips and thought about it.

Lefkowitz regarded him in silence.

Finally, Hector said, "Let's suppose it went down the way you suggest. Wouldn't Clara have heard a click? Or heard them creeping up behind her?"

"Not if they were quick. Not if Clara was running water in the sink. The sink is stainless steel. Listen."

Lefkowitz went to the sink and turned on the tap. Under the stream of water, the steel reverberated like a drum. He let it run for a few seconds to make his point.

"I figure it was when she turned off the tap," he said, "that she heard something. Or maybe she looked up and saw something."

"With her back to the door?"

"There was a full moon last night. If Doctor Whathisname—"

"Setubal."

"—Setubal is right about the time they were shot, the moon would have been"—Lefkowitz pointed—"right about there. If anyone opened the door, it would have flooded the kitchen with moonlight. Clara would have noticed, even if she'd been facing the sink."

That clinched it for Hector. He smiled in admiration.

"Lefkowitz," he said, "you are *so* good at this stuff."

"Tell my wife," Lefkowitz said. "She thinks she's got all the brains in the family."

Chapter Four

HARALDO "BABYFACE" GONÇALVES WAS looking around for a sign that would identify the building—and not finding one.

"You sure this is it?"

"I'm sure," Arnaldo Nunes said. "I used to come here on Saturdays for lunch."

"The Argentinean Club for lunch? Why?"

"They serve good meat."

"They serve good meat in lots of places. But you came here. What's the real reason?"

Arnaldo mumbled something.

"Can't hear you," Gonçalves said. "Speak up."

Arnaldo turned to face him.

"I said my oldest sister married an Argentinean."

"No!"

"Yes."

"You poor bastard."

"I think it was a sex thing. He must have been hung like a bull."

"She's still married?"

"She finally came to her senses. But, in the meantime, I went through hell. The wedding was in June of '78."

1978 wasn't the only year Argentina won the World Cup, but it was the first. And it was a year in which Brazil, already a three-time champion, had finished an ignominious third. The defeat still rankled, even for people like Gonçalves who were too young to have experienced it personally.

"Four years it lasted," Arnaldo said. "Four long years. Every time I saw him he'd rub it in my face."

"And then she divorced him?"

"No. She stuck with the bastard until 1990. The nineteenth of July. I'll never forget the date. Soon as I heard about the breakup, I went out to celebrate. It was one of the worst hangovers I ever had, but it was worth it."

"So what's with the four years? We didn't win in '82. Italy won in '82."

Arnaldo looked at him. "You don't remember what else happened in 1982?"

"Do you know how old I was back then?"

"You knew about '78. And you knew who won the Cup in '82."

"That's different. That's *futebol*."

"The Malvinas happened."

"Oh, yeah, right. The Malvinas."

In early April of 1982, General Leopoldo Galtieri, the head of Argentina's military junta, gave the order to annex the Malvinas, that small group of South Atlantic islands the inhabitants insisted in calling the Falklands. Argentina had long coveted the archipelago, and long claimed sovereignty over it.

Galtieri launched the invasion in an attempt to draw attention from a declining economy at home and to unite the nation in a common cause. In both of those things, he was initially successful.

Margaret Thatcher, the English Prime Minister, first tried diplomacy to oust the invaders. When that failed, she ordered the assembly of a naval task force, and it set out on a stately 8,000-mile voyage of liberation.

"I read about that," Gonçalves said. "The English kicked the shit out of the Argentineans, right?"

"The English did," Arnaldo said.

"So that shut your brother-in-law up, I suppose. Come on. Let's go in there and talk to those people."

He unfastened his seat belt and opened the door of the car.

"Shut it," Arnaldo said.

"What?"

"Shut the door. I'm not finished. I'm not telling this story because I enjoy the sound of my voice. I'm telling it for your edification."

"I didn't know you knew words like edification."

"You don't know a lot of things. Listen and learn."

"Learn what?"

"About Argentineans."

"What's to learn?"

"What's to learn is why it's a waste of time being here."

"I thought the Chief Inspector—"

"Mario doesn't have any more faith in this little excursion than I do. We're here because Sampaio wanted us here. Can I go on with the story?"

"Now I'm intrigued. Please do."

"A couple of weeks after the Argentineans invaded, I'm sitting in that building over there, with my wife, and my sister, and my Argentinean brother-in-law. He's all puffed up about the great victory to come. I try to point out this is the English he's talking about, and that there's a whole damned fleet on the way. 'Doesn't matter,' he says. 'We're gonna kick their asses,' he says."

"He really thought that?"

"He really did. Oh, he had all sorts of reasons, like long lines of supply, and how the Argentinean Air Force was top-notch, and how they had all these Exocet missiles they bought from the French, and how they were going to use them to sink the entire English fleet, but the point is he *believed* it."

"And the point of this whole diatribe of yours?"

"This: most Argentineans, not all, but most, have a superiority complex. They always think they're better than other people, they always think they're going to win, and they keep on thinking that way right up to the moment they get the shit kicked out of them."

"That's crap. You can't make generalizations like that about an entire people. You, Arnaldo, are a bigot."

"Am I?"

"Wait. Let me think about where you're going with this."

"Go ahead. Think."

"How's this? You believe they wouldn't bother to kidnap *Senhora* Santos to put the Artist's game off because they've got it in their heads they're going to win anyway? With or without the Artist playing for our side?"

"Bingo."

"That's crazy."

"Is it?"

"Of course it is. It's beyond all reason. The Artist can run circles around Dieguito Falabella, and he's the best man they've got."

"You know that, and I know that. But those people in there don't know that."

"You're wrong."

"Am I? Let's go see. This time of the day, they'll all be in the bar."

* * *

THE BAR of the *Clube Argentino de São Paulo* was a dim, wood-paneled room, devoid of windows, and lit by recessed lights in the ceiling. The walls were lined with photos, mostly in black-and-white. The men in the photos were playing football and dressed in striped jerseys. In the photos that had been printed in color, the stripes were sky blue and white.

Arnaldo, leading the way into the room, came to a stand-still so quickly that Gonçalves bumped into his back.

"Hey," Gonçalves said. "What—"

"You see the guy with the big moustache?"

"The one with a bald spot and the number ten on the back of his football jersey?"

"Him. That's Federico Lorca."

"Your ex-brother-in-law?"

"The very one."

Lorca, an overweight man pushing sixty, was nursing a glass of wine and swiveling his head first one way, then the other, as he held forth to the people along the length of the bar. At a given point, one of them tried to break-in on his monologue, but Lorca wouldn't have it. He raised his voice and talked right over him.

"What a windbag," Gonçalves said.

"You have no idea," Arnaldo said. "Come on. Let's get this waste of time over with."

He walked over to Lorca and tapped him on the shoulder. Lorca turned, looked at Arnaldo, and rocked back on his heels.

"Ha," he said. "Still alive? I was hoping you were dead."

"Still shooting off that big mouth of yours, are you, Federico?"

"You've got it wrong. As usual. What I'm doing is having a conversation with friends. But you wouldn't know about friends, would you? I seem to recall you never had any. What are you doing in our club?"

"Business."

"What kind of business?"

"Federal Police business."

"If you lived in Argentina, and worked for *our* federal cops, they would have fired you a long time ago."

"If I lived in Argentina, and worked anywhere, I would have killed myself a long time ago."

The Argentineans within earshot didn't appreciate the remark. There was some grumbling.

"One of the best things I ever did," Lorca said, "was to divorce Alicia."

"Watch out what you say about my sister, Federico."

"I wasn't really referring to your sister, Arnaldo. I was referring to getting rid of *you* as a brother-in-law. The day the divorce became final was one of the happiest days of my life."

"Mine too. So, finally, we've got one thing we agree on. I can't think of anything in this life that I ever wished for more."

Lorca took a sip of his wine. "You're starting to bore me. How about you get down to that Federal Police business of yours?"

"My young colleague here has some questions for you and your friends."

Gonçalves stepped in. "About the kidnapping of Tico Santos's mother."

"What about it?"

"From what I understand, the Argentinean newspapers are crying crocodile tears."

"Crocodile tears?"

"Yeah. They're saying it's a terrible thing, but they don't really mean it."

Lorca smiled a thin smile. "Really?"

"Yeah, really. So how do you people feel about it? Do you ascribe to the official line? Or are you kind of happy to see the Artist with his mind off of the game?"

Federico Lorca looked around him, as if he was taking a visual poll. Then he looked back at Gonçalves.

"We all live here in Brazil. We've got a different take on it."

"Which is?"

"We're annoyed."

"Annoyed?"

"It's like this: if Tico doesn't play, or if he plays badly when we win, people could say it wouldn't have happened if he'd been in top form."

A red flush crept up Gonçalves's neck and suffused his face.

"*When* you win. Did you say *when* you win?"

"I did."

"And you really think that's going to happen?"

"I do."

Arnaldo dug Gonçalves in the ribs. "See what I mean?" he said.

Gonçalves ignored him. "And yet, if Tico doesn't play, it would bother you?"

The Argentinean smiled. "Of course it would. It would diminish our triumph. Back home, our countrymen don't have daily contact with Brazilians. Those of us who live here do. And we'll get to rub our victory in your faces every day for the next four years."

"We were discussing the issue just before you guys came in," one of the other Argentineans said. "Somebody suggested a Brazilian did it."

"That somebody was *you*, José," one of the other men said.

"Okay, so it was me," José said. "But it's possible, isn't it?"

There was a general murmur of approval.

"Wait a minute, wait just a minute," Gonçalves said. "Are you telling me you people actually believe we'd kidnap the mother of our own best striker just to diminish the prestige of an unlikely Argentinean victory?"

"Who says it's unlikely?" one of the other men said.

"*I* said it's unlikely," Gonçalves said, his voice taking on an edge.

"Of course you did," the Argentinean said. "You're Brazilian, and therefore deluded about the outcome."

"Deluded?" Gonçalves sputtered.

"Deluded. Let me tell you how it's going to be, young man. First, we're going to make mincemeat of the three teams in our group—"

Gonçalves made a dismissive gesture. "Honduras, Greece and Nigeria. Big deal. No real competition—"

"—and then we're going on to topple the runner-up in group C, which will be—"

"The pushovers from the United States—"

"Or the brutes from the Netherlands. Take your pick."

"I don't debate any of that. Get to your point."

"My point is, we're going to play Brazil in the finals. And we're going to crush you."

"Crush us? Señor, you people have about as much chance of—"

Arnaldo gripped Gonçalves's arm.

"This isn't getting us anywhere," he said. "Ask the question."

Federico took another sip of wine and ran a finger along his moustache. "What question?" he said.

Gonçalves disengaged his arm from Arnaldo's grip and took a deep breath.

"How about this: how about a group of Argentineans snatched the Artist's mother so your country would have some chance of winning? How about that?"

"Ridiculous," José said, and laughed.

"Absurd."

That was from the Argentinean who'd called Gonçalves deluded.

"Listen to this guy," Federico said, addressing his country-men. And then, to Gonçalves, "Wishing won't make it so, young man. You people are going to have your asses kicked. But, since you've given all of us a good laugh, how about we buy you a drink?"

"And how about you all go fuck yourselves," Gonçalves said, and stormed out.

***

IN THE parking lot, Arnaldo caught up with him.

"If you're about to tell me *I told you so*," Gonçalves said, "you can just keep your damned mouth shut."

"I was about to tell you a couple of Argentinean jokes. I thought they might drive home the lesson."

"I don't want to hear any Argentinean jokes." Gonçalves kicked a stone. "Open the damned car."

"You know the one about how to make a fortune?"

Gonçalves paused, his hand extended toward the door handle. "No," he said.

"You buy an Argentinean for what he's worth and sell him for what he thinks he's worth."

Gonçalves wasn't amused.

"That's not funny," he said.

"You know what an ego is?"

"No."

"It's a tiny Argentinean who lives in all of us."

"That's not funny either."

"Argentinean jokes aren't made to be funny. They're made to be instructive."

"Get in the car and drive," Gonçalves said.

Chapter Five

RODOLFO SÁ, JURACI'S NEIGHBOR, was a florid-faced man with a big belly. His wife, Angela, was a petite woman a head shorter than her husband.

They sat Hector at their dining room table, offered him coffee and tried to pump him for information.

He fended off their questions, accepted a second cup and launched into his questions.

"Tell me about Juraci Santos."

"What do you want to know?" Rodolfo said.

"Start with her character. What kind of a lady is she?"

Rodolfo's horn-rimmed glasses had slipped down his nose. He used a finger to push them back into place, and then looked at his wife.

"You want to answer that one?"

"Not me," she said. "You go ahead."

After a pause to consider his words, Rodolfo said, "To begin with, Juraci Santos isn't a lady at all. She doesn't belong here in Granja Viana, she belongs in a slum."

"Back where she came from, is that what you're saying?"

"It sounds bigoted, I know, but *you* try living next door to someone like that." Rodolfo pointed to a set of French doors. "Our deck overlooks her back yard. Go out there and have a look. You'll see what I mean."

Through the glass, Hector could see patio furniture, a wooden rail and some greenery. He couldn't see Juraci's home.

"Why don't you just tell me?" he said.

"Garbage, that's what you'll see. When she and her friends

party out there, and they party a lot, they don't throw their paper cups, and paper plates, and chicken bones, and rib bones in the trash. They simply toss them onto the ground. We never had a rat problem before Juraci moved in, but we've sure as hell got one now. I had to put out poison, and Adolph ate some of it—"

"Adolph's your dog?"

"Yeah. He's a Doberman. It was all the vet could do to save him, and he hasn't been the same since. Intestinal problems. Believe me, you don't want to hear the details."

Angela had put a dish of bite-sized cookies on the table. Her husband put one in his mouth, masticated it and washed it down with coffee before continuing.

"Then there were the parrots," he said. "She used to have two of them over there, Macaws, a red one and a blue one. They'd squawk at dawn, and they'd squawk when the sun went down, and they were even noisier than the damned rooster she used to keep. Which, by the way, checked in every morning about half an hour before the parrots did."

"Noisy, huh?"

Rodolfo snagged another cookie.

"Noisy is an understatement. And her former menagerie isn't the half of it. She's got lousy taste in music, and she recently invested in the biggest amplifier and loudspeaker system known to man. She plays *musica sertaneja* every god-damned day, the same crap over and over again, and she plays it so loud that the glasses in our china cupboards rattle. She's got a little toy poodle that barks all night long. Which, of course, sets off Adolph, who always used to sleep through the night until she moved in. And then there are her god-damned hens."

"Hens?"

"Hens. No coop. They just wander around the yard."

"Every now and then," Angela put in, "one of them gets over the fence and goes straight for my roses."

"You've spoken to her about all of this?"

Rodolfo threw up his hands in a gesture of frustration. "Repeatedly. Nothing I say makes any difference. When I go over there to complain, she either won't answer the door, or she shuts it in my face. Juraci Santos is the neighbor from Hell. We built this house ourselves. I spent three years getting it done. It was our dream. We had great neighbors, and we were happy. And then Tiago Serra divorced his wife, and he needed to get rid of the house, and Juraci Santos moved in. Now we're thinking of selling out and leaving Granja Viana altogether. All because of that woman."

Gonçalves took a sip of his coffee. "How about her other neighbors? Do they share your opinions about the lady?"

"They sure as hell do. They don't have to put up with her eyesore of a back yard, or her hens, but all of them hear her noise. We're in a valley here. The racket carries clear over to the other side. And then there are the thefts."

"Thefts?"

"There's been a spate of thefts. I'm not accusing Juraci personally, but you gotta admit it's a hell of a coincidence that all the incidents occurred since she moved in. Nothing big, mind you. Not yet. But clothes have been stolen off clotheslines, radios and CD players ripped out of cars, TV sets stolen from houses." Rodolfo took another cookie and waved it in Gonçalves's direction. "They talk to her, the security guys do, and she claims she knows nothing about it. Maybe she doesn't. But she isn't willing to recognize that it might be the people she invites to her home, all those old friends of hers from her *favela* days." He popped the cookie in his mouth.

"Go easy on those cookies," Angela said. "You're supposed to be on a diet, remember?" Then, to Gonçalves, "More coffee?"

Gonçalves shook his head. "It was delicious, but, no, thanks. How about the Artist?"

"What about him?"

"Does he put in an appearance every now and then?"

"All the time. That's the only positive side to the whole rotten business. It's something for the kids to brag about at school. You know him personally?"

"Not yet."

"He's a nice guy, not arrogant at all, always willing to give a kid an autograph. And how about that girlfriend of his, huh? Cintia Tadesco? Now, there's a—"

"Bitch," Angela said. "The woman is a bitch. That's a known fact."

"How can you say that?" Rodolfo said. "How can you say it's a known fact?"

"Because I read about her all the time."

"In that trash magazine you subscribe to?"

"It's called *Fofocas*, and it's not trash. I don't know why the Artist puts up with her."

"Hell," her husband said, "all you got to do is to take one look and you know why he puts up with her. If I had half a chance—"

Angela punched her husband on his arm.

"Hey," he said, "that hurt."

"It was meant to," she said.

"People," Hector said, "I'm in a bit of a hurry here."

"Sorry," she said.

"Yeah, sorry," Rodolfo said—and reached for another cookie.

"Rodolfo," she said, "you want me to take that plate—"

"Last one," he said, not letting her finish.

"Tell me about the last time you saw Juraci Santos," Hector said.

"Yesterday morning," Rodolfo said. "I told you guys about that already."

"I'd appreciate it if you'd go over it again. With me."

"Oh. Okay. Sure. I was leaving for work. I drove up the ramp to the street and got out of my car to close the gate."

"What time was this?"

"Somewhere between 8:50 and 8:55," he said without hesitation.

"You seem pretty sure of the time."

"I am. That's when I always leave."

"I told him there was a shopping list on the kitchen table," Angela said, "but he forgot to pick it up. I grabbed it and ran out the front door."

"And all the while," Rodolfo said, "the Santos woman was standing next to her mailbox, arguing with a postman."

"You're sure it was an argument?"

"Hell, yes. I heard her tell him he could go fuck himself. That's the way she talks, always fuck this and fuck that. The woman has a really foul mouth. The postman saw me looking at him, and he must have said something to her because she looked over her shoulder and spotted me."

"Did she wave? Acknowledge your presence?"

"Wave? No way. Those days are long gone. All she did was lower her voice."

"Tell me more about this postman."

"What's to tell?"

"Was he your regular guy?"

"That's the thing," Angela said. "He wasn't."

"A substitute?"

She shook her head. "Not that either."

"How can you be sure?"

"They always deliver to us first. I checked the box before I came inside. There was nothing there. But, later in the day, there was."

"This postman, had either one of you ever seen him before?"

Rodolfo and Angela looked at each other, and then back at Hector. Both of them shook their heads.

"If you saw him again," Hector said, "would you recognize him?"

"I think I would," Angela said. "I've got a good memory for faces. Rodolfo is useless."

"Hey," Rodolfo said.

"You are. You know you are. It's downright embarrassing sometimes."

"I can't help it if I'm not a goddamned social butterfly."

"You could at least make an effort."

Hector picked up his spoon and tapped it on his cup.
Ding, ding, ding.

"*Senhor* Sá," he said, when he had their attention, "it's my understanding you heard a disturbance early this morning."

"Yeah, I did."

"Tell me about that."

"There was this *bang* next door. It woke me up."

"You're sure it came from next door?"

"I'm sure. Adolph sleeps in our room. He went ballistic, and that's the direction he was barking in."

"So you got out of bed to have a look."

"I did. I looked out the window—"

"Bedroom window?"

"No. You can't see much from our bedroom. I went down the hall to my office."

"Can you see her kitchen door from the office window?"

"No."

"What about her front gate? Can you see that?"

"Yes. And the road in front."

"Did you turn on a light?"

"In the office?"

"Yes, in the office."

"I did. I'm in the middle of a project. I have papers stacked up all over the floor. I didn't want to step on them."

"What did you see from the window?"

"A car driving away. He floored it. The tires squealed. He kicked up a lot of gravel."

"And that didn't make you suspicious?"

Rodolfo shook his head. "I figured him for one of her noisy friends, and I figured him for drunk."

"And you decided not to complain to the security people?"

"No point. By that time, he was gone."

"You keep saying *he* and *him*. Are you sure the driver was a man?"

"No. It could have been a woman. Truth is, I have no idea."

"How many people were in the car?"

"I couldn't say. It was too dark."

"What did you do next?"

"Nothing."

"Nothing?"

"Well, okay, not nothing. I turned off the light and went back to bed."

Chapter Six

SILVA'S FLIGHT LANDED LATE in the afternoon. It took the best part of another hour for him to get to the Federal Police's field office. Lunch, he'd told them when he called from the airport, hadn't been in the cards, so Mara Carta, Hector's Chief of Intelligence, took the initiative and had a sandwich and a soft drink waiting for him when he arrived. They updated him while he ate.

Arnaldo began by reporting on his visit to the Argentinean Club.

"You think it's enough to satisfy Sampaio," he asked when he was done, "or are we going to have to waste more time on his stupid theory?"

"It'll be enough," Silva said between bites, "provided Mara composes a report making it sound like an intensive investigation of the entire Argentinean community."

"But unfortunately unproductive," Mara said. "Leave it to me. I always wanted to write a novel."

"Hold back a day or two," Silva said, after swallowing a mouthful, "otherwise he's unlikely to believe we've done everything you're going to invent and put in there." He turned to Hector. "What did you learn at the crime scene?"

Hector shared Lefkowitz's theories.

"That Lefkowitz," Arnaldo said, "may well be the only good thing ever to come out of Manaus."

Arnaldo wasn't fond of the Amazonian city of Manaus. He hated to go there, even on the shortest of assignments, considered it a filthy and degenerate hell hole. And everyone around the table, as it happened, agreed with him. Even Mara, who usually didn't agree with Arnaldo about anything.

"He only worked there for two years," Hector said. "Long enough to inflict great suffering upon him, but not long enough to ruin him."

Silva blotted his lips and wiped his hands on a paper napkin. "And you, Mara? What have you got for us?"

"Nothing substantial," she said, "just alleged sightings. Juraci's in Porto Alegre. She's in Rio. She's in Belo Horizonte. She's all over the map. We've got twelve people working the national tip line, and they're overloaded. The average wait-time is bordering on fifteen minutes, which is an all-time record. It seems like everybody in the country wants to help. They all love the Artist."

"Joãozinho Preto doesn't," Arnaldo said.

Mara leaned forward, her shoulder brushing Silva's. "Who's Joãozinho Preto?"

All the men looked at her.

"You're being serious?" Gonçalves said. "You never heard of Joãozinho Preto?"

"If I had," she said, "I wouldn't have wasted everybody's time by asking."

"Until the Artist kicked him in the shin," Silva said, "Joãozinho was the best striker Palmeiras ever had."

"Heart and soul of the team," Gonçalves said. "A photographer from the *Jornal da Tarde* captured the moment it happened. Most horrible football photo I ever saw. Tico's shoe is against Joãozinho's shin, right at the height of his kick. From the point of impact on down, Joãozinho's leg is off at a right angle to the rest of it. His career was over just like that." He snapped his fingers. "It was an accident, but still . . ."

"The team's chance to win last year's national championship, the only one they've had in the last ten years, went right out the window when that happened," Arnaldo said. "Every single *Palmeirense* wanted to kill the Artist, and they are neither few nor noted for their passivity."

"The break never healed properly," Gonçalves said. "It was the end of Joãozinho's career, and he was only what? Twenty-seven?"

"Twenty-eight," Hector said. "But I never heard him say a word against the Artist. Not then and not since."

"Let's talk to him anyway," Silva said. "It can't hurt. Any more from the kidnappers?"

"Maybe," Mara said.

"Why maybe?"

"They're communicating through the Artist's website."

"I know. So?"

"So, before the news broke, the Artist was getting about a hundred emails a day. At the moment it's more than five thousand an hour, mostly expressions of sympathy. The kid who administrates the site is overwhelmed. I assigned a couple of people to help him. They're overwhelmed too."

"Put more people on it."

"I don't have more people."

"Can't you sort electronically?"

"We have no parameters. They didn't use the subject line when they first made contact. They wouldn't be stupid enough to use the same email address twice. And, if they run true to form, they'll log on through a wireless connection."

"And it's unlikely to be the same one they used last time."

"Correct."

"So you have to read every incoming email?"

"We do. It's a nightmare."

"Damn. How about the media? Who broadcast the story first?"

"Radio Mundo."

"Where did they get it? Sampaio wants to know."

"They won't tell us."

"Why not? What difference does it make?"

"According to them, their source insists on confidentiality."

"Probably just means she's some blabbermouth who feeds them information all the time," Arnaldo said, "and they want to make sure she keeps on doing it."

"She?" Mara bristled. "Why do you assume it's a she?"

"Uh oh," Gonçalves said. "Here we go again."

"You know any male blabbermouths?" Arnaldo said.

"I know one. He's a Neanderthal by the name of Arnaldo Nunes."

The sniping between Mara and Arnaldo was a regular feature of their meetings. Silva didn't think either one of them took it seriously. He generally ignored it.

"What's the Artist's reaction to all of this?" he said.

"He wants to pay," Mara said.

"Five million in diamonds? Just like that?"

"Five million *dollars* in diamonds. Not Reais, dollars. He doesn't even want to negotiate the amount. He's terrified, Mario. Terrified they might hurt her."

"For him," Gonçalves said, "five million dollars is peanuts. The Artist is loaded."

"I think even the Artist would miss five million dollars," Silva said. "Are his telephones being monitored?"

"His apartment," Mara said, "plus his mobile phone, his girlfriend's apartment, his house in Guarujá, his house in Campos do Jordão, his condo in Rio and his agent's office, home and mobile."

"How about the civil police? Have they brought anything to the party?"

Mara shuffled through the pile in front of her and handed him a folder. Silva perused it, and after a moment, looked up.

"Says here," he said, "that Juraci had an appointment scheduled with her hairdresser for 10:00 this morning."

"Jacques Jardin, no less," Mara said.

"Why 'no less'? Is this Jardin some kind of a big deal?"

"Yes, Mario, he's a *really* big deal. I wouldn't be able to get an appointment with him even if I could afford it."

"I fail to see," Gonçalves said, "how an appointment with a hairdresser could be of any significance."

"I wouldn't expect you to. You're a male."

"So?"

"You guys know about football players. We girls know about hairdressers. The person who wrote that report is a woman. If she was sexist pig like Nunes here—"

"Hey," Arnaldo said.

"—Juraci's appointment probably wouldn't even have been mentioned."

"And?" Gonçalves said.

"And we might have missed out on a possible lead. One of the great secrets of the sisterhood is this: we confide in our hairdressers, sometimes more than in anyone else we know. I think it might have something to do with their fingers massaging our scalps."

"Mmmm," Gonçalves said. "Sexy."

"Not at all," Mara said. "Most of the really good ones are gay."

"Who's spoken to the Artist?" Silva said.

"Only the civil cops."

"Where is he?"

"At his apartment."

"Call him. Ask if Arnaldo and I can come over."

"Now?"

"Now. We'll need his address."

Mara nodded and went out. Silva turned to Gonçalves.

"See if that fellow Jardin is at his salon. If he is, go over there and talk to him. Put him through records first, though, just in case we have something on him."

"You think a high-society hairdresser has a rap sheet?"

"You never know. Bring your cell phone."

"I always do," Gonçalves said. He stood up and took his suit jacket off the back of his chair.

"That leaves me," Hector said.

"You," Silva said, "go home and be nice to Gilda."

"And tomorrow morning?"

"Tomorrow morning, first thing, you go out to Granja Viana and have a chat with that locksmith."

Chapter Seven

"Jesus," Arnaldo said, "Look at that."

The street ahead, from curb to curb, was packed with media vans, reporters, and a horde of anxious fans.

"Back out," Silva said. "We'll park at the shopping center."

They weren't the only ones with that idea. The lot behind the Ibirapuera Shopping Center was nearly full, but they managed to snag one of the few remaining slots. They locked the car and set out for the Artist's apartment on foot.

"I read in *Veja* that a one-bedroom goes for over a million," Arnaldo said as they rounded the corner and came within sight of the building.

"And he has *five* bedrooms. I read the same article."

"What's an unmarried guy do with five bedrooms?"

"One to sleep in and four to keep his money. When he moves to Madrid, four won't be enough."

"Don't remind me about Madrid," Arnaldo said.

Wooden barriers had been put up to hold back the crowd. When Arnaldo made a move to shove one aside, a uniformed cop blew a blast on his whistle and ran over to stop him.

"Just where do you think you're going?" he said.

Silva flashed his badge. "We've got an appointment with the Artist."

Silva's badge was gold trimmed with blue enamel, a sign of high rank. In a flash, the cop's expression went from indignation to respect.

"Let me help, *Senhor*."

He completed the shoving, stepped aside—and saluted.

The salute was a tip-off to the reporters. Strobe lights flashed, only a few at first, then by the score. The people not operating cameras started shouting questions.

Silva detested attention from the media. He forced himself not to break into a run.

"I've got a new one for you," Arnaldo said, taking the reporters in stride, as he did most things.

"Later."

"You might want to reconsider that. It's about football."

"About football? Okay, tell me."

Arnaldo waited until they'd gained sanctuary in the lobby, then:

"This guy is sitting in the second row, center field, during the final game of the World Cup. Just below him, there's an empty seat."

Silva hit the button on the elevator.

"An empty seat? At the World Cup Final? You've got to be kidding."

"Of course I am. It's a joke. Next to the empty seat is an old geezer who's got his stuff all over it, program, beer, spare pair of eyeglasses, binoculars. A guy just above him, in the third row, figures he's holding it for somebody. Halftime comes. Nobody shows up. By this time, everybody is looking at that empty seat and thinking how nice it would be if their girlfriends, sisters, parents, or whatever, could be there, sitting in it. Finally, the guy in the third row taps the geezer on the shoulder.

"'Mind if I ask you a question?'

"The geezer turns around. 'What?'

"'Did you pay for that seat?'

"'I did,' the geezer says, 'I bought it for my beloved wife of fifty-eight years.'

"'And?'

"'She died.'

"'Gee, I'm sorry to hear that, but, um . . . this *is* the World Cup, after all. Surely, you've got some relative, or maybe a friend, you could have offered it to?'

"'I do,' the geezer says. 'I've got a lot of relatives, and I've got a lot of friends, and one after the other, I offered it to every last one of them.'

"'And no takers?'

"'Nope.'

"'That's amazing.'

"'I thought so too,' the geezer says. 'As a matter of fact, I thought it was downright crazy. Can you imagine? They all decided to go to her funeral instead.'"

* * *

SILVA WAS still chuckling when they reached Tico Santos's front door. Somewhat to his surprise, the Artist answered the door himself.

"Which one of you is Chief Inspector Silva?" he said.

"I'm Silva. This is Agent Nunes."

"Thanks for coming," Tico said, as if he'd issued an invitation. "The living room's this way." He pointed with his chin. "Follow me."

When Tico turned his back, Arnaldo whispered into Silva's ear, "*Football giant*, my ass."

Tico was a head shorter than Arnaldo and probably fifty kilograms lighter.

"They mean it figuratively," Silva said.

Tico heard him say something, but it was clear he hadn't understood what it was. Without stopping, he spoke over his shoulder, answering a question Silva hadn't asked.

"Maybe an hour ago," he said. "I hired a private plane to get here."

He didn't bother to explain where he'd come from; he assumed Silva would know. And Silva did. Tico had been in Curitiba, in training, with the rest of the Brazilian team.

They entered a space about the size of a small ballroom. The far wall was windows, nothing but windows, floor to ceiling. Beyond them, a thousand lights sparkled in the mansions sprinkled over the hills of Morumbi.

The view was nothing less than spectacular.

So was the woman who was sitting on one of the white leather couches. She didn't bother to get up.

"Cintia Tadesco," the Artist said, "my fiancée. Cintia, this is Chief Inspector Silva and . . . sorry, I forgot your name."

"Agent Nunes."

Side by side, Tico and his girlfriend were a study in contrasts. Both were in their mid-twenties, but it was there that any similarity stopped. One of Tico's brown eyes was noticeably darker than the other. His irregularly-spaced teeth were crooked; his forehead was a little too short; his chin a little too long; his nose a little too wide.

Cintia, on the other hand, was stunningly beautiful, taller than her boyfriend, taller than most men, with a figure that would stop traffic on Avenida Paulista at rush hour. The word *statuesque* popped into Silva's mind. He recalled some things his wife, Irene, an inveterate consumer of gossip magazines, had told him about Cintia.

Cintia was not just a beautiful face; she was a prima donna, generally disliked by the photographers and art directors with whom she spent her days. Tico followed her around like a lapdog. They were due to marry in the spring. A few of Tico's friends suggested she might be a gold-digger. Those that did were no longer Tico's friends.

She gave the cops an appraising look. "I hope," she said, "you've got some good news."

"I wish we did," Silva said. "At the moment, all we've got is questions."

"In that case," she said, taking charge, "Let me say this: Tico has had a long day. There's nothing more he can tell you. He's tired. He's stressed. He needs sleep. How about you come back tomorrow morning?"

"The first few hours are always crucial. We'll try to take up as little of his time as possible. Yours, too, *Senhorita* Tadesco."

"I'm not too tired," the Artist said. "This is my mother we're talking about. I want to do everything I can to help. Make yourselves comfortable."

Cops one, Tadesco zero, Silva thought as he took a seat.

"Discounting the ransom," he said. "Can you think of any reason why someone might have kidnapped your mother?"

"You don't think five million dollars is reason enough?" Cintia said.

If she couldn't get rid of them, she apparently intended to make her presence felt.

"It's a good one, *Senhorita* Tadesco, and it may be the only one, but we shouldn't fail to consider other possibilities."

"Like what?"

"A group of Argentineans so focused on winning the Cup they kidnapped Senhora Santos to put Tico off his game."

"That's ridiculous!"

"It probably is. How about this: someone thinks he has star quality, but Tico outshines him. He kidnaps Tico's mother. Tico doesn't play, and the kidnapper has a chance to be the big star of the Cup."

Silva put as little faith in that possibility as he had in the first. He expected Cintia to reject it out of hand.

But she didn't.

"Romário de Barros!" she said.

"Aw, come on, Cintia," Tico said, "it's not fair to accuse a guy just because—"

"Fair?" she said. "*Querido*, this is Romário de Barros we're talking about."

Romário de Barros was the Corinthians' principal striker, a brilliant player, just not as brilliant as Tico. The fans knew that, the other players knew that, everyone in Brazil knew that. Everyone except Romário de Barros. Truth be told, he probably knew it as well, he just didn't want to admit it. Had it not been for the Artist, Romário would have been Brazil's greatest star. As it was, he ran a distant second. For most people, what Romário insisted on calling the "rivalry" between himself and Tico was no more than a joke.

"Romário de Barros," Silva said, "is a distinct possibility. We'll look into it."

"I think you're gonna be wasting your time," Tico said.

"Who cares about *their* time if it pisses Romário off?" Cintia said. "He's caused you plenty of aggravation. It's time you caused him some." She yawned and looked at her gold Rolex. "How about you guys speed it up? It's getting late."

Not very concerned about our future mother-in-law, are we? Silva thought.

"And then," he said, "we also have to consider the possibility that Senhora Santos's abduction might have been an act of revenge."

"Revenge?" Tico said.

"Revenge," Silva said. "Do you know someone, anyone, who might want to punish you by kidnapping your mother?"

Tico rubbed his chin. Then he shook his head. "I can't think of anybody."

"How about Joãozinho Preto?" Arnaldo said.

"Never," Tico said. "He'd never—"

"Who's Joãozinho Preto?" Cintia said.

All the men looked at her.

"He was a striker for Palmeiras," Silva said. "Tico broke his leg just before the national playoffs."

"I still feel bad about that, but it was an accident. Ask anybody. I never even got a yellow card."

"I don't debate it. But the accident ruined Joãozinho's career. He hasn't played a day since."

"He never said a word against me," Tico said, "not then, not since. It was the fans that made a big issue of it, not him. And that photo they took at the time shocked a lot of people. Hell, it even shocked me. But we all take our chances. Joãozinho understood that."

"So we can probably discount him. Nobody else you can think of?"

"No."

"But they're out there," Cintia said. "You can count on that, *querido*, they're out there. Lots of envious bastards who earn their pissy little hundred thousand Reais a year and are jealous of people like you and me."

She gave his hand a supporting squeeze. He shot her a grateful look.

Arnaldo, whose annual salary, after almost thirty years as a federal cop, was considerably less than one hundred thousand Reais, started to cough.

"Sorry," he said. "Getting a cold."

"Maybe," Cintia said, "you should go and get it somewhere else."

"Could it have been an act directed against the lady herself?" Silva asked. "Someone intent on hurting her?"

"Impossible," Cintia said. "There's no one easier to get on with than my future mother-in-law. Everybody loves her, and she loves them right back."

Not everybody, Silva thought. *Not her neighbors, not that postman she was seen talking to. And, if the lady was fond of you, it's unlikely she'd have had a detective following you around.*

"Let's talk about Senhora Santos's house keys," he said. "Did she give keys to people who worked in her home?"

"Sure," Tico said, "but she was always careful, always changed locks when she changed servants."

"How often was that?"

Tico shrugged. "I don't know. Maybe three or four times a year?"

"So she had a problem holding on to servants?"

"She had a problem finding good ones," Cintia said. "Everybody does. Why do you care about her keys?"

"Just reviewing the possibilities."

"Wasting our time is the way I see it. They told us the kidnappers smashed her kitchen door. So where do keys come into it?"

Silva was running out of patience with the woman.

"I'm not wasting your time, Senhorita Tadesco. I have good reasons for my questions. Now, Tico, do you have any idea how many sets of keys your mother had?"

"Four. She always got four."

"Four."

"Uh huh. One for herself, one for the servants, one for us, and an extra one to keep in the house in case someone lost one of the others."

"You have yours?"

"Why?" Cintia said.

"Senhorita Tadesco, please. Tico, may I see them?"

"I gave them to you," Tico said to Cintia.

"No," she said. "You didn't."

"No? I coulda sworn—"

"You *didn't.*"

"Then I got no idea where they are," he said. "We never used the keys she gave us. We never had to. We only went out there when we knew she'd be home, and we always called before we went."

Silva took a card out of his wallet, jotted the number of his cell phone on the back and handed the card to Tico. "If you find those keys," he said, "give me a call."

Tico took the card, looked at one side of it, then the other.

"You think it's important?" he asked.

"It might be."

"Okay, then."

"The radio people, the ones at Radio Mundo," Silva said, "knew about your mother's kidnapping before we did. Any idea how that happened?"

Cintia didn't give Tico time to answer.

"Her Royal Highness," she said, "Princess Jacques Jardin."

"The hairdresser?"

"Stylist, the little *bicha* calls himself. Stylist or *coiffeur*. He *hates* to be called a hairdresser. Juraci was late for an appointment. They couldn't get her at home, so they tried here."

"And you were here to take the call?"

"We forwarded calls to my cell phone."

"Dumbo won't let me have one during training," Tico said. "He thinks cell phones are a distraction."

Danilson "Dumbo" Hoffmann was the coach of the Brazilian national team. Nobody who saw his ears ever had to ask where the nickname came from.

Cintia refused to be sidetracked. "Jardin keeps everybody waiting, but *he* doesn't like to wait for anyone. You know how much he charges for a cut? Six hundred Reais, that's how much, and he's booked back-to-back. Missing a session with Jardin is like missing a private audience with the Pope. Except the Pope probably doesn't go ballistic and Jardin does.

If you're ten minutes late, it's like you insulted him. I did it once and now the little bastard refuses to give me any more appointments."

"Showing up late really gets his nose out of joint," Tico said. "Even I know that."

"And Juraci knew that," Cintia said. "I started to worry right away. I told Jardin's secretary I'd check around and call her back. I was still trying to locate her, when the bitch called for a second time."

"How does this—" Silva started to say.

Cintia interrupted him. "You wanted to know why I think Jardin tipped off the radio people. I was telling you. Do you want to hear it, or not?"

"Please go on."

"So I was talking to this bitch of a secretary, and before I could get in a word edgewise, she started telling me how pissed off Jardin was and how, if Juraci didn't have a really, really good reason for not showing up, she couldn't be a client anymore. Jardin was going to give Juraci another fifteen minutes grace, she said, but only in deference to the fact that she was such a good client, and because he liked her. Two minutes after she hung up, Tico called me with the news that she'd been kidnapped."

"And how did you get that news?" Silva asked him.

"The kid who runs the website," Tico said. "He read the email, looked at the photo the kidnappers sent, the one of my Mom holding up the newspaper, and panicked. The note said not to contact the police, said they'd hurt her if I did."

"I remember."

"And, to tell you the truth, maybe I *wouldn't* have gone to you guys at all if the story hadn't come out on the radio."

"Understandable. Go on."

"The kid knew I was in Curitiba because it's been all over

the sports news, so he decided to try calling the training facility. They wouldn't let him talk to me, at first. But then he told them what it was about, and they called me in from the field. They still thought it was some kind of hoax, but they didn't want to run the risk that it wasn't. And it wasn't."

"Tico told me he was going to charter a plane and come to São Paulo," Cintia said. "We agreed to meet here. Then, just after he hung up, the bitch called for a third time. And, to shut her up, I told her."

"You told Jacques Jardin's secretary about the ransom note?"

"What did I just say? I blurted it out. I was nervous. So what? It's done. Jardin was probably talking to the media five minutes after his secretary hung up. He's like that."

"Probably all for the best," Silva said. "The kidnappers must know we're involved by now, and they seem to have accepted that fact. Who does the website? A kid, you said?"

"My agent's kid," Tico said.

"That's his job? Websites?"

"Nah! He studies during the day, does the sites on the side, mostly at night. He does them for most of his old man's clients. He does Cintia's too."

"These days," she said, "everybody has to have a website."

"*I* don't have a website," Arnaldo said.

"Let me amend that," she said. "Anybody of any importance has to have a website."

"Where did *you* spend last night?" Arnaldo said, his voice taking on an edge.

"Me? What's that got to do with anything?"

Arnaldo gave Cintia his cop's stare, perfected by almost three decades of facing down felons.

"At home," she said, buckling under it. "So?"

"Alone?"

"Of course, alone. I've got a part in a *novela*. I was learning my lines. What are you implying?"

"I'm not implying anything," Arnaldo said.

But he was.

Arnaldo Nunes had taken a distinct dislike to Cintia Tadesco.

Chapter Eight

JACQUES JARDIN HAD A French accent as round and thick as a great wheel of Camembert. Haraldo Gonçalves would undoubtedly accepted it as genuine—had he not discovered, before leaving the office, that Jardin did, indeed, have a rap sheet.

Jardin, the records revealed, had acquired his current name at the age of twenty-seven. Until then, he'd been Giovanni Giordano, the youngest of nine children born to an Italian immigrant couple who'd settled in São Paulo's middle-class *bairro* of Mooca.

Jardin had never spent any appreciable amount of time in France. He had, however, spent a good deal of time in public toilets. It was the time in those public toilets that had given rise to the aforementioned rap sheet. It registered half a dozen arrests, and two convictions, for indecent exposure.

When he'd first clapped eyes on the famous coiffeur, Gonçalves hadn't been quite sure whether Jardin was using eyeliner, or whether he was permanently tattooed. Curiosity about what he was actually seeing had caused him to stare long and hard at Jardin's eyes. Perhaps too long, and too hard. The stylist licked his thin lips, almost as if he could taste Gonçalves on his chops, and smoothed back his immaculately styled hair. The word *preening* came to mind.

In the initial stages of their conversation Gonçalves learned little that the Federal Police didn't already know. Revelations, however, began to surface when he touched on the subject of the Artist's girlfriend, Cintia Tadesco.

"I can well understand that you have an interest in *her*." Jardin managed to insert another oval cigarette into his ivory holder without taking his eyes off Gonçalves. "The woman is a total bitch."

"A total bitch, eh?"

Gonçalves had already learned that Jardin required only a minimum of prompting.

"I don't mean she's just a gold-digger," Jardin said. "God knows, I've known my share of gold-diggers. I don't dismiss them as a category. Some of them actually give quite good value for money."

"Value for money?" Gonçalves echoed.

Jardin's lighter was a Dupont, in black lacquer and gold. It made a musical *ding* when he lit up.

"Suppose," he said, "that you're old, and rich, and single. Divorced, maybe, or a widower. You're lonely. You haven't seen what a twenty- to thirty-year-old body looks like"—he took another puff, expelled the smoke and looked Haraldo up and down before going on—"for maybe the last quarter-century. Then along comes this nubile young thing who sells you on the idea that May-December relationships are all the rage. She tells you she loves you for yourself, not your money, or your status, or your fame. You believe it because you *want* to believe it. You say to yourself, hey, it's not as impossible as I thought. It's happened once or twice before. And now it's happening to *me*."

"Uh huh. And then?"

"And then you start bonking her, and she makes you feel like you're the most virile man she's ever met. You may have to swallow a handful of pills to get a hard-on, but when it's up, it's up, and it's glorious. She admires it, kisses it, strokes it, runs her hand up and down the shaft, tells you you're the first man who's ever made her feel truly like a woman. So you start buying her expensive jewelry, and you set her up in a nice place of her own. Why not? You can afford it." Jardin took another drag on his cigarette. Gonçalves made no attempt to interrupt. "Then, if you're really besotted, you might even marry her, marry her no matter what your family might be saying about her. If a friend opens his mouth, you'd sooner lose the friend than lose the girl."

"And you call that value for money? Estranging people from their friends and family?"

"Estrangement occurs only if the friends and family are stupid enough to question the lady's motives and start telling you things you don't want to hear. And yes, it *is* value for money if the woman has a sweet nature, is grateful for what she's being given and is willing to keep up her side of the bargain by hanging in there until you're so senile you don't recognize her anymore or dead, whichever comes first."

"You're talking about an old man. That's not the Artist's case. He's a young guy. It's different."

"Different, is it? Have you ever met the Artist?"

"No."

"Seen a photo then?"

"Well, yes, but—"

"But nothing. He's ugly as sin and, stating it kindly, intellectually challenged. What he's got going for him is the same thing that lots of old millionaires have going for *them*: fame and money. The only difference between him and them is they need their pills to get an erection."

"Don't you think you're being a bit cynical about this?"

"Cynical? My Young Innocent, you have no idea how society works, or what *real* money can buy, do you?"

"Let's get back to Cintia, okay?"

"Of course, dear boy, of course."

"Why do you think she's a bitch?"

"Two reasons. First, because I have personal knowledge of the woman. She used to be one of my clients. People say I struck her from my roster because she was late for an appointment. Not true. Between you and me, dear boy, that's one of the excuses I use when I tire of someone's company. Would you like a glass of sherry?"

"Thank you, no."

"But you won't mind if I have one, will you?"

Without waiting for a reply, Jardin balanced his cigarette holder across a large, jade ashtray and stood up. He went to a cherry wood cabinet and took out a bottle. "You're sure?"

"I'm sure."

Jardin selected a single glass, delicately cut and looking like it cost a bundle, and resumed his seat.

"Where were we?" he said, pouring the amber liquid.

"You tired of her company."

"Ah yes." He took a sip. "I did."

"Why?"

Jardin thought for a moment. "Gossip is one thing," he said. "I'm not averse to a little of it myself, but spewing venom is another. I never heard her say a good word about anyone. So I drew the obvious conclusion: she wasn't saying good words about me either."

"How about her future mother-in-law?"

"Juraci? I don't recall Cintia saying anything at all about Juraci. It would have been naïve to do so, and naïve is one thing Cintia is not. Everyone is well aware that the relationship between the Artist and his mother is a close one. If Cintia had expressed a negative opinion about her, there are *scads* of people who would have rushed off to make sure the Artist heard about it."

"How about the Artist's father? I don't recall hearing anything about him. Ever."

"You never will. Although I've been told there's a claimant every now and then."

"A claimant?"

"Juraci was . . . how shall I put this? Let's just say that, in her youth, she was quite profligate with her charms. She's never been quite sure who the Artist's father is. That's not what she gives out, but I assure you it's true. Now, however, now that her talented son has come to fame and fortune, many of the men who've passed through Juraci's life earnestly desire to be admitted back into it."

"How does she handle it?"

"Denies them, one and all; claims that the Artist's real father was a stonemason killed in a construction accident when his son was very young."

"And that's what most people believe?"

"That's what virtually everyone believes. *Fofocas* has investigated her story in some detail. They've been unable to disprove it."

Gonçalves's familiarity with *Fofocas* stemmed from the fact that it kept turning up in the bathrooms, or next to the beds, of many of the women he slept with. None of them ever admitted to purchasing it. One of their girlfriends, they'd say, must have left it behind, by mistake.

"How come you don't buy into the stonemason story?"

Jardin smiled. "Unlike you," he said, "Juraci Santos is fond of sherry. We've had a few tipples together and have, how shall I put this? Shared confidences."

"Tell me more."

"No, dear boy, I won't, not without a good deal more sherry. Do you like erotic sketches?"

"I beg your pardon?"

"Erotic sketches. Do you like them? I have a rather impressive collection."

"No. I can't say I'm much of a fan. You said you had two reasons for thinking Cintia a bitch. One of them was personal experience. And the other?"

"The opinion of the Artist's mother."

"Well, *that's* certainly relevant. Why don't you tell me about that?"

"Hmm," Jardin said. "There are limits even to *my* indiscretion, but I see no harm in telling you this much: Juraci Santos employed a private detective to check up on Cintia Tadesco's background. Unlike her son, Juraci is actually quite a perceptive woman, all too aware of the Artist's shortcomings. She never accepted that a bombshell like La Tadesco could possibly be interested in anything other than her son's money and fame. At the very least, she thought, Cintia must be cheating on him. *Mother's instinct*, she'd tell me."

"Who is this private detective she hired?"

"She told me, but I don't recall his name."

"Do you know if he discovered anything of note?"

"No."

Jardin picked up the sherry bottle.

"You mean you don't know?"

"Correct. I don't know. But, knowing Cintia, I wouldn't be in the least surprised if he did."

Jardin topped up his glass.

"Did Juraci tell her son she'd hired a private detective?"

Jardin took a sip of his sherry and breathed out a contented sigh.

"She didn't," he said. "She said the Artist would be furious if he found out."

"Unless, of course, the detective came up with something."

"True. And she was hopeful he would. At least, she was the last time I spoke to her."

"How long ago was that?"

"In the course of her last visit. Three weeks ago today. Which brings me back to *Fofocas*. Do you ever read it, by the way?"

"No. Do you?"

"Of course I do, dear boy. After all, my name is in it more often than not."

"What has *Fofocas* got to do with anything?"

"This: despite what you might think about the editorial content of the publication, they have some highly competent journalists there, always digging, digging and sifting through the dirt. Their readers like being exposed to a glittering world of which they can never hope to become a part, but they like the scandals of that world even more. The divorces, the love affairs, the drug problems, the health problems, the suicide attempts, those are the things that give impetus to circulation. It would dribble away to naught if they only printed snapshots of society parties, or interviews with air-headed show business people. Those are just the icing on the gossip cake. If there's something to find on Cintia, I daresay *Fofocas* will come up with it. The detective might not, but I assure you that *Fofocas* will—again, if there's anything to find. I told that to Juraci, told her she could have saved her money. But she said she couldn't wait. She wanted to nip the relationship in the bud, break it up before it got any more serious. The Artist was already talking about marrying the woman."

"Speaking of the ladies and gentlemen of the press, were you the one who tipped off Radio Mundo about the fact that the Artist's mother had gone missing?"

"My dear boy, why would I ever do anything like that?"

"Maybe because they give you free publicity from time to time, and you felt obligated to return the favor?"

Jardin smiled. "It must be fascinating to be a policeman,

always solving riddles. You have a talent for it, I can tell. I'll bet your superiors are proud of you."

"How about you answer my question?"

"And how about we adjourn to my place? I have a most excellent cook and a superb wine cellar. We could make an evening of it, just the two of us."

Chapter Nine

IT WAS GILDA'S NIGHT to cook. Garlic, sautéing in butter, perfumed the hallway between the elevator and their front door. In the kitchen, where Hector's fiancée was deftly wielding a chef's knife, colorful mounds of diced vegetables lined the counter.

The youngest of São Paulo's female assistant medical examiners blew a few strands of silky, black hair out of her eyes, offered a cheek to be kissed and kept on dicing.

"It's a curry," she said. "Killer hot. You're going to love it."

He came up behind her, put his arm around her waist and nuzzled her ear.

"This," he said, "is what I love. As far as your cooking is concerned. . . ."

"Finish that sentence," she said, waving the knife, "and you starve. Your uncle arrive?"

He released her, picked up the drink that was waiting for him and put it to his lips. It had become their daily ritual, a glass of wine in the kitchen.

"He did," Hector said, after taking a sip.

"Why didn't you bring him home for dinner?"

"He went to see the Artist."

Gilda rinsed her hands in the sink and dried them with a paper towel.

"Bastards," she said.

Hector didn't ask her who she was talking about. The most maligned people in the country that day were the ones who'd abducted Juraci Santos.

"I went out to her house and had a look around." He filled her in on his conversation with Lefkowitz and shared the tech's theories.

"He's good, isn't he, that Lefkowitz?" she said when he was done.

"Damned good," he said.

"He talked me into extracting the bullets before I came home."

"So that was *his* idea? I thought you offered."

"I probably would have left it until tomorrow, if he hadn't asked. They were twenty-twos. We sent them to Brasilia." She picked up her glass and took a sip of wine. "I heard the sisters were found holding hands."

"That's right."

"And I heard the bastards killed a little dog."

"They did."

She glanced at the clock on the wall.

"What kept you?"

"A meeting. My uncle, Arnaldo, Babyface and Mara."

"The usual suspects. Has she managed to get her hooks into him yet?"

"Mara? Into Babyface? She must be ten years older than he is."

"Not Babyface, silly. Your uncle."

"What are you talking about?"

Gilda added a *masala* to the pan. The aroma of the spices began to overpower the smell of garlic.

"Come on, darling," she said, "you know what I'm talking about."

"I certainly do not."

"You don't know that Mara Carta is sweet on your uncle?"

"What? No!"

"She is. Every woman in your office knows it. Even *I* know

it, and I don't work in your office."

"So how come I don't know it?"

"Because you're a male and dense."

"My uncle would never—"

"I didn't say he would. I'm just saying Mara is sweet on him."

"He loves my Aunt Irene, and she loves him."

"I don't doubt it. But I don't doubt Mara loves him as well. You come right down to it, he's pretty lovable. And she's divorced."

"With two kids."

"And your uncle has *no* kids, and he loves kids."

Gilda added the diced vegetables to the pan. Hector drained his wine, got up and poured himself another glass.

"Take it easy with that," she said.

"You want more?"

"With dinner."

"Beer goes better with curry."

"The hell it does. Ask any Indian."

"Indians aren't supposed to drink."

"That depends on the Indian. They're not all Hindus and Muslims, and they're not all devout."

He sat down again, took another sip.

"How long," he said, "do you think this has been going on?"

"Indians drinking wine?"

"Cut it out, Gilda."

"Mara being sweet on Mario? I have no idea."

"When did you first notice?"

"At last year's Christmas party. Mara had a few too many. She made it obvious."

"Not to me."

"No, and I don't think it was obvious to your uncle either. He's kind of dense that way."

"Dense? Mario Silva is the sharpest criminal investigator

in this country."

"Uh huh. But Mara isn't a criminal. Tell me this: today, during your meeting, did she sit next to him at the table?"

"Well, yes, but—"

"Did she touch him?"

"Touch him how?"

She shrugged. "I don't know. On his arm, maybe? Leaned up against him perhaps?"

"She might have."

"Might have, huh? More than once?"

"Gilda, this is silly. That's the way Mara is. She's kind of touchy-feely. It doesn't really mean anything."

"Uh huh. When was the last time she touched *you*?"

Hector thought about it for a moment.

"I don't think she ever has," he said.

"Did she hover over him, serve him coffee?"

"She . . . gave him a hot towel to clean his face when he got in from the airport, and she had a sandwich waiting."

"I rest my case."

"Case? There is no case! Mara is sadly mistaken if she thinks she can get anywhere with my uncle. He's not interested in any woman except his wife."

She grinned. "That's part of his appeal. He's a challenge."

"Gilda, this is no laughing matter. You know the state Irene is in. She's fragile."

"I know the state she's in. I know she's fragile. I also know she drinks herself insensible every night. I know she's not capable of having a conversation with anyone after six o'clock in the evening, and that your uncle is never home before six."

"She never got over their son's death. She can't help herself. You know that."

"Hector, with all due respect to your aunt, her son died

twenty years ago."

"So?"

"So maybe Mara thinks Mario has put up with Irene's dipsomania long enough, that the mourning should come to an end, that your uncle deserves a better life from here on in. Maybe she thinks she can give it to him."

"That's for him to decide, not her."

"Do you think they even make love anymore? Mario and Irene?"

"I have no idea, and I'd never ask."

"Maybe you should tell him Mara is interested, draw his attention to it, see how he reacts."

"No way," Hector said, "I know exactly how he'd react. He'd reject the idea out of hand."

"But if you—"

"No, Gilda. No and no. There is no way I'm going to get involved in this."

"And there, ladies and gentlemen, is another outstanding example of the difference between men and women. Get some plates, Hector, and set the table."

Chapter Ten

"FINALLY," SILVA SAID. "HERE we go at last. Turn that windbag off."

"Gladly," Arnaldo said.

It was nine AM, and for the last five minutes, they'd been sitting in their stationary automobile, suffering the insufferable: a radio interview with Gonzalo Bufa, the Argentinean coach. Bufa had been giving a detailed analysis of why he thought the Brazilian team was overrated.

"The man's full of crap," Arnaldo said. "We shoulda stuck with the traffic report."

"Damned traffic reports are useless," Silva said.

"So's Bufa, thank God."

After an interval of almost fifteen minutes, the beer truck in front of them had started rolling again. All around them, people were turning on the motors they'd shut off when traffic on the *marginal*, the belt road around the city, had come to a standstill. From overhead, came the constant drone of helicopters, the favored form of transport for the city's wealthy elite, and the only reliable way to get anywhere in São Paulo on a weekday morning between seven and ten.

"How about this?" Arnaldo said. "How about Juraci went to Cintia and hit her with a *Break up with my son or else?* And then—"

"Cintia, intent on making her fortune out of the Artist despite his mother's objection, kills Juraci and makes it look like a kidnapping? From gold digging to murder in one easy step? No, Arnaldo, I don't think so."

"I don't either, not really, but I still wouldn't be surprised if Cintia was involved in one way or another. Maybe for a chunk of the five million. Don't forget, she had access to a key, and up to now, we don't know of anyone else who did. How about we go back and lean on her a little?"

"Maybe later. Let's do some more digging first."

Silva glanced at the clock on the dashboard. "Damn! I'd better call Pedro and tell him we'll be late."

Before he could, his cell phone burst into life. The ID came up as *private*. Silva, averse to the practice, took the call with some reluctance.

"Silva."

"Chief Inspector, it's me, Tico."

Silva's objections vanished. Tico, of course, had to confine himself to telephones free of caller IDs. If he didn't, his contact numbers would soon become common knowledge—and he'd be deluged by calls from fans.

"Good morning, Senhor Santos."

"Tico."

"What can I do for you, Tico?"

"You know those keys you asked about?"

"Yes?"

"Cintia found them."

"Where?"

"In a drawer, in the bedroom."

"Are you at home?"

"Yeah. I don't like to go out. There's a gang of reporters at the front door. More, even, than last night."

"We'll need those keys, Tico. I'll send someone over to pick them up."

"Okay."

"One thing puzzles me. You've been in training with the team in Curitiba, right?"

"Right."

"But your mother only got those keys last Thursday, and you said she delivered them to you personally."

"She did. When I came for the party."

"Party? You broke training for a party?"

There was a long pause. When Tico finally spoke, he sounded sheepish.

"Cintia got this big perfume contract. She wanted to celebrate, said it wouldn't be the same without me, so I went to talk to Dumbo about it."

"And he agreed."

"No. He . . ."

"He what?"

"He got mad. He said some things about Cintia that I didn't like."

"And you told Cintia?"

Silence.

"Tico?"

"Yeah. I told her."

"And she convinced you to come to São Paulo, despite Dumbo's objections?"

"It wasn't like she had to convince me. I wanted to come."

"When was the party?"

"Saturday night. It was no big deal. I didn't drink a drop of alcohol, and I was in São Paulo for less than forty-eight hours. I came up on Saturday morning and went back to Curitiba on Sunday morning. And the team doesn't practice on Saturday afternoons or Sunday mornings."

"Why didn't you tell us about coming to São Paulo when last we spoke?"

"I didn't think it was important."

"Listen to me, Tico. At this stage, there's no way of knowing what's important and what isn't. You have to tell me everything, you understand?"

"I understand. I did tell you everything . . . except for that."

"I want you to think long and hard about how those keys got from your pocket to a drawer in the bedroom."

"I already did. I thought about it, and I got no idea."

"Are you going to be there tomorrow?"

"I'm not going anywhere until you get me my mother back."

"Good. Agent Nunes and I will be paying you another visit. I'll call before we come."

After Silva hung up, he called Mara and asked her to send one of her people to pick up the keys.

"Is Cintia Tadesco with him?" Mara asked.

"Probably. She was last night. Why?"

"I'll go myself. I want to see her skin."

"Her skin?"

"I can't believe anybody has skin that perfect. I think all her photos must be retouched. Is she nice?"

"No," Silva said.

* * *

ONCE AGAIN, Hector's trip to Granja Viana was against the flow of traffic. Forty minutes was all it took from his home in Pacaembu to the strip mall where Samuel Arns had his shop.

Arns's place of business was tiny, dwarfed by a pharmacy on the left and a veterinary clinic on the right. Gold letters on the glass window informed passers-by that he dealt in hardware and alarm systems as well as keys and locks.

When Hector entered, a two-tone chime heralded his arrival.

"Samuel Arns?"

"Mmmm," the man behind the counter said. Hector took it to be an acknowldgment, but the locksmith, concentrating on his work, didn't look up. He was putting the finishing touches on a key for an elderly gentleman wearing jeans and a T-shirt.

The bright brass of the blank was almost invisible between fingers thick as dinner candles, but Arns's dexterity belied his size. The file removing burrs from the metal moved back and forth, like a bow in the hand of a virtuoso.

The chime sounded again. A woman with a haughty expression and too much makeup came in. She was carrying a miniature dachshund in her arms.

Hector smiled at the woman. She didn't smile back. He looked at the dachshund. The dachshund snarled. Hector tried to remember something he'd once heard about dogs resembling their owners, but it escaped him.

Arns put the original, and the key he'd been making, into a small envelope.

The elderly gentleman laboriously counted out the exact change.

The woman started tapping her foot.

"Who's next?" Arns said when the elderly gentleman left.

"I'm in a hurry," the woman said inserting herself between Hector and the counter.

"That may well be, Senhora," Arns said, "but are you next?"

Hector liked him for that. But he'd just as soon not have anyone else in the shop while he was questioning the locksmith.

"Attend to the Senhora first," he said. "I'll wait."

The woman didn't thank him, didn't even look at him, simply slapped down a key on the glass counter.

Arns picked it up. "How many?" he said.

"One."

While Arns cut the key, the woman looked at the ceiling, the floor, and all around the little shop. Everywhere except at Arns and Hector. The dachshund, however, followed the locksmith's every move with its bulbous eyes.

When Arns was done, he slipped both keys into one of the little envelopes and put the envelope down on the counter. The woman extended a hand holding a banknote.

"On the counter, Senhora," Arns said. "Remember last time?"

She snorted, as if he'd said something offensive, and slapped down the bill. He counted out her change and put it next to the envelope. She swept up both and made her exit, nose in the air.

On her way out, she passed another woman, coming in.

"You recognize her?" Arns said when the door closed again.

"Who?" Hector said.

"The woman who just left."

"No," Hector said.

"That was Maria Luchesi," the newcomer said.

Arns nodded. "The first soprano of the São Paulo Opera Company. She thought you did. Recognize her, I mean."

"She thinks everyone does," the woman added.

"The dog's name is Gunther," the locksmith said. "It's a good thing you didn't try to pet him."

"That's why you asked her to put the money on the counter?"

"That's why. He almost got me the last time."

"He's a nasty little thing," the woman said.

Arns went to the register, rang up the diva's purchase and put her money in the cash drawer. Then he turned back to Hector.

"What can I do for you?"

"Why don't you attend to this lady first?"

The newcomer wore a white coat. It made her look like a doctor, or maybe a lab technician. She smelled of berries and spice.

"I'm not a customer," she said. "I just dropped by for a chat with Samuel. You go ahead."

Hector would have preferred to question Arns on his own, but he could hardly tell her to leave. He bit the bullet by showing his badge.

When she saw the flash of gold metal, the woman took in a sharp breath. Cops sometimes had that effect on people, particularly on people who enjoyed a juicy bit of gossip.

One of those, Hector thought—and turned his back in an attempt to exclude her from the conversation.

"Delegado Costa, Federal Police. I'm assuming you're Samuel Arns?"

The locksmith looked over Hector's shoulder and exchanged a quick glance with the woman. Hector could practically feel her eyes burning into his back.

"I am," Arns said. "What do the Federal Police want with me?"

"It's our understanding you recently changed some locks for Senhora Juraci Santos. Is that right?"

"I did, Delegado. I do it all the time. She's a regular customer, changes locks every time she changes servants."

"And that's often?"

"Fortunately for me, it is."

"This particular job was on Thursday of last week."

"I remember."

"How many sets of keys did you make?"

"Four. It's always four."

"This time as well?"

"This time, every time."

"You sound very sure."

"I am. Senhora Santos always buys the best. The locks on all her external doors are Medecos. They're imported, virtually pickproof, but they're expensive, and I don't sell a lot of them. They come with two keys. If you want to make extras, you need special blanks. I stock them just for her."

"Suppose someone wanted to make another copy of one of those keys. Suppose you weren't here, and they needed the copy in a hurry. How could they go about it?"

"They'd go into town."

"Where in town?"

"Their best bet would be one of the big locksmiths on Avenida São João. Those guys keep blanks for every conceivable type of lock, Medecos included. Why are you asking?"

"We think the kidnappers used a key to get into Senhora Santos's house."

"But . . ." It was the woman again, speaking from behind Hector's back.

Hector turned to face her. "But what?"

"I read in the paper they'd smashed the door to her house."

"They did."

"Then why did you want to know how many keys Samuel made?"

"Yeah," Samuel said. "Why? You think maybe they got in some other way? You think they used a key?"

"Maybe."

The locksmith shook his head. "Sounds crazy to me. If that's what they did, why would they go to the trouble of smashing the door?"

"He knows something," the woman said, pointing at Hector. "Something that wasn't in the papers. Is that right, Delegado?"

"It's just a theory we're working on."

"But what would make you think—"

"Please, Senhora. With all due respect, I'm not here to answer your questions. I'm here to ask them of this gentleman."

She reddened. "Yes, yes, of course," she said. "Sorry."

Hector turned back to the locksmith. "Any idea why she always asked for four sets of keys?"

"One for her, one for the servants, one for her son and one extra."

"And anyone who had one of those keys could have had it duplicated?"

"Yes, they could. There are certain keys that you *can't* duplicate, and other ones you aren't *supposed* to duplicate, but Medecos don't fall into either category. The only problem in duplicating a Medeco is to get your hands on a Medeco blank."

Hector thought about it. Lefkowitz had found three sets of keys in Juraci's house. One had been in her office. That must have been the extra set. One was in the purse of one of the maids. That would be the servants' set. One was in Juraci's purse. Her set. That left the set that had been made for her son. He sure as hell wouldn't kidnap his mother. But who was to say that someone hadn't used Tico's set? Or copied it?

Perhaps a line of inquiry into Madeco blanks might lead to something. If they couldn't come up with anything else, they could always try that.

"Who do you get the blanks from?" he said.

"The importer."

"There's only one?"

"Only one. That's how they manage to keep the prices as high as they do."

"Can you give me the name and address of those people?"

"Sure."

Samuel Arns went into the back. The woman, visibly chastised, didn't say a word while he was gone. A minute or so later the locksmith came back with a piece of paper. He held it out to Hector.

"It's a reliable firm," he said. "One of the oldest."

Hector took the paper and glanced at it. Arns had printed out an address and telephone number in a clear, legible hand. The importer was in São Paulo. That, at least, was a break. Hector couldn't think of anything else to ask the locksmith, so he bid him and the red-faced woman a good day, went out to his car and called-in a report to his uncle.

Chapter Eleven

PEDRO CATALDO LOOKED TO be five kilograms heavier than the last time they'd seen him, maybe more. The extra weight was straining the buttons on his shirt.

"Jesus, Pedro," Arnaldo said, eyeing his gut, "you—"

"—need an exercise bicycle. Yeah, I know. How are you guys?"

"More important," Silva said, "How are you? You deserve a medal for putting yourself through all this."

"Forget the medal. I'd settle for a day on the beach, or even a walk in the park. Maybe it's some kind of poetic justice. I've sent away a lot of people in my time. Now, I'm getting a taste of my own medicine."

"Poetic justice, my ass," Arnaldo said. "They deserved it. You don't."

Cataldo flashed him a sad smile. "There's that," he said. "Coffee?"

"No sugar," Silva said.

"I remember. I remember yours, too, Arnaldo. Lots of sugar, lots of milk, right?"

"Right."

Cataldo, busying himself with the cups, pointed with his chin.

"You guys take those chairs. I'll sit on the bed."

Pedro Cataldo was forty-two years old, a federal judge condemned to death by the people he was trying to bring to justice. In over a year, he'd left the office—where he worked, slept and ate—only twice, both times because it was strictly necessary, both times wearing a bulletproof vest, and both times riding in an armored car accompanied by armed guards.

In the course of the previous eighteen months, he'd condemned 114 people to a total of 919 years and six months of prison. He had, in addition, confiscated twelve *fazendas* totaling 12,832 hectares, three mansions, one valued at almost six million Reais, three apartments, three houses, dozens of vehicles and three aircraft, all bought with money generated by organized crime.

To protect his wife and three daughters, Cataldo had moved them to a secret location. His food was prepared under strict controls. The head of his seven-man security detail was Nirvaldo Evora, hand-picked by Silva, incorruptible, and currently standing on the other side of a steel door only Cataldo could open.

The price on Pedro's head was a million US dollars, up from three-quarters of a million three months ago and half a million six months before that. The people who wanted him dead kept upping the ante, trying to make killing him more attractive.

"How the hell do you stand it?" Silva asked after taking a sip.

"You don't like my coffee?"

"You know what I'm talking about."

Cataldo abandoned his attempt at humor.

"Forcing me to live like this," he said, "is backfiring on the bastards. I've got nothing to do but work, so I work day and night. I get up early, I go to bed late, and I'm bringing them down like never before. It's driving them nuts."

"So I've heard," Silva said, "but it must be hard."

"It's hard," Cataldo admitted, "but it's my choice. Somebody's got to do it. I only wish more of my colleagues thought the way I do."

"As do we, Pedro, as do we."

"What brings you? I don't suppose it's purely social."

"I need information."

"You came to the right place. These days, I got information coming out of my ears."

Silva set down his cup. "So I've heard. I've also heard that you're not sharing much of it."

"With good reason. Last time I did, some stupid bastard said the wrong thing to the wrong people. The source got whacked, and all my other sources dried up. It took me months to get back to square one."

"I heard that, too."

"But I make exceptions. I'll make an exception for you, because I know you can keep your mouth shut." He pointed to the pot. "More coffee?"

Silva shook his head. "No, thanks."

"What, specifically, do you want to know?"

"I'd like you to speculate on who might have abducted Juraci Santos. Have you heard any rumors? Anything at all?"

"Ah, you're handling that one, are you? Well, look, I don't want to bitch and moan, but I will tell you this: one of the few pleasures I have in here is watching football on television. I can't tell you how much I was looking forward to the Cup, looking forward to seeing us kick Argentinean ass. And then some *filhos da puta* go out and kidnap the Artist's mother. I hope to hell the day will come when they'll appear before me. I'll put the bastards away for the rest of their lives."

"Amen, Pedro. But we've got to catch them first."

"I'll put the word out, see what I can pick up. I'll call you if I hear anything. Keep me posted on your progress, okay?"

"Gladly. Nothing for us at the moment?"

Cataldo rubbed his chin.

"Maybe one thing worth following up," he said. "What do you know about Jordan Talafero?"

Silva shrugged. "Not much. He owns the Spartans. He just sold the Artist to *Real Madrid* for a bundle of money. He's a big shot in the administration of some samba school. That's about it."

"That's almost enough. You touched on the three critical issues, but you didn't link them. So let me do it for you. First of all, Talafero doesn't *own* the Spartans. He's the president of the club, which means he makes most of the business decisions, but he's only a minor stockholder."

"So?" Arnaldo said.

Cataldo looked at him. "So he isn't as rich as a lot of people think he is."

"Okay," Silva said, "go on."

"Second, yes, he did sell the Artist to the Spaniards, which is pissing a lot of people off, but the question nobody seems to be asking is this: why did he choose to do it now? The Artist has been playing with the Spartans since the beginning of his career. Talafero could have sold him two years ago, even three years ago, for the same price he sold him for last week. But he didn't. He sold him *now*."

"And your conclusion is?"

Cataldo drained his cup and set it aside before he replied.

"He needs money. And he needs money because of that samba school. It's called Silver Carnations, and it's Talafero's baby, his passion. They've won first prize for the last three years running, and it's all because of Talafero."

"Or, rather, because of Talafero's money."

"Correct. You can't make money with a samba school, you can only spend it, but in glory and fame they pay off, big time. Talafero never got the glory and fame out of the Spartans. His players did, but not him. Lots of people in this town don't even know who he is. But, with Silver Carnations, it's different. He's the man. He made them, and if he takes his money away, it will break them. That appeals to him as no football team ever did. He has an ego the size of Spartan stadium."

"Spell it out, Pedro. Where are you going with this?"

Cataldo responded with a question of his own: "Until the day before yesterday, what were the odds of Argentina beating us?"

"Virtually nil."

"Correct. So, if you laid down a bet for the Argentineans to win, and took the odds against that on the day before yesterday, and Argentina *did* win, you—"

"—would stand to earn a considerable amount of money."

"Right again. And who, of all people, would best know what might unbalance the Artist and skew the results?"

"Jordan Talafero."

"I rest my case."

Silva stood up.

"Leaving so soon?" Cataldo said.

"We'll be back. Right now I have an overwhelming desire to have a chat with Jordan Talafero."

Chapter Twelve

WHEN SILVA'S GRANDFATHER WAS a lad and football was a game played almost exclusively by the English, the Tietê River was a pellucid stream on the outskirts of São Paulo. As a child, Silva had heard stories from the old man about transparent waters where people went to fish and boat and bathe.

On one stretch, so straight it appeared to be a canal dug by the hand of man, a rowing club had sprung up. At the time, no man could consider himself educated unless he was steeped in Greek and Roman lore, and the founders of the club were all so steeped.

They'd chosen to call their organization the Spartan Rowing Club. In those days, to be a Spartan meant simply to be a great warrior. The word hadn't yet taken on the more recent connotations of frugality and austerity.

The battles those warriors fought were on the lazy current of the river, and they consisted of racing each other in sculls of one, two, or four men.

Time brought radical change. By the last years of the twentieth century, and on into today, no one would think of entering the water, boat or no boat. The Tietê had become little more than an open sewer, devoid of fish and poisonous to man.

As the quality of the water degenerated, the rowing club evolved. Females were admitted, and the members began to take up other sports. The boats disappeared, replaced by tennis courts, swimming pools, athletic fields and a clubhouse, in which there was a ballroom and a restaurant.

Most important of all, in the northernmost corner of the complex was the football stadium, capable of seating 78,420 people and home to the CFS, the *Clube de Futebol Espartense*, the Spartan Football Club, nine times national champions.

Twenty-five city blocks had been demolished to construct the building and the parking lot that surrounded it. Packed to capacity on game days, the lot was largely empty when Silva and Arnaldo drove in. The two federal cops were able to find a spot not fifty meters from the main entrance.

They passed through portals hung with the club's flags (red Grecian helmets on a white field) and approached a security checkpoint. Seated there, in a uniform as grey as his hair, an old man was reading a newspaper. He looked up when Arnaldo leaned on the counter.

"Senhores?" he said.

"Jordan Talafero," Silva said. "We want to see him."

* * *

DESPITE THEIR surprise visit, Talafero didn't keep them waiting. Within five minutes of their arrival, the two cops were in comfortable chairs, sipping coffee.

Talafero sat with his elbows propped-up on a desk that appeared to have been made out of a solid plank of jacaranda. A picture window in the wall behind him overlooked the playing field. The other salient feature of Talafero's office was his clocks.

They were of all sizes and types. There were clocks sheathed in plastic, in wood, in different kinds of metal, in domes of glass. There were clocks on the walls, clocks on the desk, clocks on the side tables, clocks on the bookcase.

"Little hobby of mine," Talafero said in a high, squeaky voice ill-suited to a man of his considerable height and bulk. "Good thing you guys arrived just before the hour."

"How so?" Silva asked.

Talafero held up a hand. "Wait for it," he said.

Just then, one of the clocks started to chime. It was still chiming when another clock kicked in. In seconds, the office was filled with the sound of clocks tolling the hour. Talafero sat listening with a smile on his face.

"That first one was a little bit off," he said when the ring of the last chime had died away. "I gotta adjust it."

"Quite a show," Silva said.

"That was nothing," Talafero said. "You want to hear them pull out all the stops, stick around until noon."

Silva studied a model standing on his side of the desk. Inside a crystal case, three spheres, supported by a central axis, rocked back and forth. They were fashioned of the same gilded metal used for the hands.

"How many have you got?" he said.

"Seventy-four. When I got my sixtieth, my wife made me bring them into the office, said they were driving her nuts."

"Some look quite old."

"Some are. See that one over there? That's from 1873. The date of manufacture is inside, etched into the frame."

"I'm impressed."

"I don't just collect them, I repair them. I even build them, make 'em for Christmas presents. See this one? It's one of mine."

Talafero was in his mid-forties and running to fat. A Spartan T-shirt was tightly stretched over his bulging belly. It wasn't particularly warm in the room, but his underarms were soaked with sweat. So was his forehead. He seemed to be agitated about something.

"Enough about clocks," he said. "We got more important things to talk about. You're here about the Artist's mother, right?"

Silva raised an eyebrow. "What makes you think so?"

"Stands to reason. Who else would you talk to first? Who's closer to the Artist? Answer me that."

"Frankly, Senhor Talafero—"

"Nobody. Nobody's closer. I've known him since he was twelve. I know his mother. Hell, I even know that girlfriend of his, although sometimes I wish I didn't. You guys are federal, right?"

"Right."

"Good. Because, if you were from the Civil Police, I wouldn't talk to you. He's got all of those guys on his payroll."

"Who?"

"The man who did it. Captain Miranda."

"Miranda, the *bicheiro?*"

By bicheiro, Silva meant a mobster, a banker for the *jogo do bicho*—the animal game. Brazil's illegal lottery was an import, with minor variations, of a similar form of illicit gambling run by organized crime interests in the United States. There, it was referred to as the "numbers racket."

"Him," Talafero said. "He's the one. He snatched Tico's mother. I'm sure of it."

"You may be sure of it, Senhor Talafero, but can you prove it?"

"No, I can't."

"So why do you think he did?"

"I don't *think* he did, Chief Inspector, I *know* he did. He takes the whole carnival thing very seriously. He—"

"Wait," Silva said. "Back up. What's carnival got to do with it?"

"It's got *everything* to do with it. He's not just a bicheiro, he's the patron of Green Mangos."

"The samba school?"

"Of course, the samba school. You know anything else called Green Mangos? We've beaten the bastards three years running. Miranda doesn't want it to happen again."

Silva scratched his head. "Miranda wants his school to win the competition, so he decides to kidnap the Artist's mother? I don't get the connection."

"Maybe I'm getting a little ahead of myself," Talafero said, mopping his brow. "Let me lay it out in terms that even your muscle man here will understand."

"Hey," Arnaldo said.

Talafero ignored him—as he'd been doing since the beginning of the conversation. "You heard about my deal with Real Madrid?"

"I heard about it," Silva said with distaste.

"You got no call to be looking at me like that," Talafero said. "It's just business."

Business that had become front-page news, business that had caused a great deal of discontent among Brazilian sports fans. The Artist's pending transfer to the Spanish club, Real Madrid, was immensely unpopular.

"People got no right to be so pissed off," Talafero said defensively. "It's not like it's going to fuck up our chances of winning the Cup."

It didn't. In the World Cup, players always represented their home countries. The Artist would play for Brazil no matter who owned his contract.

"Yeah," Arnaldo said, "but from here on in we only get to watch him on television."

"Most people watch him on television now."

"That's because he's playing here, for the Spartans. How many people really care what he does in Spain?"

"How many? Forty million Spaniards, that's how many. Listen, you guys aren't here to question my business decisions. You're here because it's your job to get the Artist's mother back."

"Thanks for reminding us," Arnaldo said. "We almost forgot."

Talafero ignored the sarcasm. "Let's not get off on a tangent."

"You were talking about—"

"I know what I was talking about. Here's the thing: I haven't got Real Madrid's signature on the dotted line. They can still back out."

"Why should they?" Silva said.

Talafero threw up his arms, revealing sweat-stained armpits. "Give me a break! Isn't it obvious? When the Artist finds out his mother is dead—"

"What makes you think she's dead?"

"That's the way Miranda works. That bastard kills people, and when the Artist finds out he's done it to his mother, he'll go all to pieces. Believe me, I know. I know how Tico is, and I know how he thinks about her. There's no way he's going to get over it in time."

"*If* she's dead," Silva said, "I'd have to agree with you. We have less than two weeks before—"

Talafero, impatient, cut him off in mid-sentence.

"You think I'm talking about the Cup?"

"Aren't you?"

"Hell, no. I'm talking about the option with Real Madrid. It's only got twenty-seven days to run. If they don't sign before then, the deal is off."

"But not for long," Silva said. "There's only one Artist. He may be distraught right now, but sooner or later, whatever the outcome, he'll get over it. Then the scramble will start all over again. Now that the other European teams know you're willing to sell, you might even get a bidding war going."

"You don't have to tell me my business. I know all that. Thing is, I don't need the money in three or four months. I need it *now*. I need it for Carnival."

"Carnival? Carnival is eight months away."

"You got any idea how long it takes to put together a first class *desfile*? Eight months is cutting it short."

"Let me make sure I've got this straight. You think Miranda snatched the Artist's mother so he can ransom her for five million dollars, so he can invest it in his samba school, so he can win next year's competition? With all due respect, Senhor Talafero, nobody takes Carnival that seriously."

"Miranda does. He hates Silver Carnations, and he hates me. And he's not doing it for the five million. By snatching the Artist's mother, he queers the deal with Real Madrid and makes sure I don't have the money to invest in costumes, or floats, or dress rehearsals. Meanwhile, the prick already has a business that nets him hundreds of thousands every month. He doesn't need the ransom money. That's just gilt on his fucking lily."

"So, according to you, the kidnapping of the Artist's mother is an ego thing? It's all about who can put on the best show?"

"What the fuck is wrong with that? The public wins, right? You think they go to the Sambadrome to see poverty? You know who likes poverty? The fucking intellectuals and bleeding-heart liberals, that's who! Them with all their bullshit about the integrity of the common man, the noble worker, all that crap. If that's what you think, Chief Inspector, I got news for you. What the common man wants is luxury. That's what they go to the Sambadrome to see, the kilometers of skirts wrapped around the *Bahianas*, the sequins on the bikinis of the *destaques*, the floats as big as a ten-story building. They want to see luxury. And luxury costs money."

"So by snatching the Artist's mother—"

"Miranda fucks up my deal, prevents me from getting my hands on the money we need, and Green Mangos wins. To top it all off, he pockets five million dollars. It's that simple."

Chapter Thirteen

THE RUA AUGUSTA WAS once a fashionable place to shop. But that was once. In recent years, it had become a strip of potholed asphalt and broken sidewalks lined with down-market snack bars, second-class boutiques, and third-run cinemas.

Caio Prado's office was two flights up, above a store that sold cheap Chinese knickknacks. The hand-painted sign in the flyblown display window read, *Sale! Everything less than two Reais.*

The sale must have been going on for a long time, because the letters were faded, and the paper was curling at the edges.

Prado's receptionist looked to be in her late teens and, like most females of any age, seemed happy to find Gonçalves standing in front of her. Her smile revealed braces.

"Help you?"

"Here to see the boss." Gonçalves flashed his badge. "Agent Gonçalves."

She fluttered eyelashes heavy with mascara. "You have a first name?"

"Haraldo."

The smile got wider. "I'm Ana."

"*Prazer*, Ana. As much as I'm enjoying our little tête-à-tête, I'm in a bit of a hurry."

"Okay," she said, reaching for her telephone, "keep your shirt on. Or maybe not."

Less than a minute later, Gonçalves found himself being led into the presence of an elderly gentleman in a faded blue suit. Prado was thin, almost frail, had an ingratiating smile and looked rather like everyone's favorite uncle. He offered coffee. Gonçalves accepted, and kept his eyes on Ana's undulating derrière as she left to fetch it.

"How old is she?" he asked when she was gone.

"Eighteen, going on thirty-five," Prado said, "and before you get any ideas, she's my niece."

"Ah," Gonçalves said. "Seems like a sweet girl."

"Seems that way to a lot of people," Prado said. "It's an illusion. But mostly those people are a lot younger than you are, which is the way my sister and brother-in-law prefer it."

"How old do you think I am?"

Prado looked at him speculatively. "Twenty-two?"

"Thirty-four."

"Really? You don't look it."

Gonçalves sighed. "I know," he said.

Ana returned with two cups on a tray and stood there, fluttering her eyelashes until Prado told her to leave.

At which point Gonçalves got down to business: "It's my understanding you undertook some inquiries on behalf of Juraci Santos."

Prado stroked his chin. Gonçalves was beginning to think he didn't intend to answer at all. But then he said, "Did you read the brass plaque next to the front door?"

"*Caio Prado. Confidential Inquiries.* That one?"

"That one. *Confidential*, Agent Gonçalves, is the operative word. My clients prize discretion."

"In this case, Senhor Prado, I think your client would value release from captivity over discretion."

"There's nothing I could tell you that would lead to her release."

"We already know you were investigating Cintia Tadesco, and we know you were doing it on behalf of Juraci Santos. What else is there to know?"

"Very little. Senhora Santos largely wasted her money. And you, Agent Gonçalves, are wasting your time."

"I'd like to be the judge of that."

"I'm sure you would. But no one wants a private investigator who spreads their business all over town. It's not your welfare I'm considering, it's mine."

"Talking to the Federal Police can hardly be characterized as spreading it all over town. Look, Senhor Prado, your client is in trouble. Do we agree on that?"

Prado nodded. "Of course."

"Then it should be clear you can best serve her interest by telling me what you know."

"Her interest, perhaps, but not mine. If it got out that I—"

"It's not going to get out," Gonçalves said.

"Isn't it?"

"No. We're quite accustomed to dealing with confidential sources. You can count on me not to go bruiting your name about."

"Can I?"

Gonçalves's patience was wearing thin. He threw aside the carrot and picked up the stick.

"Listen to me, Senhor Prado. Let me make something clear. We, and by *we* I mean the Federal Police, have got everybody in the goddamned hierarchy right up to the President of the Republic on our backs. I'm not asking you anymore, I'm telling you: you're going to brief me on everything you know, and you're going to do it right now."

Prado shook his head. "What I know is of no relevance, no relevance whatsoever, to your case."

"You're not *listening*. Now, we can do this the easy way, or the hard way. You decide."

Prado was probably an ex cop, certainly knew how the system worked. He was going to have to give Gonçalves something, but he made a last attempt to give him as little as possible.

"Here it is in a nutshell: Juraci Santos neither liked nor trusted her prospective daughter-in-law. She asked me to investigate her background. I found nothing incriminating. That's it."

"That's nowhere near enough. I want more than the nutshell, I want the nut. Let's start at the beginning. How did you acquire Juraci as a client?"

Prado gave a deep sigh—and crumbled.

"The Artist's mother was recommended to me by one of her friends, a lady who'd employed me in a divorce action. Juraci called me and asked me to drop by her home to discuss a matter she described as being highly confidential. I told her I'd consult in my office for free, but a house call was something I'd have to charge for. She told me money was of no import. It was a statement, I confess, that aroused my immediate interest. Clients like that don't come along often."

"What was her brief? Exactly."

"To discover whether the Tadesco woman was doing, or had done, something that might damage the Artist in any way. A romantic liaison with someone other than Tico, for example, or if there was something in Cintia's past that might engender a scandal."

"Do you think Juraci was simply being cautious, or did she give you the impression she'd be pleased if you could come up with something negative?"

"The latter. It was evident from the way she spoke about Senhorita Tadesco that she'd taken a dislike to her."

"So her true objective was to find some way to encourage the Artist to break off his engagement?"

"I believe that to be the case, yes."

"And your investigations revealed . . . what?"

"I told you. Nothing. Nothing she could use."

Gonçalves took note of the qualification and pounced.

"But there *was* something."

Prado paused to consider his words.

"I'll say this much, Agent Gonçalves: I wouldn't want *my* son to contemplate a marriage with the likes of Cintia Tadesco."

"Explain."

"I'm about to. I do a good deal of my work with people in show business. In the course of time, I've learned a lot about it."

"So?"

"Do you remember Marco Franco?"

"Franco, the actor?"

"Him."

"He was pretty big once. Whatever happened to him?"

"Cintia Tadesco happened to him. Marco had an agent by the name of Leo Marques. Marques is every performer's dream. He's not only a shark when it comes to negotiations; he's also adept at making stars."

"The public does that."

"I disagree." Prado had turned a corner from laconic into loquacious. "The public most definitely does *not* do that. Manipulators like Marques do that. There's no truth to the expression *a star is born*. Stars are made, not born. Stars are constructed article by article, sound bite by sound bite. The more an actor is exposed to the public, the more famous he or she becomes, the more press coverage they get. It's a snowball effect, but somebody has to get the snowball rolling. That's what people like Marques do, they get the snowball rolling. Am I boring you?"

"Not in the least. Keep talking."

"Essentially, actors and sports stars are little more than entertainers, but many of them, deluded by the adulation of the masses, become convinced they're much more. They begin to believe their opinions have validity in realms that go beyond their area of expertise, that they're authorities on government, culture and art, and that they're qualified to give advice on everything from child-rearing to where you spend your vacation. The public, by and large stupid, and the press, who earn their daily bread by pandering to the public, lap up their advice like dogs lap up vomit."

"That's pretty distasteful, Senhor Prado."

"Divulging asinine pronouncements as if they're gospel truth is even more distasteful, Agent Gonçalves."

"What's all this got to do with Cintia Tadesco?"

"I'll get back to Cintia in a minute. At the moment, I'm still talking about Marco Franco. Franco, then, largely due to Marques's efforts, achieved star status. People admired him, people took his advice. He did testimonials for everything from toothpaste to cars, and the masses went out and bought whatever he recommended. For Leo Marques, who got ten percent of every centavo he earned, Marco Franco was a gold mine."

"I still don't—"

"Bear with me. I'm almost there. Now, actors come and go. They age; they lose their charms; they fall out of fashion. Marques is an old fox. He's been around a long time. He knows his continuing success depends upon constantly developing new people, getting new snowballs rolling. He spotted Cintia Tadesco at some party or other and told her to drop around and see him."

"Sexual interest?"

"Not at all. Leo Marques is of an age where the only thing that gives him a hard-on is money. So Cintia shows up with her book . . . you're familiar with the term book?"

"Portfolio?"

"Right. She shows up with a book which has only a few photos in it, and second-class photos at that. He leafs through it. They have a little conversation. He tells her she's got the basics, and if she does *exactly* what he tells her, they'll make a lot of money together."

"You know this for a fact?"

"I'm making a few assumptions, but I'm not far off the mark."

"Okay. So Cintia agrees."

"Cintia agrees. Marques orchestrates a campaign to get her picture into *Fofocas* and all the other magazines and tabloids. He gets her into gossip shows on television. He gets her invited to parties where she's photographed next to the rich and famous."

"But you can't just mandate that kind of stuff," Gonçalves said. "Why should the magazines and television shows go along? Why should they give her free publicity? I mean, there must be hundreds, maybe thousands of people who are clamoring for it. There are probably tens of thousands of beautiful women in this country. The competition is fierce."

"It is. But that's where Marco Franco came in. In him, Leo Marques was representing a well-established personality. The readers of *Fofocas* like to read about who's courting who, who's divorcing whom, who's running around with someone else behind whose back. But all those *whos* have to be people the readership already knows. They only begin to care about nobodies when they become somebodies. So one of the ways to get a new snowball rolling is to link the person you're trying to promote with someone who's already famous. A man with a man, a woman with a woman, a man with a woman, it doesn't matter. Before long, the unknown person becomes known. Got it?"

"Got it. And in Cintia Tadesco's case—"

"Leo Marques linked her to Marco Franco."

Gonçalves scratched his head. "But Marco was already famous. Why did he go along? What was in it for him?"

"Two things: first of all, no matter how famous you are it never hurts to have a photogenic female on your arm. It generates more pictures."

"And the second thing?"

"Timing. Marco Franco's public was overwhelmingly female. There was a rumor going around he was gay. It could have killed him. He needed somebody like Cintia Tadesco."

"And is he? Gay, I mean?"

"Let's say he's sexually confused."

"Which means?"

"It's never been clear, even to him, if he's bisexual, or homosexual. But one thing's for sure: there was truth to the rumor. At the time, Marco was having an affair with a male tennis pro and the news was getting out and it was *bad* news for him because most of that huge female audience of his had fantasies about being in bed with him. There was no way they'd take kindly to a gay tennis pro being in there with them."

"Understandable. So, as far as the press is concerned, Marco and Cintia became an item?"

"It started out that way, but before long, so the story goes, Marco is boffing Cintia and loving it. He buys her a BMW. He gives her a weekend place out in Granja Viana. He takes her on a tour of Europe. He rejects his old ways and becomes a raging tower of testosterone."

"But?"

"But Cintia has no sense of gratitude. She's hard as a diamond, and she's always looking for ways to better herself. She's introduced to the Artist. She doesn't hesitate. She makes a play for him, and she snags him. He's not only a step up; he's a whole flight up. He's famous all over the world. He can buy and sell Marco Franco twenty times over."

"And he's ugly as sin and dumb as a post."

"That's why I said I wouldn't want my son to get involved with her. It's obvious to everybody, as it was obvious to Juraci, that what her son has going for him has nothing to do with physical beauty or intelligence, both of which Cintia has in abundance. Of course, she *might* love the Artist for the kind and gentle soul he is. But how likely is that? Juraci didn't buy it. She'd already pegged Cintia as a social-climbing, mercenary harpy. As far as I was able to learn, so has everyone else who's ever had contact with her. Everyone except the Artist, that is."

"And Franco? What happened to him?"

"She returned his letters, wouldn't take his phone calls, told him to get lost. She humiliated him in public and in private, leaked to the press that the rumors about his being gay were all true. Then, when the reporters came to talk to her about it, she did this teary-eyed television interview saying that she really loved him until she found out he was cheating on her with the aforementioned tennis pro."

"Which he wasn't."

"Which he wasn't. That was all before Cintia came along. The tennis pro, though, felt jilted and wanted to get back at Marco."

"So he said it was true."

"He did, and the gossip press had a field day. They went on about it for weeks, every sordid exchange, every scandalous revelation. Well, the rest of the story is quickly told. Marco couldn't get any more work. He's still got money, but fame is an addictive thing. He misses it, and he's drinking heavily. People in the know tell me he's drinking himself to death and won't last out the year. Cintia, sweet thing that she is, has allegedly said she doesn't give a shit."

"Did you report all of this to Juraci Santos?"

"I did. But think about it for a minute. What did I really get? Nothing, Agent Gonçalves, nothing that Cintia couldn't easily refute. If she sticks to her side of the story, and if the Artist believes her, Juraci really has very little that she can condemn her for, nothing she can go to her son with."

"When did you make your report to Juraci?"

"I called her the day before she was abducted."

"No written report?"

"I prepared one. I was going to mail it this morning. But then there didn't seem to be much point."

"Will you make me a copy?"

"If I must."

"You must. Were you able to find out anything else about Cintia? Does she have other boyfriends?"

"I'm not sure."

"But you wouldn't rule it out?"

"My recommendation to Juraci was to put Cintia under around-the-clock surveillance."

"Around the clock, eh? It wouldn't have been cheap."

"It certainly would not have been. But I think she was going to agree to it."

"You could have earned a bundle."

"I most certainly could have. If you catch those people, and it is my earnest hope that you do, would you do me a favor?"

"What?"

"Give each and every one of them a kick in the balls from me."

Chapter Fourteen

"BACK SO SOON?" PEDRO Cataldo said. "What happened with Talafero?"

Silva told him.

"You believe him?"

"I'm suspending judgment. Meantime, what can you tell me about Miranda?"

"Captain Miranda? Now, there's a piece of work. I've been after him for years."

"How close are you to nailing him?"

"Not close. He's a slippery bastard."

"Why 'Captain'?"

"Because he was."

"Military?"

"An army officer. During the dictatorship, he worked in Section II."

Silva's mouth crinkled in disgust. Section II was a torture squad, the most notorious of them all. The Section's members received monetary rewards for capturing, or killing, left-wing militants—and they'd sooner kill than capture. After the country reverted to democracy, it became known that many of Section II's victims weren't militants, or even left-wingers.

"While he was busy killing people for the government," Pedro continued, "he also got involved in contraband."

"Smuggling?"

Pedro nodded. "Whiskey and cigarettes, but it didn't work out. He and a dozen of his buddies got busted."

"He confessed?"

"He confessed, but when he got in front of a judge, he claimed it was beaten out of him."

Silva snorted in disgust. "And?"

"His case was thrown out on appeal."

"Grounds?"

"Torture, if you can believe that."

"How's that for irony," Arnaldo said.

"In fiction," Pedro said, "nobody would believe it. By the time he was acquitted, though, Miranda had become a *persona non grata* to his army buddies. They cashiered him."

"So," Arnaldo said, "the army promoted him for killing people, and threw him out for smuggling. What a country we live in!"

"So there he was," Pedro said, "thirty-five years old, no marketable skills, and looking for something to do with his life. Apolidoro Nasca gave it to him."

"Who's Apolidoro Nasca?"

"Was, not is. He's been dead for years, but he was a big man once, a crook who controlled the animal game in the four biggest towns in the state of Minas Gerais. You're in a job like that, you need killers to work for you. Miranda was a killer with credentials, so Nasca hired him. For a while, so they say, Miranda only killed the people Nasca told him to kill. Rivals, deadbeats, people who were skimming money."

"And then?"

"And then, one day, Nasca disappeared."

"Miranda took over his operation?"

"Uh huh. What you're thinking is what everybody thinks—but nobody can prove it. Then Uncle Scrooge—"

"Uncle Scrooge?"

"Nelson Catto, the chief bicheiro. His nickname was Uncle Scrooge. So Uncle Scrooge starts keeping a close eye on what Miranda is doing in Minas Gerais. Within a year, he

doubles the income of the business, which means he doubles
the cut for Uncle Scrooge. Within three years, the Captain
is up there on the Council of Seven, the guys who run the
operation for the entire country. As soon as they put him
in the chair he moved from Belo Horizonte to São Paulo. It
took him less than six months to consolidate the market."

"Consolidate the market?"

Cataldo nodded. "Before Miranda came along, São Paulo
was divided into three districts, all about equal in size. Now
it's just one."

"How did he pull it off?"

"Easy. He was already on the Council. All he had to do
was assign dead men's territories to himself."

"Except, first, he had to make them dead?"

"Exactly. By the early-nineties, he was into his golden
years, having a great run, walking around dressed in expensive Italian suits. It annoyed the hell out of Lili Norunha.
She spent years building up a case against him."

"I knew Lili well," Silva said. "I liked her. A lot."

"I did too. She told me, before she died, that she'd managed to implicate Miranda in sixty-two murders. But in the
end, the whole thing fell apart. He only got six years."

"Wait a minute," Arnaldo said. "This guy kills sixty-two
people and he only gets six years in prison?"

"Miranda got to the jury. And then he went after Lili. I
know it, but I can't prove it."

Judge Lili Norunha had been found in her apartment, shot
dead, on the 27th of November, 1998. Her husband and two
sons were murdered with her. Officially, the case had never
been solved.

"Uncle Scrooge died in 2001," Pedro went on. "Natural
causes, they say. Maybe it's even true. Miranda stepped up,
became the boss of bosses. He still is."

"Still wearing his Italian suits?"

"No more. He learned his lesson. These days, he keeps a much lower profile. But he's the one guy nobody screws with. Not that anybody would want to. He's making lots of people tons of money. He's the best manager the bicheiros ever had, the head of the whole rotten organization."

"So, when you finally get him, you'll be able to stamp out the game?"

Pedro laughed. "I'm not that naïve, Mario. The game is here to stay; it will be with us forever. As soon as Miranda is out of the picture, some other bicheiro will step up and take his place."

"If it isn't going to change anything, why are you so set on putting him away?"

"The game is secondary compared to the other stuff he's up to."

"Murders?"

"The murders don't bother me all that much, because the people he kills are mostly crooks. I'm focusing on the other stuff."

"Corruption?"

"Big time. Everybody knows the bicheiros have a deal going with the civil police. They've had one for years. There's no way they could operate if they didn't, but Miranda has taken it to a whole new level. He's gone beyond bribing cops and judges. He's investing in political campaigns, fattening the bank accounts of senators and deputies. He's even got the governor of São Paulo on his payroll."

"Jesus. I had no idea."

"Most people don't. Since Miranda took over, it's not just the game anymore. Now it's bingo parlors, casinos and slot machines. Every day it's something new, every day it's something worse. The man's greed is monumental."

"You try going after him for his taxes?"

"I did, and he's covered. He now makes his living, he says, as a"—Pedro used his fingers to make quotation marks in the air—"*financial consultant*. He takes in upward of a half-million a month in so-called *commissions* from people he claims to be advising on investments. And he pays taxes on every centavo. Meanwhile, he's squirreling away millions in Uruguay, or the Caymans, or some other place I don't know about."

"But you're trying like hell to find."

"You bet I am."

"Getting back to Talafero for a minute, do you buy into his story about Green Mangos?"

"No, I don't. Bicheiros like Miranda are *supposed* to support samba schools. People expect it of them. When Miranda inherited the São Paulo bank, he inherited the obligation to support Green Mangos along with it."

"So it's not like his heart is in it?"

"Miranda doesn't have a heart. Green Mangos, for him, is a cost of doing business. He does it to generate goodwill, keep his customers satisfied. That's what I think. Mind you, I could be wrong."

"Talafero was pretty convincing." Arnaldo sounded doubtful. "You shoulda heard him."

"If I had," Pedro said, "I still wouldn't buy it. Since you guys were here last, I've been doing some digging about Talafero. There's a reason why he might want to sick you guys onto Miranda."

"Which is?"

"To distract Miranda, get him off his back."

"Why would that be necessary?"

"Talafero's setting up a new business, one Miranda doesn't like."

"What is it?"

"Making book on football games."

"What's new about that? You can do that now."

"Not the way he's doing it. With the lotto you have to bet on the outcome of a series, and with the Internet you have to use a credit card."

"Uh huh. So?"

"So, if you want to bet on an individual game, and you don't have a credit card, which most people in this country don't, you can't do it. And you can't bet small amounts."

"Talafero is taking centavo bets?"

"He is, which opens it up to kids and pensioners and people living in favelas."

"Just like the animal game."

"Which is why Miranda doesn't like it. And, since the whole country is football crazy, folks are flocking to Talafero and his football action."

"And away from Miranda and his animals."

"Exactly."

"Stupid," Arnaldo said. "Miranda isn't going to take it lying down."

"But Talafero didn't get where he is today by being stupid," Silva said.

"You think he's worked out a plan for neutralizing Miranda?"

"I think it's likely. But let's not get sidetracked. Our primary objective is to recover Juraci Santos and to see that the people who murdered her maids get what's coming to them. Miranda and Talafero only merit investigative time if they can contribute to that objective. We're not going to waste more energy on Talafero until we've explored a few other avenues."

"How about Miranda?"

"We'll talk to him. But what Pedro just said makes sense. His samba school is unlikely to be as important to him as Talafero seems to think it is or, at least, told us it was. With all of his other businesses absorbing his attention, I don't think it's likely he'd set out to kidnap Juraci if it was only for the money."

"If you don't think he's involved in the kidnapping," Pedro said, "why do you want to talk to him at all?"

"Because a man in his position would have more under-world connections than anyone. He'll be plugged in. People will tell him things. He'll know where to go to get answers."

"So?"

"So I'm going to ask for his help in bringing the Artist's mother home alive."

"I see two things wrong with that," Pedro said.

"Tell me," Silva said.

"Miranda is a selfish bastard. He's not likely to help with-out getting something in return."

"That's one. What's the other?"

"We have no reason to believe Juraci Santos is alive at all."

Chapter Fifteen

JURACI AWOKE TO A splitting headache, her body drenched in sweat, her heart beating wildly in her chest, the nightmare fresh in her mind.

Except it wasn't a nightmare. A man wearing a hood *had* broken down her door, *had* pinned her to her bed, *had* stuck a hypodermic needle in her arm. Now she was . . . she was . . . *where the hell was she?*

The place reminded her of nothing so much as a windowless prison cell. Except for the door: no bars, solid wood. The walls smelled of fresh cement. On one of them, held in place by a single nail driven into the concrete, was a typewritten piece of paper. She stared at it until the letters came into focus:

THE RULES

Do not talk to us. We will not answer you.

Do not shout, or scream. No one will hear you.

This is about money. You are being held for ransom. When your son pays us, you'll be released unharmed.

When you stretch out on the floor, your hands will come within twenty centimeters of the door. This will enable you to reach your food trays and exchange used buckets for clean ones.

The bucket is your toilet. After use, put it against the wall to the right of the door. It will be removed and exchanged for a clean one. We will do this when we bring you food.

You will be fed three times a day. We will knock. You will sit on the bed. We will open the door wide enough to put the tray on the floor. Only after the door has closed again may you stretch out and drag the tray toward you. After eating, put the tray back in the same place you got it from.

If you violate any rule, you will spend the next twenty-four hours without food or water.

AFTER SHE'D READ THE seventh rule, she'd curled herself into a ball and wept.

Hours later, it seemed, they'd given her food for the first time. It consisted of a ham and cheese sandwich and a bottle of water.

There'd been no eating utensils, no cup, or glass. The bread, at least, had been fresh.

While she'd been unconscious, they'd changed her clothes, taken off her urine-stained nightgown and dressed her in a track suit. It pinched at the waist, in the armpits, in the crotch. They could have abused her when she was naked, but they hadn't.

Maybe, she thought, *because I still stink of piss.*

She'd wanted to use some of the water to clean herself, but she was so thirsty, and there was so little of it, that she'd drunk it all.

There was a chain around her ankle, loosely fastened with a small padlock. Another padlock linked the chain to an eye bolt set into the wall. The loop around her ankle was beginning to chafe her skin.

Her cell was square, the walls about four meters apart. In the middle of the ceiling, a bare bulb hung from a wire. What they'd referred to as a bed was, in reality, no more than a mattress on the floor, no frame, no spring, no sheets. The air was warm and stale. The only source of fresh air was a single aluminum vent set into the top of the door.

There was no radio, no television, but they'd left her a stack of old magazines. She was grateful for that.

Her captors were two, one tall and broad-shouldered, one of less than average height and girth for a man, but average on both counts if the captor was a woman. Their outfits were identical: blue coveralls, a hood made of blue cloth, black tennis shoes and vinyl gloves.

They rotated, first one, then the other, never coming into her cell together, never speaking.

Except once.

That time, they *had* come in together. The big one had handed her a newspaper, and told her how to hold it, while the smaller one took a photograph.

That incident happened shortly after she awoke. The flash had made her headache worse. They'd taken the newspaper with them when they'd left.

Were they people she knew?

The thought disturbed her.

Something else disturbed her, too.

Back in her bedroom, before the big oaf put the needle in her arm, she'd heard two sharp reports.

In the *favela* of her childhood, such sounds were everyday events, background noise, like birdsong in the countryside, or surf on a beach. She'd heard them many hundreds of times.

Gunshots.

Chapter Sixteen

IRENE ASKED HIM WHEN he'd be coming home.

"We talked about that yesterday," Silva said, and then regretted it. It would pain her to know she'd been so drunk she couldn't remember.

"I . . . I miss you," she said, in a small voice, slurring her speech. He took it for what it was—a drunken attempt to apologize.

"And I miss you, Irene. Now, let me talk to Maria de Lourdes."

Silva no longer felt comfortable about leaving his wife alone, not since the day, almost three months ago, when he'd come home to find her in a stupor on the kitchen floor. She'd hit a corner of the table on the way down, and the gash had bled profusely. He thought, at first, that she'd been shot, there was so much blood on the tiles.

He'd promptly hired Maria de Lourdes Krups, their former cleaning woman, as Irene's full-time companion.

Despite her somewhat Teutonic surname, Maria de Lourdes was a *mulata* from Paraná, fiercely loyal to Silva and infinitely patient with his alcoholic wife. The loyalty stemmed from a favor he'd done her once, an affair linked to her only son, like Silva's, now dead.

"Senhor?" Maria de Lourdes said.

"I should have called earlier, shouldn't I?"

"I'm sure you've been busy, Senhor."

"It's early in the day for her to be that far along. Has she had any more than usual?"

"No, Senhor. Sometimes it's just. . . ."

"I understand. Call me on my cell phone when she's gone to bed."

"*Sí*, Senhor."

Silva hung up. Mara stopped typing on her laptop. Arnaldo put down his pencil.

"How is she?" Arnaldo said.

"The usual. Hasn't had a fall, though, for almost a month."

"Because Maria de Lourdes follows her around like a mother hen."

"Maybe. She's a jewel, that woman."

"Why don't you just cut her off?" Mara asked. "Stop buying it for her. Don't give her any money."

"Doesn't work," Silva said. "You can't force a cure on an alcoholic. They have to *want* to get cured."

"Irene doesn't want to get cured?"

"Not yet." Silva changed the subject. "That call you took while I was talking to her? Was it about the keys? The ones you picked up at the Artist's place?"

"It was. They fit. No useful prints other than those of Cintia and the Artist."

"And Cintia Tadesco's skin?"

"Perfect. The bitch."

"Bitch is right," Arnaldo said. "I do *so* hope she's mixed up in this. If she is, I want to be the one to cuff her."

"Get in line, Nunes," Mara said. "Ladies first."

"What was in the syringe?" Silva asked.

"We don't know," Mara said. "Not yet."

"Hurry the lab along."

"I'm on it."

"Ballistics?"

"The bullets that killed both maids were fired from the same weapon."

"Surprise, surprise," Arnaldo said, and would have said more, but just then, they heard footsteps approaching in the corridor, a woman's high heels, moving fast. They all looked at the door.

Celeste, one of the Mara's people, bustled into the room. She was clearly excited.

"A tip," she said. "There's a warehouse in Bom Retiro—"

"That neighborhood is nothing *but* warehouses."

"Let her talk, Nunes," Mara snapped. "Go on, Celeste."

"This particular warehouse has been abandoned for ages. Then, yesterday, at about seven in the morning, a truck pulled up in front. Two men got out, unloaded a packing crate, and carried it inside."

"Big crate?"

"Big enough to contain a human being. The truck drove off. The men stayed. They've been there ever since."

"Who called it in?"

"A neighbor, a widow lady, name of . . ."—Celeste consulted the paper she was holding— "Garcia."

"Who took the call?"

"Marlene. She says Garcia sounds like an old biddy, a self-appointed watchdog of the neighborhood."

"Nothing terribly suspicious in what you've told us up to now," Silva said. "There must have been more, something that prompted the Garcia woman to pick up her phone"

"There was," Celeste said.

"What?"

"She heard a woman scream."

* * *

LESS THAN an hour later, a hostage rescue team headed by Gloria Sarmento had taken up positions around the warehouse. Gloria, dressed in gray coveralls, wearing a headset, and carrying an H&K MP-5, was peeking out through a gap in Senhora Garcia's curtains. From the old lady's living room, she had a clear view of the warehouse's front door.

Hector was on Senhora Garcia's roof with three of Gloria's snipers. Gloria's number two, Raul Franco, and three other members of the team, were on a parallel street, covering the rear exit.

Silva studied the lady who'd called in the tip. She looked like a friendly grandmother, appeared to be about eighty, had watery eyes and thick eyeglasses.

"It was more than one scream," she said. "It was a whole lot of shrieking. I called right away, but your answering system put me on hold for almost fifteen minutes." She stuck an accusing finger in Silva's face. "That screeching, Chief Inspector, was almost an hour and a half ago. It sounded like they were torturing the poor woman. God knows what they've done to her by now."

"We're short-staffed, Senhora Garcia. Sometimes it creates problems."

"If you ask me, the law enforcement in this country is getting worse and worse. You can say what you like about the dictatorship, but if you called the police in those days, they showed up right away."

"Really?" Arnaldo said. "Did you have occasion to call them often?"

"What are you?" she snorted. "A goddamned pinko?"

"Tell us about the packing crate," Silva said.

"It was wood," she said, "and plenty big enough for a person."

"Painted?"

"No, and nothing written on it either. What are you standing around talking to me for? Why don't you just go in there, grab those bastards and kick the shit out of them?"

"Will you be my grandma?" Arnaldo said.

"How would you like my cane shoved up your ass?"

"What do you remember about the men who were carrying the box?" Silva said.

"Did I tell you they were men?"

"You told the lady who took your call."

"They were men. I'm just keeping you on your toes."

"How were they dressed?"

"The shorter one was wearing a coverall like Superwoman's over there, except hers is gray and his was blue."

"Who are you calling Superwoman?" Gloria said, fingering the trigger on her machine pistol and looking as if she'd like to use it. She'd been in the room with Senhora Garcia longer than any of the others.

Senhora Garcia ignored her question.

"I couldn't see his face very well," she said. "My eyes aren't what they used to be, and by the time I'd fetched my binoculars from the windowsill upstairs he'd gone inside."

"And the other man? What was he wearing?"

"Slacks and a blue shirt. Short sleeves."

"You haven't seen either one of them since they went in there?"

"Did I say that? Did I say I hadn't seen either one of them since they went in there?"

Silva sighed.

"No, Senhora Garcia, you didn't."

"You're damned right, I didn't. The one with the blue shirt has been out of there three times. The first time was just after he went in. He was away for about ten minutes and came back with a box of bottled water, Minalba, the one with the red label, the one without gas. The second time, he went down to the *padaria* on the corner. He came back carrying a paper bag."

Senhora Garcia's vision might not have been quite as sharp as she would have liked, but it wasn't all that bad either. And there didn't appear to be anything wrong with her memory.

"What about the third time?" Silva asked.

"He came back with a couple of plastic bags, looked like they were from the supermarket around the corner on Rua Francesco Bellini."

"Did you see either one of them with a gun?"

"No, I didn't."

"What do you think, Gloria?" Silva said, turning to the head of the hostage rescue team.

"We checked with the power company," she said. "They haven't got electricity in there. If anyone comes out, we pounce on him. If not, we wait until five in the morning and go in with night-vision scopes."

"You're the expert," Silva said, "but I really hate the idea of waiting that long."

"Hate it, but you're going to do it, eh?" Senhora Garcia said. "Bunch of goddamned pussies."

∗ ∗ ∗

IN THE end, they didn't have to wait at all. Fifteen minutes after adopting Gloria's strategy, the man in the blue shirt walked out the front door of the building.

Her people grabbed him as soon as he'd rounded the corner. Minutes later, he was shackled to a metal table in the RV that the team was using as a mobile command post.

Silva kicked off the interrogation: "What's your name?"

"Tulio Santiago, Senhor."

Santiago was scared, short, and hunger thin. His brown eyes, big behind steel-rimmed glasses, kept oscillating from the MP5 in Gloria's hands to the Glock on Arnaldo's belt.

"Who else is in that warehouse, Tulio?"

The prisoner squirmed. "Just my *companheiro* Elvis, Senhor."

"Elvis, is it? Elvis what?"

"Pinheiro, Senhor."

"You weren't armed. Is Elvis?"

"Armed, Senhor?"

"Is he carrying a gun? Or a knife?"

"Oh, no, Senhor. We never carry those kinds of things."

"If you don't carry weapons, Tulio, how do you control your victims?"

"Victims, Senhor?"

"Stop beating around the goddamned bush, Tulio. The game is up. Someone heard her scream. So save us the trouble of roughing you up. Tell us what we'll find in there when we break down the door."

Santiago hung his head and sighed. He was ready to cooperate.

"Did you torture her?"

Santiago's head snapped up.

"Torture her? Of course not. What kind of people do you think we are?"

"If you didn't torture her, why did she scream?"

"They all scream, Senhor. That's just the way they are. We try to keep them quiet, but it doesn't always work."

"Keep them quiet? Really? And what do you do to keep them quiet?"

"We give them nuts, Senhor, and sometimes a piece of fruit."

* * *

THE HOSTAGE in the warehouse wasn't the Artist's mother. She was a Lear's macaw.

One of Gloria's men put in a call to the IBAMA, the Brazilian environmental agency. A no-nonsense female wearing a bush shirt and sporting a nose stud showed up about half an hour later. She introduced herself as *Doutora* Kipman.

"Physician?" Hector asked.

"Biologist," she said. "Who's Silva?"

"That would be me."

She stuck out a hand. "Congratulations, Chief Inspector. You did a great job today. We've been after these two characters for quite some time."

"What's going to happen to them?"

"You caught them *em flagrante*." She rubbed her chapped hands together in glee. "They're gonna get at least five years, maybe even seven."

"Five *years*? For smuggling birds?"

Kipman bristled. "The Lear's macaw is the second rarest macaw in the world. Do you know how many of these birds survive in the wild, Chief Inspector?"

"I have no idea."

"Then let me tell you. There aren't more than eight hundred of them, eight hundred in the wild and maybe another fifty in captivity. That's it. There are no more. That one preening itself over there represents more than one-tenth of one percent of the entire species."

Silva looked at the blue bird with new respect. "Is that so?" he said.

"That's so," she said. "And God knows whether it would have survived the journey to wherever they were sending it to. They pack them in boxes, tape their beaks shut so they can't squawk, tie their feet together so they can't move. Jail is too good for those two bastards. They should get a taste of their own medicine."

Kipman looked angry enough to tape their mouths and tie their legs herself.

"How much money are those things worth?" Silva asked.

"We have strict legislation against keeping them in captivity, even stricter legislation against their export. No permit has ever been issued. I'd estimate they would have realized at least twenty-thousand Reais for this one."

"Twenty thousand Reais? For a parrot?"

"You think that's a lot? There's one collector in Singapore who'd pay double that if they could get the bird to him. Poor thing. Look at her. She's so nervous."

"How can you tell?"

"She's picking at her breast feathers."

Chapter Seventeen

"CRAP," SAMPAIO SAID. "I already told the minister about that warehouse."

"Told him what, Director?"

Silva was holding the telephone several centimeters from his ear. Sampaio wasn't quite shouting, but it was close.

"I assured him it was just a matter of hours until we had the Artist's mother back. What do I tell him now?"

"Perhaps, Director, it was a little premature to have assured the minister—"

"If I want your advice on how to do my job, Chief Inspector, I'll ask for it. You have no idea what kind of pressure I'm under. What's Godofredo's take on this?"

"I haven't spoken to Godofredo yet."

"Call him. Call him right away. You should have involved him long before now."

Godofredo Boceta was the Federal Police's profiler, an academic blowhard hired by Sampaio himself. Silva was never averse to asking for expert advice from people he respected, but Boceta was a man for whom he had no respect at all. The profiler had never been of help in the solving of any case.

"I'll call him as soon as I get back to the office," he lied.

"Where are you calling from?"

"A car. We're on our way to see Fiorello Rosa."

"Rosa? What the hell do you want to talk to Rosa for? Rosa has been in jail for five years!"

"Seven."

"Seven, then. What can you possibly expect from him?"

"He re-wrote the book on kidnapping. He's the best that ever there was. He might have some ideas about how this one went down."

"Even if he does, why should he talk to you?"

"Because he has a parole hearing coming up."

"How do you know that?"

"I received a letter. I've been asked to testify."

"Don't waste your time with Rosa. It's not going to get you anywhere. Godofredo is the guy you have to talk to. How about that network of snitches Pedro Cataldo's got?"

"He's working it, but there's no word on the street."

"And that bicheiro, Miranda?"

"I'll speak to him before the day is out."

* * *

Fiorello Rosa, PhD and master kidnapper, was a most uncommon felon. He'd been a professor of criminology and had published seven books on the subject. His work had earned him high praise in the academic community, some notoriety in law-enforcement circles, and far too little money.

So, sometime in the late nineties, Rosa set his mind to bettering himself—and chose kidnapping as the most lucrative and least violent way of achieving his objective. At the time of his arrest, he'd been abducting people for almost six years and hadn't once, in all that time, missed a single university lecture because of it.

Throughout his criminal career Rosa selected his victims based upon their ability to pay, a strategy he considered wise at the time, but one which, when he was brought to justice, added to his troubles. Rosa's furious and resentful ex-victims used all of their influence to make sure the judge threw the book at him. The judge, eager to please the power elite, did just that. The miscreant was sentenced to fourteen years.

To Rosa, the severe sentence came as a most disagreeable surprise. He'd never committed murder or mayhem on his victims. Indeed, he'd never touched a hair of their heads. He'd expected to get away with a sentence of no more than eight, which might have put him out in four.

The prison where Rosa was being held was in Guarulhos, not far from the international airport of that name. After Silva hung up with Sampaio, he and Arnaldo chatted about Rosa's arrest.

"Refresh my memory," Arnaldo said. "I took the kids to the beach for a few weeks. When I got back, you had the whole thing wrapped up."

"Luck," Silva said, and told the story.

The last of Rosa's victims had been a wealthy advertising man, a partner in a successful agency. Rosa's gang had kept him in captivity for almost three months while the terms of his release were being negotiated. As day followed day, with few developments to break the monotony, one of Rosa's henchmen had gotten sloppy. Against all instructions, he'd left the prisoner alone and gone down to the local padaria for a coffee and a *cachaça*.

The place where the gang had been holding their victim was a semi-detached house, rented specifically for the purpose. It wasn't soundproof and, if the guard had followed his instructions, there was no reason why it should have been. But when the captive heard movement next door, he called out to his guard and, getting no response, raised his voice and hazarded a cry for help. Before long, he managed to attract the attention of a student living in the adjoining garret.

When the guard got back from his recreational excursion, he found Silva and his men waiting for him. The guard, in exchange for leniency, fingered Rosa as the mastermind.

The abduction of the ad man had been the last in a series that Silva, as a professional, admired for meticulous planning and execution. It had taken place in broad daylight at what was, ostensibly, a police roadblock. False cops, cars and uniforms correct in every detail, were checking licenses and registrations of vehicles. They'd established their trap between the home and the office of their victim.

In the subsequent interviews, it appeared everyone noticed the strange accent of the cop who was doing all the talking, but such was the power of his uniform that no one questioned his authority.

The false cops had gone through the motions of attending to almost a hundred other vehicles by the time the man they were after pulled up to the checkpoint. They left him fidgeting and looking at his watch for a full five minutes. His impatience kept building, and building, and when his turn came, he rolled down the three centimeter thick bulletproofed window without a squeak of protest.

It was all over in a heartbeat. No one died; no one was shot; no one was manhandled. Rosa's thugs simply bundled their victim into a vehicle and took off with him. They left his driver shackled to the car's steering wheel with two pairs of handcuffs.

The getaway car was indistinguishable from any other police cruiser in the city. As soon as they were around the corner, they stopped to remove their license plate, revealing another already in place. Then they drove four kilometers to a garage, where they switched the police car for a van. Fifteen minutes later, they arrived at the hideout.

The little room was ready and waiting, with a television and a stack of books. On a tray sat a bottle of the ad man's favorite whisky, a bucket of ice, and a cut-crystal glass of the kind he liked to do his drinking from.

Rosa had done his research well. He knew their victim was an alcoholic. He didn't want to put his life in danger by exposing him to withdrawal symptoms—and he even provided him with the proper pills for his hypertension and type 2 diabetes.

The "cops" he'd hired, the only members of the gang who might be recognized, were immediately flown to Argentina, the place they'd come from. They embarked, by private plane, less than an hour after the commission of the crime. None were apprehended.

* * *

"Chief Inspector Mario Silva," Rosa said, when they led him in. "What an agreeable surprise."

"Hello, Professor. You seem happy to see me."

"I am."

"Why?"

"I'm not stupid, Chief Inspector. We aren't exactly friends. We haven't seen each other in seven years, and when they told me you were coming, I could only think of one reason for your visit. You want something."

"I do indeed."

"As do I. You're aware that I'm coming up for a parole hearing?"

"I've been invited to testify."

"So my attorney told me. And this gentleman is?"

"My colleague, Agent Arnaldo Nunes."

"Pleased to meet you, Agent Nunes. I'd offer you a hand, but . . ." Rosa held up his shackled wrists.

"I think we can dispense with those," Silva said, and nodded to the guard.

The guard removed Rosa's handcuffs and left without a word.

"Sit down, Professor."

Rosa rubbed the red marks on his wrists and shook hands with both Arnaldo and Silva before taking a seat.

"It's the Artist's mother, isn't it?" he said.

"Yes," Silva said, "it is."

"Just before the game with Argentina, too. Rather unpatriotic, don't you think?"

"That's exactly what I think."

Silva dropped a sheaf of papers on the table. Rosa looked at it, but he didn't extend a hand to pick it up.

"What's this?" he said.

"Copies of all our reports, everything we've done up to now."

Rosa raised his eyes to Silva's, then lowered them again to study the height of the stack.

"Not very much, by the look of it."

"It's early days yet. I'd like you to look at this material as a professor of criminology, but also in the light of your . . . more recent experience."

"With the objective of uncovering something you might have missed?"

"And anything else that might help us to apprehend the people who did it.'"

"Such as?"

"Profiles of the kind of people we might be dealing with."

Rosa gave a slow, deliberate nod and leaned back in his chair. "You recognize, of course, that I can make no guarantee other than to try my best?"

"Yes."

The kidnapper narrowed his eyes. "If I undertake this, can I count on your help in getting me out of this place?"

Silva, expecting the question, had the answer ready. "You can."

Rosa's expression didn't change. "Even if my contribution, in the end, doesn't help you in any substantial way?"

"As long as I'm convinced you tried your best."

"Good," Rosa said, picking up the papers and removing a pair of reading glasses from his breast pocket. "Then we have a deal. Let me peruse all of this. I might have some questions for you."

Arnaldo and Silva sat in silence while Rosa read. The file was very short, and the reading didn't take long. When he finished, Silva said, "Any initial impressions?"

"The people behind it definitely had someone on the inside."

Silva nodded. "I concur, but I'd like to hear why you think so."

Rosa looked at Silva over his glasses. "Who's this fellow Lefkowitz?"

"Our chief forensics technician. A *Paulista*, who was working with the local police in Manaus. We discovered him, concluded that his talent was wasted up there and hired him."

"Manaus." Rosa shuddered. "Why would any self-respecting individual abandon São Paulo for Manaus?"

"His wife is a biologist. She thought working in the Amazon would be paradise."

"I'll bet that didn't last long."

"It didn't. Once they discovered what Manaus is really about, they were desperate to get out."

Rosa snorted in agreement. "Of course they were. Your gain, I'd say. He seems a perceptive person, this Lefkowitz."

"He is."

Rosa tapped the file with a forefinger.

"I agree with him. The kidnappers had a key. Smashing the door was a mere ruse to conceal that fact. If you don't have a key, there are easier and quieter ways to get into a locked house, ways that don't entail making anywhere near as much noise."

"Indeed. Anything else?"

Rosa removed his reading glasses, folded them, and put them back into his breast pocket.

"Another salient point is the killing of the maids," he said. "Why would they do that if not to reduce the danger of recognition? It occurs to me that Senhora Santos's maids might have known and recognized the kidnappers. And I'm strengthened in that belief by a feeling that the people who committed this crime weren't professionals."

Silva leaned back and crossed his arms. "Why?"

"True professionals always carefully consider what they're getting into. They don't embark on a project unless they're reasonably sure of being able to escape unscathed. That said, they always retain their fear of being apprehended. They set limits for themselves, avoid unnecessary risk, plan for the worst-case scenario."

"That's what you did."

Rosa grinned. "Except at the last," he said, "when I chose the wrong man to do a simple job." The grin vanished. "But I wasn't speaking as a kidnapper. I was speaking from the point of view of a criminologist. I studied hundreds, probably thousands, of cases before I was arrested. I've continued my research here in prison."

"You're an expert, Professor. That's why I'm here. Explain to me, exactly, why you're convinced these people weren't professionals."

Rosa shook his head. "I didn't say I was *convinced*, Chief Inspector. I said I had a feeling. Criminology isn't an exact science."

"Noted. Go on."

"Murder bears a much heavier penalty than kidnapping. Professionals would have been aware that, with proper planning, murder would have been superfluous. And it certainly wouldn't have been desirable. So they wouldn't have done it. These perpetrators, on the other hand, either didn't plan properly, or got rattled and forgot what they'd planned, or allowed one, or both, of the maids to get a glimpse of someone they knew. Or perhaps they'd already decided upon murder before they entered the house, or simply killed out of impulse. I can't see any other possibilities. Any one, or any combination of them, would mark the abductors as amateurs."

Silva rubbed his chin. "Interesting. Anything else?"

"The diamonds."

"What about the diamonds?"

"They've obviously been requested for some specific purpose. But what purpose?"

"Portability. Large denominations would be difficult to negotiate. Five million dollars in small bills, even hundreds, would make quite a bundle."

"Perhaps. But think about it. If I'm right, and they're amateurs known to Juraci, or someone in her circle, it follows that they live here, that they have a life here."

"And?"

"And, if they want to *stay* here, they'd wind up selling those diamonds here. The risk of them being traced through the people who buy them, it seems to me, offsets the convenience of portability."

"Also interesting."

"Does Juraci have any medical condition that might require special treatment or special drugs?"

"No."

"But you *have* inquired?"

"Yes."

"So that's a dead end. You won't be able to trace her through physicians or drug purchases." Rosa closed his eyes and rubbed them. "I really have to get a new prescription for those reading glasses," he said.

"Any further questions?" Silva said.

"Not at the moment. You'll send me updates as your investigation progresses?"

"By email. From Mara Carta. She's our intelligence officer here in São Paulo—"

"And collates the various reports into a unified whole. I know how it works, and I well remember the charming Senhora Carta. Tell me, Chief Inspector, did you ever think we might someday work together?"

"Not in my wildest dreams."

"Well, think about it now. I'll be seeking employment when I get out of here. The university is unlikely to have me back."

"You're asking for a job?"

"You think that's absurd?"

Silva rubbed his chin. Rosa had been one of the best criminologists in the country—and one of the best criminals. He had a profound knowledge of both sides of the fence.

"What do you propose to do for us?" he said.

"What I will attempt to do for you now. Profiling. Criminal profiling."

Arnaldo and Silva looked at each other.

"What?" Rosa said, looking from one to the other.

"We already have a profiler," Silva said.

"No, you don't," Rosa said. "You have that incompetent ass, Godofredo Boceta."

"Professor," Arnaldo said, "I like your style."

Chapter Eighteen

LEO MARQUES'S PARENTS HAD named him well. There was, indeed, something leonine about him. His massive head, with its thick mane of gray hair, seemed set directly upon his broad shoulders. He glided around his desk with feline grace, shook Gonçalves's hand and gave him an appraising up-and-down look.

"Do you mind me asking how old you are?"

"Thirty-four," Gonçalves said.

"Really?" Marques's voice conveyed disappointment. "You don't look it." He turned around and walked back to his chair.

Gonçalves had the feeling that he'd been judged and found wanting. Instead of saying I *know*, his customary response to someone telling him he didn't look his age, he said, "What difference does it make?"

"After thirty-five," Marques said, "the camera becomes a hard mistress. She's crueler to women than to men, but still . . ."

"I'm not here for a modeling job, Senhor Marques."

Marques smiled an apologetic smile. "Sorry," he said. "Of course you're not. But when a fine-looking young man like you walks in here, my professional instincts kicked in. You're not at all what I expected."

"What *did* you expect?"

"Some grizzled veteran, I suppose. You know how it is. When your secretary says you have a visitor from the Federal Police . . ."

"I've don't have a secretary, Senhor Marques, so I really wouldn't know."

"No. No, of course not. But tell me honestly, Agent Gonçalves, have you never considered a career in modeling?"

"Never."

"Seriously?"

"Seriously."

"Perhaps you should have. Not now, but certainly when you were younger. Even now, you must still be quite a hit with the girls, or the boys, if your preference goes in that direction."

"Girls."

"I'll bet you have to beat them off with a stick."

"Well . . . not really."

"No need to be modest. I'm an expert on these things. Coffee?"

"No, thank you. I had one just before I arrived."

"Then what can I do for you, Agent Gonçalves?"

"You can talk to me about your client, Cintia Tadesco."

"Ex-client," Marques said, the smile vanishing from his face. He looked like he'd just taken a mouthful of something sour.

"A recent development?"

"We parted ways a month ago."

"Amicably?"

"Not in the least."

"Two of my colleagues met her yesterday. They found her . . . difficult. Would you concur with that assessment?"

Marques leaned back in his chair and folded his hands over his grey waistcoat.

"In my line of work, Agent Gonçalves, difficult goes with the territory. I often take on demure young beauties and mild-mannered young Adonises only to see them evolve into raging egomaniacs. It happens all the time and no longer surprises me."

"But, with Cintia Tadesco, you got something that *did* surprise you?"

The agent stuck out his jaw, as if Gonçalves had questioned his judgment.

"I'm good at reading character. Ask anyone. But for her, purely out of spite, to kill a goose that was laying golden eggs? Well, that, I confess, I never expected."

"The goose being?"

Marques's belligerent attitude vanished in the wink of an eye. He broke into a sheepish grin.

"The goose being me, I suppose."

His self-deprecation showed another facet of the man; Gonçalves began to like him.

"It's this way," Marques said. "I don't expect my clients to become intimate friends, but I do expect a modicum of loyalty."

"And you didn't get it from Cintia?"

"No, Agent Gonçalves, I didn't. Do you read *Fofocas?*"

"I've seen it around."

"It's trash, and it's full of lies, but I find it a useful tool. I'm only asking because there was a recent article about Cintia's new agent and his stable of clients. All of those clients, until last month, were clients of mine. Cintia was quoted as saying I'd been a good agent once, now become but an aged shadow of my former self. She went on to state that anyone truly concerned about their career shouldn't consider employing me."

"Ouch."

"Ouch, indeed."

"Do you think she believed what she was saying?"

"I do not."

"Why, then, would she do it?"

"I have a supposition."

"Nothing concrete?"

"No. Simply a supposition."

"Something to do with money?"

"Money?" Marques scoffed. "No, Agent Gonçalves. Nothing at all to do with money. Cintia is greedy. She loves money. She can never get enough of it. But, as far as our relationship is concerned, it's no longer a factor. She has achieved what physicists call critical mass. She's hot and getting hotter. She no longer needs external impetus to fuel her growth. Despite her disagreeable personality, Cintia is getting more offers of work than she can possibly accept. Money she could make with me or with any other agent. Money wouldn't be a motive for her to switch."

"What then?"

"I could be wrong, but I suspect a romantic liaison with her new agent."

"If that's so," Gonçalves said, "she's being discrete about it."

Marques smiled. "You've been talking to Caio Prado."

"How did you know?"

"After that damned article appeared in *Fofocas*, the Artist's mother came to see me. By that time, it was apparent there was no love lost between me and her potential future daughter-in-law. Juraci wanted to know if I had any dirt to dish, told me she'd hired a detective, told me it was Prado. Not a bad choice, by the way."

"He doesn't make much of an impression."

"That's one of his strengths. People don't notice him; he fits in anywhere; he's never perceived as a threat. Prado is a sly old fox. Lots of people in the entertainment industry use him, and he knows a good deal about it. Juraci could afford the best. In Prado, she got it."

"So you told Juraci your supposition about this new agent of Cintia's?"

"Actually, I didn't."

"Why?"

"I was still in a state of shock, still trying to understand *why* Cintia did what she did. Since then, I've given it a great deal of thought. Frankly, I can't come up with any other explanation."

"Who is this guy?" Gonçalves asked. "This new agent of hers?"

"A young man by the name of Tarso Mello. Actually, his name *isn't* Mello, or even Tarso, but it's the one he goes by, a stage name, one that was chosen for him."

"What's the name he was baptized under?"

Marques scratched his head. "I'm not sure he *was* baptized. I think he's Jewish, but that's beside the point. He never uses his original name. Tarso Mello is the only name you'll need to locate him."

Gonçalves made a note of it and said, "Okay, go on."

"He was an actor once, a bad one, but he was extraordinarily good-looking when he was younger, and he had a reasonably good run as a photo model. But then, when he started pushing thirty-five . . ." Marques held out two hands palms upward.

"His bookings started to dry up?"

"Indeed they did, and he was without a single prospect of a role in television or cinema, so he started casting about for another career."

"And that's when Cintia and Mello started a relationship?"

Marques nodded.

"That's not a fact, mind you," he said, "only an assumption. All I can tell you with certainty is that Cintia came to me and asked me to take him on as an assistant. I said I didn't need an assistant. What I *didn't* tell her was that, even if I *had* needed an assistant, I would never have considered Mello. To be a good agent you have to have a modicum of sensitivity, and you have to be intelligent. Mello has no sensitivity at all, and he's astoundingly stupid."

"Cintia took it badly? Your refusal to hire Mello?"

"She got nasty, as she always does whenever she doesn't get her way. But I stood firm. I thought, and I continue to think, that Mello would do me more harm if I accepted him than if I rejected him, even if Cintia did get her nose out of joint."

"Even if you lost her as a client?"

"That aspect of it didn't enter into my deliberations. I thought the storm would blow over."

"Had you known then what you know now, would you have acted differently?"

"I would have acted in exactly the same way. My days have been less lucrative since Cintia left, but they've been far more peaceful. At this stage in my life, peace is of more value than money."

"From everything I've heard of the woman, I can understand why you're happy to be rid of her. But I detect a certain inconsistency."

"What's that?"

"You're telling me she switched her business for emotional reasons. That doesn't sound like the Cintia Tadesco I'm learning about. From everything I've heard, she's nothing if not calculating. She doesn't let emotion get in the way of her goals."

Marques leaned back in his chair. "We humans are complex creatures, Agent Gonçalves. We're hardly ever one hundred percent this or that. Cintia Tadesco may be largely a calculating bitch, but she's still capable of an emotional act. In this case," he said, "I think she's committed two of them. I think she did what she did to favor Mello—but also to spite me."

"To spite you? Simply because you wouldn't give her what she wanted?"

Mello nodded, and a lock of mane tumbled in front his eye. He lifted a hand and brushed it aside. "When Cintia Tadesco doesn't get what she wants, she reacts like the spoiled child she is. She's extraordinarily impulsive. I've seen her turn on people in a heartbeat. One moment she loves you, and the next she's ready to destroy you. It happened to me. In time, it will happen to Mello."

"Convinced of that, are you?"

"I am. And for Mello it will be worse than it was for me. She brought him *all* of his clients. When she takes them away, it will destroy him."

"Could she do that?"

"Of course she could."

"Doesn't he have them under contract?"

"Big clients, Agent Gonçalves, the ones that really matter, resent signing contracts. It makes them feel constricted. They want to be free, at the drop of a hat, to distribute their largesse to whomever they wish."

"Do you continue to manage Marco Franco, Cintia's former boyfriend?"

"I do. Not that it's doing either one of us any good. He's quite unemployable at the moment."

"Took it hard, did he?"

"Terribly hard. And with good reason. She hurt the poor bastard in just about every way she *could* hurt him. He not only gave her his heart, he also gave her a BMW, one of the big ones, and a house. She kept the car and the house, stabbed him in the heart and went on to torpedo his reputation."

"I think I know the answer to this, but let me ask you anyway."

"Yes?"

"Why is Cintia Tadesco hanging around with the Artist? Do you think she loves him?"

"Certainly not. She's with him for what he can do for her, and for what she can take from him."

"Do you think she might be involved in this kidnapping business?"

"I think not."

"Why?"

"Why would she be? She can get everything she wants from the Artist without involving herself in a crime."

"Just bear with me for a minute. Suppose Juraci had the goods on her. Suppose she could prove that Cintia was betraying Tico, and she was planning to go to him with the information."

"Then you'd have to assume that Cintia knew ahead of time that Juraci was going to do it."

"Okay, assume that as well."

Marques reflected for a moment. "Perhaps. But . . ."

"But what?"

"But I hope, for the Artist's sake, that Cintia Tadesco had nothing to do with the disappearance of his mother."

"You *hope*? Why?"

"Because, if Cintia *is* involved, I'd virtually assure you that we're not going to see Senhora Santos again in this life. And that's the truth."

Chapter Nineteen

"I'M GONNA NEED YOUR guns," Captain Miranda's chief bodyguard said. "Nobody who's carrying gets in to see the boss."

Silva and Arnaldo were in an anteroom accessible only through two steel doors. One led to the elevator, the other to Miranda's inner office. The bodyguard was a tall black man wearing a single gold earring and a blue pinstripe suit of impeccable cut. His number two was a thug with a low forehead, nowhere near as well dressed, and missing an ear.

Arnaldo and Silva surrendered their pistols.

"And now," the black man said, "my partner here is going to frisk you."

"We're federal cops, for Christ's sake," Arnaldo said. "You saw our goddamned IDs."

"If you are who you say you are, then you know how easy it is to fake IDs. The rule is I gotta frisk you. You don't want to submit to it, that's okay. But then you leave without seeing the boss."

Arnaldo turned to Silva. "I think he's outsmarted us. This calls for a change in plan."

"What plan is that?" the black man said.

"We were gonna walk in here, shoot your boss and go to lunch."

The black man smiled. "Never gonna happen," he said. "Not on my watch. Put your hands on the wall and assume the position."

"Been with him long?" Silva asked as the guy without an ear frisked him.

"Eleven years," the black man said.

"Good job?"

"Boring. The boss hardly ever sends me out to kill people any more."

"I can understand how you'd miss it," Arnaldo said. "Why not do it in your spare time? Kind of like a hobby?"

"I only do it for money."

"Like your mother?"

The hands playing over Silva's body stopped moving. They remained on his left leg, motionless, during a long silence—and only finished the act of frisking him when the black man started speaking again.

"You calling my mother a whore?" he said.

There was no change in the inflection of his voice. But, somehow, Silva knew he was furious.

"I thought we were talking about killing," Arnaldo said, a hint of satisfaction creeping into his voice. Obviously, he'd sensed the same thing Silva had. "But, come to think of it, there used to be a black slut working the Rua Aurora who looked just like—"

"Can be really fucking dangerous telling jokes like that. Could be you need a tour of the collection."

"Collection?"

The bodyguard inclined his head toward a glass-fronted cabinet butted up against one wall.

The thug who'd been doing the frisking stepped back and said, "Clean."

Arnaldo strolled over to the cabinet. The black man came to stand beside him.

Beyond the glass, and distributed over three shelves, were several dozen instruments of torture.

"Some of this stuff is almost five hundred years old, was used during the Inquisition." The black man pointed.

"See those pincers? How they're blackened at the tips? That's because they used to heat them up red hot before they used them. That thing over there? It's called a thumbscrew. Supposed to hurt like hell, but I wouldn't know, would I? Me and Luis, we never use any of this stuff, do we Luis?"

Luis gave an appreciative chuckle. Their little joke.

"Some of the people I show this stuff to," the black man said, "get really scared."

"Which ones do you use on people who tell bad jokes?" Arnaldo said.

"Like you?"

"I never told a bad joke in my life," Arnaldo said. "You must have a lousy sense of humor."

"Wrong," the black man said. "I got a great sense of humor. Sometime, maybe, I'll get a chance to show you a few things I think are funny."

The exchange of pleasantries was cut short by a voice emanating from a speaker in the ceiling.

"When you two comedians are finished with your act," the voice said, "maybe the lot of you might like to step in here."

There was a *click*, and the door to the inner sanctum opened. It turned out to be a square room, not particularly large, with no windows and only the single door.

Miranda got up to greet them. He was a handsome man in a pink short-sleeved shirt.

"You guys want coffee?" he asked.

"No," Silva said.

He despised people like Miranda. He didn't want anything from the man except information. The bicheiro seemed to sense Silva's hostility.

"Sit," Miranda said, managing to make it sound like he was giving orders to a dog.

"How about if your two colleagues here go and stand where we can see them," Silva said. "I don't like them breathing down my neck."

"Do it," Miranda said. And they did, taking positions behind him, leaning against the wall.

Silva took his time sinking into one of the two chairs Miranda used for guests. Arnaldo waited a beat and followed suit.

Last of all, Miranda reassumed his seat.

"So what do you want?" he said.

"What can you tell us," Silva said, "about the kidnapping of the Artist's mother?"

Miranda's voice took on an edge. "I can tell you that it was a fucking unpatriotic thing to do, and if the bastards who did it fall into my hands, I'll have Gaspar here string them up by the balls."

Arnaldo looked at Gaspar. The black man was smiling at him.

"That your name? Gaspar?"

"That's my name," he said. "And stringing people up by the balls is one of the things I think is funny. Hard to do, though, to people as fat as you are, on account of the fact that their scrotums rip right out."

"You know what?" Arnaldo said. "If you were doing the ball-stringing to one of the guys who snatched the Artist's mother, I'd stand by and let you do it. I wouldn't even take out my handcuffs until you were finished."

"First sensible thing you said since you came in here," the black man said. "Now you know my name. What's yours?"

"Arnaldo Nunes."

"Huh," Gaspar said, as if he was storing the name away for future reference.

"I hate to break up this little love fest," Miranda said, "but I'm busy. Is that all you came for? Just to ask me that question?"

"Not just for that," Silva said.

"What, then?"

"How about you put the word out that you'd be grateful for any information that helps us to find the lady?"

"You know what? I already have. But don't count on me passing the information along to you."

"All we want is to get that woman back," Silva said. "That's all. I don't give a damn what happens to whomever kidnapped her."

"Well, that's good," Miranda said. "It's good you don't give a damn about what happens to whomever kidnapped her, because *I* do. And I don't want any conflict between us on that score. I don't need any more trouble with the law; I got enough already. Speaking of which, what brought you here so early in the investigation? Why did you think of me?"

Silva considered telling Miranda about Talafero's accusation—and decided not to.

"You have a lot of contacts," he said, "more than most people. I'm talking to everyone who might be able to help."

"You know what, Cop? I don't believe you. Somebody's spreading rumors about me, and I got a good idea who it is."

"Do you?"

"It was that *canalha* Talafero, wasn't it?" Miranda was looking deeply into Silva's eyes, hoping for a reaction. He didn't get one.

"Football is just a business to him," Miranda went on, "a way of making money. You know he's selling the Artist to Real Madrid?"

"Everybody knows it," Silva said. "What's your point?"

"Talafero goes around saying things about me," Miranda said, "so let me say this about him. I happen to know he placed a bet in London this morning, a bet for a hundred thousand English pounds *against* Brazil. What does that say to you?"

"It suggests he has a hundred thousand English pounds offshore. That would be illegal unless he declared it on his tax statements, which he probably hasn't. How did you find out about it?"

Miranda waved the question aside.

"That's none of your goddamned business," he said. "You know what it says to me? It says he arranged to have the Artist's mother snatched so he could place that bet with a good chance of winning it, that's what."

"Could be," Silva said, "that he's just betting against the likelihood of getting her back."

"If I needed any further prompting to get involved in this," Miranda said, "he gave it to me with that bet. I'd love to see him lose his hundred thousand fucking English pounds."

"But you don't want to see him selling the Artist to Real Madrid, because that would mean he'd have a lot of money to invest in this year's carnival."

"You figured that out all by yourself?"

"All by myself."

"You're lying. How about you get out of here and let me get back to business? Your welcome just dried up."

* * *

BACK AT the office, Mara was waiting for them. "That Sá woman knew more than she let on."

"Sá woman?" Arnaldo said.

"Juraci's neighbor."

"Didn't she already tell all to Hector?"

"No."

"Why not?"

"She didn't want to appear nosy."

"So you. . . ?"

"Played nosy myself."

"Watcha mean, *played?*"

"Shut up, Nunes. You want to hear this or not?"

"We want," Silva said. "Ignore him."

"I got her to gossiping."

"Kindred spirits," Arnaldo said.

"One more remark like that, Nunes—"

"Let her talk, Arnaldo," Silva said. "Go on, Mara."

"After her husband left," Mara said, "Angela went to an open window and stood behind the curtain."

"To eavesdrop on the conversation?"

"Uh huh."

"And then?"

"She heard Juraci call the postman José."

"A name? You got a name?"

"I did."

"Excellent."

"It would be," Arnaldo said. "if the guy's name was Nicodemos or Lemuel. But José? José has got to be the most common name in this country."

"For once," she said, "you're right. Statistically, it is. There are one hundred and twenty six postmen in the greater metropolitan area with the name José. But I'm going to find us *our* José."

"How?"

"I had one of my girls go through the post office's personnel records. She brought me photographs and home addresses of every damned one of the hundred and twenty-six."

"Which you're going to show to Senhora Sá?" Silva said.

"Correct."

"Good. What else are you working on?"

"A girl's best friend."

"That would be me," Arnaldo said.

"That would be the diamonds, Nunes. The words *friend*

and *nightmare* are not synonyms. On the off-chance they try to sell the stones here in Brazil, I'm getting detailed specifications on the ones the Artist bought."

"He bought them already?"

"He did, and I've got a diamond expert going over them as we speak. We'll circulate the results to every registered jeweler in the country. If we get lucky, we'll be on those guys like flies on a big smelly pile of Arnaldo Nuneses."

"That," Arnaldo said, "was uncalled for."

Mara smiled. "I thought you'd like it if I talked dirty."

Chapter Twenty

WHEN TARSO MELLO MADE a minute adjustment to his Hermés necktie, one of his French cuffs slid back to reveal a gold Rolex. That, Gonçalves suspected, was what the adjustment was designed to do—allow him to display his expensive watch.

"As I told you on the telephone," Mello said haughtily, "I never discuss my clients' personal lives with anyone."

"And as I told *you*," Gonçalves said, "I find that commendable. But, in this specific instance, I'm going to have to insist on your cooperation. What you tell me will be held in the strictest confidence."

"I don't propose to tell you anything," Mello said.

Gonçalves leaned back in his chair and crossed his arms. "How would you like to have your taxes audited?"

Mello blinked. His eyes were a striking shade of blue, but didn't seem to have much behind them. It took a moment for him to grasp the significance of the non sequitur.

"Are you blackmailing me?" he said.

"Not at all. I asked you a simple question. How would you like to have your taxes audited? Gone over, in fact, with a fine-tooth comb? You think I can't get a court order to access your bank accounts? Think again."

"This is preposterous!"

Gonçalves shrugged. "The choice is yours. You either talk to me about Cintia Tadesco, or I'm out of here. But I won't be gone for long, and when I come back, it will be with accountants from the *receita federal*."

Mello took in a deep breath and looked out the window, as if something outside had captured his attention. Not likely, as Mello's office was on the twenty-third floor of a highrise on Avenida Paulista. All the buildings on his block were skyscrapers, and his view didn't extend any further than the other side of the street.

"What do you want to know?" he asked, sullenly.

"There's a rumor going around that you have a personal relationship with Cintia Tadesco. True or false?"

"Define *personal relationship*," he said.

"That the two of you are lovers."

Mello met Gonçalves's eyes, broke into a broad grin, and then into an outright laugh.

"What's so funny?" Gonçalves said.

"What's funny, Agent Gonçalves, is that you couldn't be more misinformed."

"Couldn't I?"

"I'm gay, Agent Gonçalves, gay and out of the closet since my mother died."

"My condolences."

"Condolences? Are you a homophobe?" Mello said it with a straight face, tried to make Gonçalves believe his question was a serious one.

Leo Marques had been right. Mello was a very bad actor.

"When did she pass away?" Gonçalves said.

"Not that it's any of your business, but it was at the end of last year."

"You live alone?"

Mello looked petulant. The interview had taken on overtones of an interrogation. "I live with my partner."

"Where?"

"Granja Viana."

Gonçalves gave Mello his best suspicious stare. Marques would have been impressed.

"Juraci Santos lives in Granja Viana," he said.

"A lot of people live in Granja Viana. What's your point?"

"It wasn't a point. It was an observation. What's your partner's name?"

Mello's eyes got big. Outrage, maybe. Or fear?

"Edson Campos. Leave him out of it."

"Why should I?"

"He has nothing to do with my work or my clients. He doesn't know Cintia. He isn't even involved in the entertainment industry."

Mello's voice had turned shrill. Gonçalves decided it was outrage.

"No?"

"No. He's a veterinary technician."

"Tell me more about Senhorita Tadesco."

Taking the spotlight off his partner had an immediate calming effect. Mello seemed to relax.

"What do you want to know?"

"Do you like her?"

"Do I *what?*"

"Like her. Not as a client. As a person."

"What's that got to do with—"

"Just answer the question, Senhor Mello."

"Like her? Actually, I do."

"The way I hear it, most people hate her."

"I'm not most people. I find her candor and single-mindedness refreshing. I don't hate her a bit, and she knows I don't. She wouldn't continue to retain me if I did."

"How's her relationship with her prospective mother-in-law?"

"Cintia doesn't discuss her personal life with me."

"Never?"

"Never!"

"You wouldn't be lying to me, would you, Senhor Mello? I don't like lies."

"I'm not lying, and I resent the implication that I am."

"You don't recall Cintia saying *anything* to you about Juraci Santos?"

"No."

"How important to Cintia is her relationship with Tico Santos?"

"Very important. She loves him."

"How can you possibly be sure?"

"What?"

"If, as you've just alleged, Cintia doesn't discuss her personal life with you, how can you be sure she loves Tico?"

"It's . . . it's been in the newspapers, in the magazines."

"And you believe everything you read in the magazines?"

"I . . . I . . ."

Mello's gape reminded Gonçalves of a fish. Gonçalves disliked fish.

***

"He was nervous as hell." Gonçalves was on the street again, calling Silva to report. "I think he's hiding something, and the dumb bastard isn't good at it."

"So you don't think Mello is particularly intelligent?"

"Hell, no. He's a dumb fuck. You think it's true? That part about his being gay?"

"I think it must be. He'd know how easy it would be to check. He even encouraged you to do so."

"Yeah, that's true I guess."

"And if he's nervous, it doesn't necessarily mean he's hiding something. Let's put Mello on the back burner for a minute. Remember that postman?"

"The one Juraci's neighbors saw her talking to?"

"Correct. The Sá woman has identified him from a photo. Come back to the office. You and Hector are going to pay a visit to the gentleman."

Chapter Twenty-One

THE POSTMAN'S NAME WAS José Afonso Lyra. He lived in Penha, a lower-middle class neighborhood in the northern suburbs. The narrow, one-way streets were unpaved, the signposts few, and Hector and Gonçalves had to stop several times for directions. The sun had set by the time they arrived.

The Lyra manse turned out to be a tiny, free-standing house, located on an equally tiny lot and constructed of unpainted concrete blocks. A dim glow shone through the shutters. The front door was ajar. From within, they could hear the audio of *Radio Mundo's* third soap opera of the night.

Hector took a picture out of his pocket, a copy lifted from Lyra's personnel records.

"This is him."

Gonçalves brought the photo close to his face and studied it in the light of a street lamp. "Scrawny little runt like that isn't going to give us any trouble."

"No? I ran into a fellow once who was even smaller and scrawnier. He had a shotgun. He killed three cops before they brought him down."

Gonçalves handed the photo back and loosened the Glock in his holster. He kept one hand on the grip, as he followed Hector up the concrete path.

There was no doorbell. Hector balled a fist and rapped on the wood.

"Senhor Lyra?"

There was a rustling from inside, and a skinny scarecrow of a man holding a drinking glass in one hand and a cigarette in the other appeared in the opening. His personnel records from the post office had given his age as forty-two, but he looked older. His only garment was a ragged pair of shorts. Gonçalves took his hand off the butt of his gun.

"Who are you guys?" the scarecrow said.

"Federal cops," Hector said. "Are you José Lyra?"

"Yeah, I'm him." Lyra frowned. "What do you want with me?"

"We want to talk to you about the argument you had with Juraci Santos," Hector said.

"Ah, crap. What did she tell you? That I was blackmailing her, or some such shit?"

"She didn't tell us anything," Hector said. "She's been kidnapped."

"Really?" Lyra said raising his eyebrows.

He was either the last person in Brazil who didn't know what had happened to the Artist's mother, or he was lying.

"You don't watch the news?" Gonçalves said. "Read the papers?"

"I get home too late for the news, and I get all the reading I want from addresses on envelopes. So she got her ass kidnapped, did she? Hell, I wouldn't wish that on anybody, not even that selfish bitch."

"Why do you call her that?"

"Because she is. Come on in. Have a drink. I'll tell you all about it."

All Lyra had to offer was cachaça, but the cachaça was out of a jug, and it was amber-colored. A jug meant domestically produced; amber that it was aged. Both cops accepted a glass, sipped, made appreciative noises.

"Yeah," Lyra said, "smooth, isn't it? Made on a *fazenda* near Riberão Preto. A friend of mine brings it to me whenever he's in town. Okay, you asked about Juraci? Well, here it is: she was my sister-in-law."

"Wait a minute," Hector said. "Did I hear you right? Did you say sister-in-law?"

Lyra settled back in his chair, as if the story was going to be a long one.

"My first wife's name was Graça," he said, "and she was Juraci's sister. She'd just turned fifteen when she got pregnant. I was six months older. Our parents said we had to get married. We were just kids, used to doing what we were told, so we did. We moved in with my parents. I left school and got a job."

"And Juraci?"

"Juraci was a year younger than Graça, only fourteen, but she was a woman already, if you know what I mean."

"Uh huh."

"She had this long brown hair that hung all the way down to the crack in her ass. I was in love with that hair. Hell, I was in love with *her*."

"How about your wife?"

"I was in love with her, too. For a while. But then we lost the kid, and it hurt her, and she didn't want to screw anymore. Meanwhile, here's Juraci, giving me the eye every time we go around to her parents' place for Sunday dinner. I could see she was keen. I heard she'd had a couple of boyfriends, wasn't a virgin or anything like that, so I went around one day and tried my luck. Her mother and father both worked, but she was still going to school. I knew she got home around three. I told my boss I was sick and went over there."

Lyra took a final drag on his cigarette, extinguished it, and took a sip of his cachaça.

"And then?" Gonçalves prompted.

"It was like she was expecting me. We fucked right there in the front room, her bending over one end of the couch, me standing behind her, looking through a crack in the curtain to make sure nobody walked in on us."

"So you became your sister-in-law's lover?"

"Best piece of ass I ever had. The best ever. She'd do everything, let me stick it anywhere. And she loved it! If I forget everything, I won't forget that. As far as I was concerned, it could have gone on forever."

"What happened? Did you get caught?"

"No. We never did. But one day, out of a clear blue sky, she told me not to come around anymore. She was tired of me, she said. Later, I found out she had this thing going with some kid at school."

"How did you find out?"

"She got pregnant, that's how. You'd think she would have learned, right? I mean after what happened to her sister and all? But no, she went out and got herself pregnant. Stupid, I thought at the time. But Juraci never did stupid stuff, even when she was a teenager, so when I looked back on it later, I got to thinking she did it on purpose."

"Because she loved him? Because she wanted him to marry her?"

"That's what I figure. It was good for me in a way, though, because the baby could just as well have been mine."

"One minute you say *she* was stupid, and the next you say the kid could have been yours. What's with that?"

"What's with that is I broke a condom. I learned my lesson with Graça, and always used them with Juraci, but I never broke one. Only that one time. Never before and never since. The way I figure it, my ex-wife found it in my wallet. And she sure as hell knew I wasn't using condoms on *her*. So the bitch stuck a pin through it, or something. She wouldn't have done it if she'd known it was gonna wind up in her sister. And the fact she never knew was really lucky for me. If she, or her parents, had ever found out who I'd planned to use that condom on, they would have killed me."

"What happened to the baby?" Hector asked. "Did Juraci have it?"

Lyra was about to take another sip of his cachaça. He took the glass away from his lips and smiled. "You mean you still don't get it?" he said.

Comprehension dawned for both cops at the same moment. "Are you telling us the baby was Tico?" Hector said.

Lyra nodded. "You think he looks like me?"

"Frankly?" Hector said. "No."

Lyra sighed. "No," he said. "Me neither. *Caralho*, that boy's even uglier than I am. But now it's all these years later, and here's Juraci giving out that the kid's father died in an accident, and here's Rafael—"

"Who's Rafael?"

"Rafael Souza, the boyfriend she had at school. And here's Rafael, not stepping up to claim he's the kid's old man. And nobody else either. So I figured—"

"Why do you think Rafael didn't put in a claim to be the father?"

"Probably because he doesn't think he is. Rafael's father had a good business, an *oficina mechanica*. He was well-off, and he didn't want his son marrying some slut. When Juraci got pregnant, he checked around and discovered a few things."

"Like what?"

"Juraci was screwing a whole bunch of other guys. At least three, probably more. If any of them knew then what they know now, it would have been different. I mean, who wouldn't want to be the father of the best striker in the world, right? But back then, nobody wanted to be the husband of a slut, and nobody wanted to assume responsibility for somebody else's baby. All of them bowed out."

"And you?"

"Nobody ever found out about me, thank God. Like I said, her parents would have killed me. Well, as to the rest of it—hey, you want another drink?"

"No, thanks," Hector said.

Lyra turned to Gonçalves. "You?"

Gonçalves shook his head. "I'm driving," he said.

"Yeah, okay, where were we?"

"How did it all end?" Hector asked. "What happened to your wife? Your in-laws?"

"My wife died last year. Cancer. She was only forty-one. We never had any more kids. She was scared to death of getting pregnant again. Her parents are dead too, killed in one of those bus crashes on the BR116 when they were going to Paraná to visit her brother. I hadn't seen Juraci in years. Graça wouldn't have her in the house, said she couldn't forgive her for what she did to their folks, getting pregnant and all."

"But Graça got pregnant herself."

"Right. But she snagged a husband out of it, and Juraci didn't, so that made Graça the passionate wife who just couldn't wait for the wedding, and her sister was the slut. You want to hear the truth?"

"Tell us."

"Graça and Juraci never really got along. I figure it was just an excuse to keep her out of the house."

"I think I see where this is going," Hector said.

"Where what's going?"

"What the argument was about."

"Well," Lyra said, defensively. "Wouldn't you do the same thing? I mean, here's the kid sitting on a pile of money. And it could be my kid. I couldn't approach him directly. Why should he believe me? But if Juraci admitted she was fucking me, and the kid would agree to take a blood test, hell, to me it was like playing the lottery. You know your chances of winning are pretty slim, but you play anyway, right?"

"Uh huh."

"It wasn't hard to find out where she lived, but it was hell to get there. I took a bus to Cotia, got off on the way, and walked to her place. Musta been a good ten kilometers."

"You didn't try to call her first?"

"She's unlisted."

"So you just showed up on her doorstep and asked to see her?"

"And was she surprised! She was nice enough at first, thought I'd just dropped by for old time's sake, but when I told her what I wanted, she started treating me like shit. *Where were you when I needed you?* Stuff like that."

"She refused to even consider the blood test thing?"

"She did."

"And it made you angry?"

"Sure it did. Hey, you're not suggesting that I had anything to do with this kidnapping, are you? Just because of a thing like that?"

"Did you, José? Did you have anything to do with it?"

"Hell, no. I wasn't happy about her attitude, but I gotta admit she was right. I didn't step up when she was accused of being the family whore. I didn't go out of my way to stay in touch. I haven't even seen her in what? Twenty years? And, besides, she's getting long in the tooth. Maybe she'll be looking for some company in a few years. I could always try again, right? Hey, you sure you don't want some more cachaça?"

Chapter Twenty-Two

AT NINE IN THE evening, Silva was sitting at Hector's desk, re-reading Mara's most recent summary of the team's activities, when the author put in an appearance.

"That guy, Miranda?" she said. "The bicheiro?"

Silva put down the folder and looked up expectantly.

"What about him, Mara?"

"He's on the phone. He wants to talk to you."

Silva looked at his watch.

"What are you doing here at this hour?"

"Waiting for you to take me to dinner." She smiled, but Silva didn't think she meant it as a joke. "Line five."

Silva picked up the receiver and pushed the appropriate button.

"Silva."

Miranda began without preamble. "Just one question," he said. "Did the kidnappers tell you they wanted to be paid in diamonds?"

Silva stiffened.

"Where did you get that information?" he said.

"I'll take that as a yes," Miranda said. "Get this: Somebody's checking out the market in illegal gemstones. They want to know how they can best convert diamonds into cash. And they want to know details about the most marketable stones, their size and quality."

"Names, Miranda. I need names."

"I don't have any. Not yet."

"But you will?"

"By tomorrow morning."

"And when you get this information, are you going to share it?"

"It depends. I do something for you, maybe you can do something for me. Tit for tat. Let's talk about it."

"When and where?"

"Noon. My office."

Silva thought about it, concluded he had nothing to lose. "There will be two of us, myself and Arnaldo Nunes."

"Nunes, huh? That the gorilla who was with you last time?"

"I'll be sure to tell him you said that."

Miranda laughed. "And I'll tell my boys you're coming. Gaspar, particularly. He's got a thing for your buddy Nunes."

Miranda hung up. Silva took out his notebook and looked up the Artist's unlisted number. When he called, Cintia Tadesco picked up the phone.

"Tico's sleeping," she said. "I have no intention of waking him up."

"A question for you, then."

"What?"

"The kidnapper's demand that payment be made in diamonds . . ."

"Yes?"

"Who have you told about it?"

"Me? Nobody."

"And the Artist?"

"You guys asked to keep it quiet. That's what we did."

"You're sure you didn't confide in anyone else?"

She gave an exaggerated sigh. "Yes, I'm sure." Then, more sharply: "I don't like repeating myself. What's this about?"

"Captain Miranda called me. He knows about the diamonds."

"That bicheiro? What's he got to do with it?"

"He's helping us with our inquiries."

Helping you with your inquiries? Oh, *please.* You trying to sound like you're Scotland Yard?"

Silva, with an effort, managed to keep his temper.

"We're meeting tomorrow. He hopes to have more information by then. Meantime, please continue to keep quiet about the diamonds."

"It's gonna get out anyway. The kid who runs the website knows, which means his father, Tico's agent, knows, which means a lot of other people know, because a bigger-mouthed *filho da puta* was never born. And then there are all the cops that know."

"I don't think—"

"The cops would let it slip? Ha! Don't make me laugh. From what I hear, cops are cheap. You buy them a meal, or a drink, and they spill their guts. Oh, hey, sorry, it didn't occur to me until just now that you're a cop."

"Are you trying to be offensive, Senhorita Tadesco?"

"I'd say I'm succeeding. Wouldn't you?"

She hung up.

Silva slammed down the phone.

"Bitch," he said.

"Who?" Mara said, coming in from the corridor.

"Cintia Tadesco."

"Why were you talking to her?"

Silva told her.

"Sounds like that visit you two made to Miranda paid off," Mara said.

"He called Arnaldo a gorilla."

"Maybe he's not such a bad guy after all," Mara said. "How about that dinner?"

Chapter Twenty-Three

SILVA WAS STAYING AT the Sorrento, a small hotel within walking distance of Hector's office. When his cell phone rang just before seven the following morning, he was sound asleep. He groped for it and put it to his ear.

"Silva."

"I'm at Miranda's place," Hector said. "His home, not his office. I sent a car to pick you up."

"What happened?"

"Turn on the television."

"Which channel?" Silva said, reaching for the remote.

"Take your pick," Hector said. "It's on all of them."

The coverage of the explosion, and the fire that followed, was being carried live. Silva watched the images while he dressed. He was knotting his tie when the reception desk called to tell him his car was waiting.

He arrived to find Arnaldo, Hector and Gonçalves surrounding the man in charge of quelling the blaze, a fire captain named Godoy.

"So that's all I can tell you," Godoy was saying, "but we should have some answers soon."

Silva was introduced, shook hands with the captain, and squinted upward into the morning light.

"Miranda lived in the penthouse," Hector said.

The building had been eight stories tall. Now it was seven.

"Bomb?" Silva asked.

Godoy shrugged.

"Give me another explanation then."

"It's like I just told these guys, I don't want to speculate. I've got an examiner up there now. Go have some coffee. Come back in half an hour."

The cops went to a nearby padaria and took their cups to a table.

"Miranda was there when it happened," Hector said.

"That's confirmed, is it?" Silva asked.

"He got home at around ten-thirty last night. He never left."

"That based on surveillance tapes?"

Hector nodded. "Time-coded. Security is, if anything, even tighter than at his office."

Silva drained his coffee. "Run me through it."

"To start with, Miranda's elevator goes directly to his penthouse."

"*Went* directly to his penthouse," Arnaldo said. "That elevator doesn't go anywhere anymore."

"Went, then," Hector said. "The point is, no stops along the way. You could get on, or off, either from the garage or the penthouse, no other options."

"Stairwell?" Silva asked.

"Sealed with a grate and rigged with an alarm. The grate is on the floor below, steel, hinged, triple-locked and set into a steel frame. The frame is embedded in the wall. Godoy's examiner couldn't open the locks, so she had to cut her way through it."

"She? A woman?"

"Either that, or a guy with long hair, a high voice and breasts," Arnaldo said.

Silva ignored him.

"Only the one elevator?"

"There are two others," Hector said, "social and service, running upwards from the garage, but programmed not to go any further than the floor below Miranda's. And to make damned sure they didn't, steel girders were welded across the shafts."

"He'd be good and stuck, wouldn't he, if there was a power failure."

"He had a generator in his apartment."

"Big enough to power the elevator?"

"So I'm told."

"Security cameras?"

"The building runs one on every entrance, including the garage. Miranda had two more of his own, one in the stairwell, one in the elevator."

"The recorders for those two?"

"Upstairs, in the apartment."

Silva glanced upward at the smoldering ruin.

"So they're toast?" he said.

"They're toast," Hector confirmed.

"Guards?"

"Two in the apartment, one in the garage. The guy in the garage survived."

"Other fatalities?"

"Miranda's wife and two kids."

Silva narrowed his eyes. "Kids? There were kids?"

"Third wife. Eight and six, both girls."

Nothing affected Silva so much as the murder of children.

"You figure this is business related?" Hector said, breaking a short silence. "Some rival trying to take over Miranda's bank?"

"Maybe," Silva said. "But . . ."

Arnaldo caught his meaning and shook his head. "A job like this," he said, "takes time to set up, lots more time than just a few hours. Besides, who knew Miranda was going to talk to us?"

"Cintia Tadesco," Silva said. "Cintia Tadesco knew Miranda was going to talk to us."

"She couldn't have done it on her own. She would have needed help."

"Five million dollars buys a lot of help. How about access to the garage from the outside?"

"Two sets of gates, on tracks, motor controlled. You go down the ramp and honk your horn. They check you out on the TV camera and open the first gate. Then they close it behind you before they open the second."

"Who's 'they'?"

The doormen in the lobby."

"Is that the only switch?"

"It is."

"Can both gates be opened at once?"

Gonçalves shook his head.

"Do they issue remote controls to the residents?"

"No, and they don't open the gates to anyone but them— or people they authorize—in person."

"Other entrances?"

"The social entrance faces the street. The service entrance faces a parking lot in the rear. Access to the lot is via a driveway that runs along the side of the building."

"The tapes?"

"I looked at the ones of the front door and the service entrance. I haven't had time yet for the garage."

"Anything suspicious?"

"Not yet. The images are lousy. The recorders are VHS devices, older than my grandmother. They run on a twenty-four hour loop. I shut the system down as soon as I got here, but by then it was hours after the explosion."

Silva glanced at his watch. "It's time. Let's go back and hear what that fire examiner has to say."

***

Elisabeth Correia had a smudged face and looked to be in her mid-thirties. Her heavy yellow coat was two sizes too big. When she took off her helmet, spiky black hair protruded in all directions.

"A bomb," she said. "Almost certainly."

"What kind?" Silva asked.

"I can't tell you without chemical analysis. You want a guess?"

"Please."

"Ammonium nitrate and fuel oil, or maybe kerosene."

"A fertilizer bomb?"

"Yes. The fruitcake's weapon of choice. They're bulky, but they're oh-so-easy to make. The detonator would have been the most sophisticated part of the package. If I'm lucky, I'll find some trace of it."

"In that mess? Seriously?"

"Seriously. Something else: they used an accelerant, probably gasoline. Liters and liters of the stuff. They poured it all over the place."

"Did you find the children?"

"Yes."

"Were they—"

She put up a hand, as if to fend him off. "Please, Chief Inspector," she said. "I'm a mother, and I'm very close to losing it, and if I talk about what I just saw, I *will* lose it. That wouldn't do either one of us any good, now would it?"

"I understand."

"Do you?" She was looking up at the building.

"Believe me, I do. I once had a son."

She met his eyes. He could see, now, that she had tears in hers.

"I'm sorry," she said.

Commiseration or apology, Silva wasn't sure which.

"Any idea how they got the bomb into the penthouse?" he asked.

"They *didn't* get it into the penthouse."

"How so?"

"The bomb was *under* the penthouse. It was set off in the master bedroom of the apartment below."

Chapter Twenty-Four

THE DOORMAN ON DUTY at the time of the explosion was in his fifties. He was still in a state of shock.

His relief man, recently arrived on the scene, was much younger, probably well under thirty. He was smiling, talkative and seemed to be enjoying all the excitement.

Silva positioned them side-by-side on a couch in the lobby.

"Who lived on the floor below the penthouse?"

"Atilio Nabuco, Senhor," the younger man said.

"Married?"

"Married, Senhor."

"Children?"

"Two."

"Boys? Girls?"

"One of each."

"Ages?"

The younger man shrugged and looked at the older one.

"Vanessa was eighteen last week," the older one said.

"And you know that because . . ."

"She was excited about getting her driver's license. She kept talking about it."

"How about the boy?"

"You think he's dead, Senhor?" the younger man asked.

"If he was in his parents' apartment at the time of the explosion, he is. How old?"

"Older."

"Twenty-one," the older man said. "Lito was twenty-one. A nice kid. Always polite."

"My understanding," Silva said, "is that you don't open the garage gates to people you don't know, people who aren't residents of the building."

"Correct, Senhor," the younger man said.

"What happens if there's a delivery of some kind, furniture or some such?"

Silva looked from one to the other. The older man seemed to tune out, stared at the wall, let his younger colleague answer the question. "It has to be brought upstairs in the freight elevator, but before that happens, a resident has to okay it. Nobody's allowed in the garage otherwise."

"There's a TV camera down there, right?"

"There is, Senhor."

"Where?"

"To the left of the ramp."

Silva was concentrating, now, on the younger man. "Does it capture the faces of the drivers?"

"Yes."

"But only when they come in?"

"Correct, Senhor."

"How do people signal when they want to leave?"

"It's not necessary, Senhor. There are sensors. On the way out, the gates open automatically."

"Do you keep a log of comings and goings in the garage?"

"Yes, Senhor."

"Bring it, please."

The older doorman seemed to snap out of his reverie. He got up, went into a room opening off the back of the reception desk and came back carrying a ledger. Resuming his seat on the couch, he made a gesture for Silva to sit down next to him. Then he opened the book and laid it across Silva's knees.

"Here, Senhor, you see?" he said, leaning in, putting the tip of one of his index fingers on the book. "The times are on this side, and, here"—his finger moved to the right of the page—"the numbers of the apartments. Senhor Nabuco lives in Apartment 7."

Silva raised a critical eyebrow.

"Times and apartment numbers? That's all? You don't identify the vehicles?"

"We used to have a camera that recorded them. But then the camera broke down, and we never had need of the recordings, so the owners decided not to replace it."

"No 7A or 7B?"

"This is a luxury building, Senhor. Only one apartment to a floor."

* * *

THE VIDEOTAPE was time-coded. The times corresponded closely to notations in the log. That made it possible to fast-forward between entries and quickly locate all of the comings and goings associated with Apartment 7.

They watched Nabuco leave for work, his wife leave and return with shopping bags, his son and daughter leaving and returning with books, and at 7:14, exactly, Nabuco returning home at the wheel of a white Volkswagen mini-van. It wasn't the same vehicle he'd left in that morning.

Silva froze the tape. Nabuco, his eyes wide with fear, was looking directly at the camera.

"Look at that," the older doorman said. "What a god-damned idiot."

"Idiot is right," his colleague agreed.

"Who?" Silva said.

"Antonio. The four to midnight man."

"And the supervisor's nephew," the older man added heatedly, "or he would have gotten his ass fired a long time ago. Look at Senhor Nabuco. Anyone can see he's scared out of his wits."

"Call this Antonio fellow and get him over here," Silva said. "Now."

* * *

"How the fuck was I supposed to know there was anything wrong? What am I, a mind reader?"

"Just look at him," the older doorman said, pointing at the image frozen on the screen. "Look at Senhor Nabuco's face. It's obvious he's frightened to death. How you could have missed it is a mystery to both of us."

"The two of you ganging up on me again, huh? As usual? Assholes!"

"Asshole yourself," the older man said.

"Shut up," Silva said. "Both of you. Look at it again."

He hit the rewind, then the play button. On the front seat next to Nabuco, seated well back, face in deep shadow, was a man. Or maybe a woman. It was impossible to tell.

Silva froze the image in approximately the same place he'd frozen it half a dozen times before.

"No good to keep playing it," Antonio said. "I already told you. I wasn't paying attention."

"Brought that little TV of yours along, didn't you?" The older man said. "Watching it, weren't you?"

"No," Antonio said, but he flushed.

"You've been told not to do that," his other colleague told Antonio. "And now look what happened."

"Easy for you to talk," Antonio said. "You weren't here. If you were, the same thing could have happened to you."

"Never. I'm like Cristiano here. I take my job seriously, I do."

"That's enough!" Silva said. "You recall what time the van left?"

"It didn't leave," Antonio said. "Not when I was here, it didn't."

"About three in the morning," the older doorman said.

"And you didn't find that strange?"

He shrugged. "Not particularly. Folks come and go at all hours."

"When the van reached street level, could you see who was driving?"

"No."

"Was it a man or a woman?"

"I couldn't even see that. It was too dark and, besides, it turned right. It didn't pass in front of the building."

"Let's have a look at it," Silva said.

He put the tape on fast-forward. When the van appeared again, the time code read 03:19. Silva froze the image. They all leaned in for a closer look.

An indistinguishable shape sat behind the wheel. On the screen it was no more than a featureless blob.

"Have you ever seen Senhor Nabuco driving this van?" Silva said.

All three men shook their heads.

"People here don't drive vans," the older man said. "They drive BMWs and Mercs, stuff like that. I remember thinking a van was funny."

"Funny, but you were too lazy to get off your fat ass and have a closer look, weren't you?" Antonio said.

"Don't try spreading the blame for your incompetence to me, you fuck."

Silva's phone rang. He left them sniping at each other and stepped into the lobby to answer it.

"Chief Inspector Silva?"

He didn't recognize the voice.

"I'm Silva."

"Chief Inspector, this is Warden Fuentes."

Fuentes ran the penitentiary where Fiorello Rosa, the

ace kidnapper, had been incarcerated for six of the last seven years.

"Rosa wants to talk to you, wants to know if it could be this afternoon."

"Even sooner," Silva said.

"No hurry," Fuentes said, "He isn't going anywhere."

* * *

THEY WERE heading toward their car when Arnaldo came to a sudden stop.

"Look," he said.

Gaspar, the black man who'd been Miranda's bodyguard, was standing next to one of the trucks, talking to a firefighter.

Money changed hands.

The federal cops changed direction.

"Gaspar, isn't it?" Silva said when they came within earshot.

"Yeah," the black man said, "that's right. Gaspar."

No broad grin this time. He looked angry as hell.

"I gotta get back to it," the fireman said and hurried off.

"I suppose you told him you were a reporter," Silva said.

"None of your damned business."

"What did he tell you?"

"That some filho da puta put a bomb under the boss's apartment and blew him, and his wife, and his two kids, and some friends of mine all to hell."

"How come you weren't in there with them?" Arnaldo said.

"Not that it's any of your fucking business," Gaspar said, "but it was my night off. You know how old those kids were?"

"We know," Silva said.

"Come on," Arnaldo said, "give us some help here. Who did it?"

Gaspar exploded. "You think I know? You think I don't *want* to know? What kind of a sick fuck does something like this? What kind of a callous bastard kills kids so they can get at their old man? You and me, cop, we're asking ourselves the same questions."

"You sound as pissed off as I am," Arnaldo said. "You got any kids?"

"I got two. Girls. Just like the boss had."

"Did you know," Silva said, "that your boss called us and scheduled a meeting?"

"I knew," Gaspar said. "There's a roster. Your names were on it."

"Any idea what he wanted to talk to us about?"

"No," Gaspar said. "It was none of my business. My business was to keep him safe, that's all." He turned to Arnaldo. "And spare me any wise-ass remarks. I already told you. It was my night off."

"It's gonna surprise you to learn that I wasn't gonna make any wise-ass remarks," Arnaldo said. "Who might know what he wanted to talk to us about?"

"Nobody. The boss didn't blab his business to anybody."

"Speaking of business," Silva said, "what's likely to happen to Miranda's operation now that he's dead?"

"Even if I knew, you think I'd tell a federal cop? I will tell you one thing, though."

"What's that?"

"The guy who did this is dead meat. And it won't matter a damn if you're the first ones to catch up with him. People can always be got to—wherever they are, jail or anywhere else."

"A comforting thought," Arnaldo said.

"Maybe not for you," Gaspar said, "but it sure as hell is for me."

Chapter Twenty-Five

"KILLING MIRANDA IS ONE thing," Fiorello Rosa said. "He was a cold-blooded murderer. But his two little girls? That, Chief Inspector, is way out of line. Whoever did it should rot in hell."

"I agree," Silva said.

"His wife, now, that's another matter. She was an adult. She had a choice. She must have known what kind of a man her husband was."

"Did your wife know about you?"

"Ex-wife. Yes, she did. She told everyone she didn't, but she did. Before I took my first customer, I told her what I was planning to do. Share the benefit, I said, but be aware there's a risk—and you'll be sharing that as well."

"And she accepted that?"

"She said she did. But the truth is Carolina is a person incapable of sharing. I clung to some illusions to the contrary before I was arrested, but she disabused me of them in short order. I wasn't in jail for twenty-four hours before she'd emptied our joint bank accounts. Less than a week after that, she filed for divorce. Fortunately, I'd lived with her long enough to . . . well, never mind. Enough about her. Have you given any thought to my proposition?"

"I have."

"And?"

"And we'll discuss it if you're granted a parole."

"*When* I'm granted a parole."

"You're that confident?"

"Oh, yes, Chief Inspector, I am. I'm extremely confident."

"Because?"

"Because, with a few exceptions, like yourself, this country has the best justice system money can buy."

"I'm all too aware of that. But haven't you been telling everyone you're broke?"

"I have, haven't I?" Rosa sighed. "Well, I suppose I'll just have to find the money somewhere."

"I think," Silva said, "you're likely to have more luck than we did when looking for the same money."

Rosa responded with a smile.

"Why did you want to talk to me?" Silva said.

"To share my knowledge of Ketamine."

"Ketawhat?"

"Ketamine. The substance found in the syringe. Didn't you read the lab report?"

"I've been busy. What's Ketamine? I've never heard of it."

"There's no reason why you should have. But *I*, before being totally reformed by this excellent penal system of ours, made it my business to familiarize myself with drugs that might have been of use to me in my former profession. Ketamine was one of them."

"You have my full attention, Professor."

"Ketamine was developed by Parke-Davis back in the early sixties. Initially, it was employed as an anesthetic by American medics during the Vietnam War. Small doses of it will make you high, medium doses will knock you out, large doses will kill you."

"Did you ever use it?" Silva asked.

"No. I wrote it off as too dangerous. Psychotomimetic effects have been observed in its use."

"*What* kind of effects?" Arnaldo said.

"Psychotomimetic. Delusions, hallucinations, the reactions we've come to expect from opiates."

"How easy is it to get, this Ketamine?"

"Very. In the days before my total transformation into an honest citizen, I could have acquired the drug with no difficulty whatsoever. Ketamine is still widely used in veterinary medicine. A single visit to my local unethical veterinarian would have provided me with enough to treat a dozen unwilling patients. I think it's unlikely that the situation has changed very much over the course of the last seven years."

"Interesting," Silva said, "but I don't see how knowing any of this is going to be of help. As you say, any veterinarian who'd provided the stuff to Juraci's kidnappers would, by definition, be unethical—and unlikely to come forward. Where else would one get Ketamine, if not from a veterinarian?"

"From narcotics dealers. The street name is Special K."

"We can hardly expect any of those people to come forward either. Other sources?"

"Pharmacies. I imagine a number of them would stock it to serve veterinarians in their area."

"Maybe. Other thoughts?"

"On Ketamine? No."

"Something else then?"

"It's occurred to me that the gang you're after is probably quite small."

"On what do you base that supposition?"

"I've been reading Senhora Carta's summaries. You're not getting any tips. Your informers aren't feeding you a thing. There are no rumors on the street."

"So? Connect the dots."

"The larger the gang, the more likely it is that *someone* will talk. You never add just one member to a gang. You add that person's lover, family and friends as well. People like to be in the know. They like to gossip. Not only for gossip's sake, but also to *prove* they're in the know. But nobody's gossiping, are they?"

"No. So your conclusion—"

"*Preliminary* conclusion."

"—*preliminary* conclusion is that we should be looking for a person or persons with ties to a veterinarian—"

"—or a pharmacist, or a drug-dealer."

"Wait, wait, wait," Arnaldo said. "Didn't Babyface—"

"Who's Babyface?" Rosa said.

"Haraldo Gonçalves," Silva said, "one of our agents. We call him Babyface."

"But never to his baby face," Arnaldo said.

"I know where Arnaldo's going," Silva said. "Tarso Mello." Rosa looked perplexed. "And he is?"

"I guess Mara hasn't written up that one yet. Mello is Cintia Tadesco's current agent."

"Cintia the top-model? Cintia the girlfriend of the Artist?"

"That Cintia. When Gonçalves interviewed Mello, Mello told him he was gay, and that he lives with a partner."

"So?"

"The partner is a vet tech."

"If I was a judge," Rosa said, "and you appealed to me for a search warrant based upon that coincidence, I wouldn't give it to you."

"But if you were a federal cop, would you follow it up?"

"I certainly would."

"You mentioned a small gang. How small?"

"I can't see the job being done with less than two: one to start the car's engine while the other smashes the kitchen door; one to dispatch the maids while the other subdues Juraci. Yes, I think they could do it with two."

"Or three," Arnaldo said. "Mello, his partner the vet tech, and that bitch, Cintia Tadesco."

"I take it," Rosa said with a smile, "that you have met the beautiful Senhorita Tadesco—and been less than enchanted."

"You take it right," Arnaldo said.

"Tell me this, Professor," Silva said, "do you think Juraci is still alive?"

"I'd virtually guarantee it."

"Why?"

"Proof of life. Until they get their hands on the ransom, they could be asked to provide it at any time."

"And *after* they get their hands on the ransom?"

"At that point, Chief Inspector, the situation will change radically."

"I share your opinion, but I'd like to hear your reasoning."

"The murder of the maids clearly demonstrates the ruthlessness of the people responsible. The choice of such a high-profile target illustrates their audacity and resolve. They won't want to risk recognition. They won't want to leave loose ends. Juraci Santos *is* a loose end. The conclusion, therefore, is inescapable."

"They're going to kill her."

"Yes, Chief Inspector, they're going to kill her."

Chapter Twenty-Six

ON THE STREET IN front of the Artist's building, media people had settled in for the duration.

Canopies now afforded protection from inclement weather; tents and chairs had been set up; the smell of cigarettes and coffee was in the air; high wooden platforms supported long-lensed cameras.

Silva, as before, ignored the questions that assailed him from every side. This time, many were in English. The international press had arrived in force.

Upstairs, roiling grey clouds hung mere meters above the Artist's windows. Rain was beginning to sprinkle on the panes.

Cintia was curled up on an L-shaped divan, a fashion magazine on her lap. She raised her eyes and gave the two cops a blank stare. Then she went back to the article she was reading. The Artist was more cordial.

"How about those keys?" he said. "Did they fit?"

"They did," Silva said. "Still no idea how they wound up in that drawer?"

The Artist shook his head.

Cintia turned a page "You don't have to be a rocket scientist," she said, without looking up, "to figure that out."

"You have a theory?"

Now, she did look up. But it was with the air of someone being put upon.

"When Tico empties his pockets," she said, "everything goes on the dresser. His wallet, small change, everything.

A maid picked the keys and put them in a drawer. End of mystery."

"Why would they do that?"

"Why are you wasting your time on a set of keys?"

"Because it could be important. Please answer the question."

For a moment, he didn't think she would. Then she said, "Tico's maids are too lazy to put things where they belong. When they tidy up, they just shove things out of sight."

The Artist looked shamefaced. "I didn't grow up with maids, so I don't know how to handle them. That's what Cintia says."

"And it's true," she said, closing the magazine and tossing it aside. "But now they've got *me* to deal with. And they'll either get with the program, or be looking for new jobs."

"Tell me this," Silva said. "Has anyone other than yourselves, or your servants, had access to that drawer?"

"You think we invite people to come and inspect the contents of our drawers? You think—" She broke off in mid-sentence and blinked as if something had just occurred to her.

"Senhorita Tadesco?" Silva prompted.

She shook her head.

"Nothing," she said.

"The drawer in which you found the keys, what do you use it for?"

"Underwear."

"Tico's or yours?"

"Mine. And the answer is no."

She was back to her usual unsympathetic self.

Silva frowned.

"The answer to *what* is no?"

"You may *not* look in my drawer. I hate the idea of people pawing through my things, particularly my underwear."

"I had no intention of asking," Silva said.

"No?"

"No. When we spoke on the phone Tico mentioned a party you held on Saturday evening."

"What of it?"

"I'd appreciate it if you and Tico would make a list of the people who attended."

"No problem," Tico said.

"I'd also like to know if you've received more than one visit from anyone between Friday and the day of the kidnapping."

"Wait a minute," Cintia said. "Are you suggesting some-one came up here, took those keys and later returned them?"

"I'm not suggesting anything. But we can't discount the possibility."

"Oh, yes, we can. We can discount it right now. We didn't get more than one visit from anybody."

"Except for my mother," Tico said. "She came on Friday for dinner and again on Saturday, for the party."

"On which of those two occasions did she give you the keys?"

"Friday," Cintia said, answering for him.

"Did your guests on Saturday include Jordan Talafero?"

"Yes."

"How about your agent, Tarso Mello?"

"Yes. Ex-agent."

"I beg your pardon."

"Tarso doesn't know it yet, but he's no longer my agent. I'm going to fire him."

"Rather sudden, isn't it? Saturday you invite him to a party, and now you intend to fire him? Why the sudden change of heart?"

"That, Chief Inspector, is none of your business."

The Artist looked at her. "You didn't tell me you had a problem with Mello," he said.

"Didn't I? I thought I did."

Silva cleared his throat. "Does the name Edson Campos mean anything to you?"

"He's Tarso's boyfriend," she said.

"What, if anything, can you tell me about him?"

"Not a thing. I've only heard the name. I never met him."

"Do you know what he does for a living?"

"No idea."

"He's a veterinary technician."

"So?"

"Do you know what Ketamine is?"

"What?"

"Ketamine. Ever heard of it?"

"No. Where are you going with all of this?"

"We found a syringe in Senhora Santos's bedroom. It contained traces of Ketamine, a drug used in veterinary medicine."

"Used for what?"

"To anesthetize animals."

"Animals?" Tico said, shocked. "And the bastards used it on my mom?"

"We think they did," Silva said.

"Could it . . . could it have hurt her?"

"We don't think so. It was originally developed for human use."

"Well, thank God for that," Tico said.

"I can't see that wimp Tarso getting involved in something like this," Cintia said. "He wouldn't have the balls. You done?"

Silva got to his feet. He'd had quite enough of Cintia Tadesco for one day.

"We're done," he said.

"Good," she said, and picked up her magazine.

Chapter Twenty-Seven

SILVA HAD SWITCHED OFF his mobile phone while they were in the Artist's apartment. After they were back in the car, he remembered to turn it on again. There were three missed calls and a voicemail, all from the Director. He listened to the voicemail and spat out an expletive.

"What?" Arnaldo said, starting the engine.

Before Silva could respond, the phone started to vibrate. Still annoyed at what he'd just heard, and without glancing at the caller ID, he pushed the button and took the call.

"Director?"

"I thought my promotion was supposed to be a secret."

It was Hector, not Sampaio.

"Not funny," Silva said.

"I thought it was."

"Really? Well how's this to take the smile off your face? The reason I addressed you as Director was because Sampaio is anxious to get in touch with me. When you called, I thought it was him, making another attempt."

"I'm still smiling."

"You won't be when I finish. He left a voicemail. The *reason* he called was to tell me he's coming to São Paulo."

"You're right. I've stopped smiling. He's coming to stick his nose into the investigation?"

"He's coming to attend a cocktail party at the governor's mansion."

"That's a relief."

"Not entirely. He has to be prepared to hold forth on the great job he's doing."

"Meaning we'll have to give him a briefing."

"Meaning exactly that. Second floor meeting room. Four PM the day after tomorrow. Tell Mara."

"I'm sure she'll be as pleased as I am. Where are you?"

"We just left the Artist. We're on our way to you."

"So is that fire inspector, Elisabeth Correia."

"She's an examiner, not an inspector. What does she want?"

"Says she found something important."

"What?"

"She wouldn't tell me, says she has to show us."

"Give her some coffee. Arnaldo and I will be there in twenty minutes."

They weren't. But neither was Elisabeth Correia.

"Tractor-trailer jackknifed on the Limão bridge," she said when she bustled in a quarter of an hour later. "I had to make one hell of a detour."

She wore jeans, a denim shirt and rubber boots. She smelled of citrus perfume, smoke and ashes. She was carrying a paper bag.

She put the bag on the conference room's big table and helped herself to coffee from the thermos flask on the sideboard. "Most people have no idea what we can find by sifting through the detritus of a fire. We can usually determine where it started, and how it started. The *how* can occasionally lead us to the *what*, the object that actually set it off. Knowing the *what* can sometimes lead us to the *who*." She added a packet of sugar, and dissolved it with one of the stirring-sticks. "It seldom works like that, but sometimes we get lucky."

"Thanks for the lecture," Arnaldo said, "but what's the point?"

"The point," she said, taking a sip, "is this." She thrust
her free hand into the bag and took out a fistful of plastic
envelopes. "These are all components of the device used to
detonate the bomb. The timer was purely mechanical. There
were no electronics involved."

"So it was like a clock?" Silva said.

"It was *exactly* like a clock, not a digital clock, but an old-
fashioned clock driven by a spring. And it wasn't an off-the-
shelf item. It was built from scratch."

Silva turned to Arnaldo. "Are you thinking what I'm
thinking?"

"Talafero."

Elisabeth looked from one to the other. "How about you
guys share? What's with the knowing looks?"

"In confidence?" Silva asked.

"Absolutely," she said. "Dish."

"Have you ever heard the name Jordan Talafero?"

"Who hasn't? He owns the Spartans. And the bastard just
sold the Artist to Real Madrid for a gazillion dollars."

"A woman who likes football," Arnaldo said. "Marry me."

She looked him up and down.

"I don't think so," she said. "I'm a single mother, but I'm
not that desperate."

"Talafero is an expert on clocks," Silva said. "His office is
full of them. They're his hobby. He collects them, he repairs
them, and he undoubtedly knows how to build one."

"This might be easier than I thought," she said. "I've got
a present for you."

"What kind of present?"

She selected an envelope from the pile. "I was saving this
one for last," she said, handing it to Silva. "Look close. No,
not on that side, on the other."

Silva put on his reading glasses and squinted. The object

in the bag was a blackened strip of something that looked like plastic. On one side, clearly delineated, was a fingerprint.

"I already made a photograph of that," she said. "Unfortunately, it's not a thumbprint."

Thumbprints, like photos, were an integral part of all national identity cards. The Federal Police had thumbprints on file for the vast majority of the adults in the country. But only thumbprints, not prints of any of the other fingers.

"Visualize a clock," Elisabeth said, "that, instead of an hour hand and a minute hand, had two contact points. The points, in turn, were wired up to a battery and a blasting cap. When the two points came together they closed the circuit. That sent an electrical impulse to the blasting cap and boom!"

"I understand. Go on."

"The wires from the detonator were fastened to the power source, in this case a battery, with electrical tape."

"And this," Silva said, holding up the bag, "is a piece of that tape?"

"Uh huh. The part wound around the battery was protected from the explosion by what remained of the battery wall. It was blown into the toilet, where the water prevented it from burning up. When I unwound it—voilá—I found the print."

"Great work," Silva said. "It's as good as a signature."

"It is, isn't it?" she preened. "If it's Talafero's print, I'd say he's gonna have a pretty hard time explaining how it got there."

"I'd say you're right," Silva said. "Now, when first we spoke, you suggested the bomb might have been set off in the apartment below Miranda's."

"No *might* about it. It *was* set off in the apartment below Miranda's."

"That apartment," Silva said, "was owned by a man named Atilio Nabuco. He had a wife and two kids."

"*Had* is the correct tense. All four of them died in the explosion. It was murder."

"How can you be sure?"

"Because we found all four of them together. They were handcuffed and shackled to the plumbing."

∗ ∗ ∗

"WHAT A bastard that Talafero is," Arnaldo said when the fire examiner had gone. "I didn't like the prick from the moment I set eyes on him."

"Ask Mara to see if there's a complete set of his prints on file," Silva said to Hector. "Maybe they were archived for some reason, a weapons permit perhaps."

The Federal Police had, long since, digitalized and centralized fingerprints from every law enforcement organization in the country. In the early days of his career, Silva had spent a great deal of time lobbying for the establishment of such a database. Now, some thirty years on, the system was almost as good as the American FBI's IAFIS.

"Going in by name is quick," Hector said as he returned the handset to its cradle. Mara says it shouldn't take more than half an hour."

It didn't. Twenty-five minutes later, Mara came in with an answer. The result was negative. "The only one on file is his thumbprint."

"We'll visit him," Silva said, "give him something to handle that won't arouse his suspicions, a photo or some such, and get his prints that way. I hope we're having better luck with the van?"

"Ah, yes, the van," Mara said, letting out a long breath. "Well, we're not. It's a Volkswagen Kombi, just about the most common type ever made. It's white, too, which is the most common color. There are tens of thousands of the damned things out there."

"And the person sitting next to Nabuco on the front seat?"

She shook her head. "You saw the original recording, right?"

"I did. Did you try enhancing it?"

"Tried, but it was a waste of time. The quality wasn't good enough."

"Could it have been a woman?"

"You're thinking Cintia Tadesco?"

"We can't discount her, but I'm beginning to think the two cases are unrelated."

"Miranda's murder and the kidnapping?"

"That's my feeling."

"So Talafero killed Miranda for business reasons?"

"If, indeed, he killed anyone at all."

"Come on, Mario," Arnaldo said. "The detonator was a *clock*, for Christ's sake."

"The signs seem to point to him, either as the perpetrator or the contractor, but it's still unproven. Miranda had lots of rivals, not just Talafero."

"Once he's confronted with the print, he'll talk."

"Maybe."

"One more thing about that van," Mara said, "There's a scrape along the left-hand side. Not just the paint; the metal is indented."

"How many auto repair shops are there in this city?"

"Almost as many as there are white Volkswagen Kombis."

"Surely not."

"Okay, I'm exaggerating. But we're not talking dozens, Mario, we're talking hundreds. And God knows how many more Mom and Pop operations run out of backyards and home garages. We've lifted a photographic image of that indentation from the video, and we'll circulate it, but it's a long shot."

"I assume you've checked to see if Talafero owns a white Kombi?"

"I have. He doesn't."

"Get the word out. We'll cross our fingers and hope we get lucky. Is Gonçalves here?"

"Babyface? Downstairs, trying to discover how someone might unload five million dollars in diamonds."

"Get him up here."

Gonçalves, looking relieved at the prospect of something more interesting to occupy his time, appeared three minutes later.

"Chief Inspector?"

"Did you interview that partner of Tarso Mello's?"

"Edson Campos? No. Should I?"

"He's a vet tech, right?"

"So Mello said."

"The substance used to subdue Juraci was Ketamine. It's an anesthetic; its principle use is in veterinary medicine."

"The plot thickens."

"Thickens?" Arnaldo said.

"Thickens. I am a reader of the classics."

"Classics? The last thing I saw you reading was that piece-of-trash magazine, *Fofocas*."

"That," Gonçalves sniffed, "was research."

"Where exactly does this Campos fellow work?" Silva asked.

"I don't know," Gonçalves said. "But I'll find out."

Chapter Twenty-Eight

"HE'S NOT IN," TARSO Mello's secretary said.

"When will he be back?" Gonçalves said.

"I don't know."

"Where is he?"

"I don't know that either."

"Come on, lady. This is the Federal Police you're talking to, not some wannabe actor in need of an agent."

"I'm not being evasive, Agent Gonçalves. Really, I'm not. Something strange is going on. This morning, Senhor Mello was in a great mood, but then he took a call from one of his clients and—"

"Was that client Cintia Tadesco, by any chance?"

"As a matter of fact, it was. What do you—"

"Never mind. What happened next?"

"He came out of his office, passed my desk and walked out without a word. He looked ill. I called out to him, but he didn't answer me, didn't even turn around. You might try him at home. Do you have the number?"

The woman, it was now apparent, wasn't being obstruc-. tive. Gonçalves regretted he'd taken a tough line.

"Maybe you can help," he said.

"If I can."

"It's my understanding that Senhor Mello's partner, Edson Campos, works at a veterinary clinic."

"That's right."

"Do you know which one?"

"It's called the Clinica Polo. It's in Granja Viana."

***

ONLY LATER, when he was on his way, did it occur to Gonçalves that the name Polo sounded familiar. And it wasn't because of the explorer. No, something else, but he couldn't call it to mind.

Two women and a bird were in the vet's waiting room. One of the women was the receptionist, the other, a client. The client smiled and said hello. The cockatoo on her shoulder lifted its crest and said hello as well.

The receptionist stared at him suspiciously.

"I don't see an animal," she said. "What are you selling?"

She was a woman with steel-rimmed glasses, grey hair tied back in a bun and pictures of her grandchildren on her desk, a type impervious to Gonçalves's charm. Her nametag identified her as Calestra Polo.

"I'm not selling anything," Gonçalves said, "and I haven't got an animal. I'm here to speak to Edson Campos."

"Ah," she said, "so you're the one who called. Well, sorry, you'll have to wait."

She didn't sound sorry at all. She said it, in fact, with a considerable degree of satisfaction.

"I'm in a bit of a hurry."

"Too bad. Doctor needs him."

"So do I," Gonçalves said, flashing his badge.

She wasn't impressed. "You," she said, "are not paying his salary. My son, the doctor, is. Take a seat."

"I—"

"A seat."

She picked up her pen and opened a ledger. As far as Calestra Polo was concerned, the conversation was over.

Gonçalves didn't like her attitude. "How about I cite you for obstruction?" he said.

Behind her glasses, Calestra Polo drew her eyes into a squint.

"And how about," she said, "if I arrange to have my other son, the lawyer, ask his wife, the public prosecutor, to bring you up before my husband, the judge, on a charge of abuse of authority?"

Gonçalves suddenly remembered where he'd heard the name Polo. Judge Nemías Polo was reputed to be one of the nastiest bastards ever to sit on a Brazilian bench. And no friend of the police.

Gonçalves gritted his teeth—and took a seat.

***

"THERE'S A new e-mail from the kidnappers," Mara said, barging into Hector's office with nary a knock. "It just came in."

Arnaldo and Hector broke off their conversation. Silva, about to call Irene, put down the receiver.

"Where is it?"

"Being forwarded. But the gist is that they want to schedule the payoff for tomorrow morning," Mara said.

"We'll need a proof-of-life question," Silva said. "Get the Artist to formulate one."

"The usual drill? Something only he and his mother would know?"

"The Artist is a delightful man, but his brilliance is confined to football pitches. If we leave it to him, he'll come up with something too easy to guess. Help him with it."

"Will do."

"And don't tell him about that email until the press conference is over. We don't want him inadvertently blabbing payoff information to the press."

"I'll call him now."

Silva held up a hand. "Call the technical people first. We'll need a tracking device for the diamonds, something small, so it's hard to find, and powerful, so it will work over a considerable distance."

"Small and powerful," Mara said. "Got it."

* * *

THE WOMAN with the cockatoo was gone. So were the man with the cat who came in after her, and the kid with a toy-sized Yorkshire terrier who came in after him. The reception area was now empty, except for Gonçalves.

The vet's mother, after an absence of almost five minutes, came back through the door that led to the consulting rooms and beckoned to him.

"Doctor will see you now," she said.

"I don't want to see the Doctor," Gonçalves said. "I just want to see Edson Campos."

"Then you should have gone to his home. Instead, you chose to come here. That makes it Doctor's business as much as it does Edson's."

"That's ridiculous," Gonçalves said.

"He's waiting," she said.

Gonçalves stood up and marched in, ready for a fight.

He didn't get one.

Doctor Polo was a soft-spoken fellow with unruly hair and friendly eyes. The first words out of his mouth were an apology, but he waited until his mother closed the door before he offered it.

"She thinks she's helping me," he said. "I'm a good vet, really I am, but a lot of people visit me once, and never come back. I'm convinced it's because of her."

"Why don't you fire her?"

"Fire her? Ha! My brother would sue me, and my father would send me to jail."

"Protective of her, are they?"

"Protective?" Polo smiled, but it was a rueful smile. "It has nothing to do with protective. They don't want her in *their* hair any more than I want her in mine. If she was out of here, she'd split her time between my brother's law offices and dad's chambers. There's no way either one of them would take that lying down. But enough of my troubles. You want to see Edson, right?"

"Right. Also—"

The vet didn't let him finish. "I'll call him in a minute. Chat with me for a while first. I know her. She's out there waiting for me. She's going to grill me, and I'll need some kind of a story to tell. By the way, I'd offer you coffee, but I'd have to ask her to bring it."

"For God's sake, don't."

"Yeah, that's what I figured. You were saying?"

"There's something else you might be able to help me with."

"Shoot."

"We're investigating the kidnapping of Juraci Santos, the Artist's mother."

"I sure hope you catch those bastards."

"We're doing our best. Now, what I'm going to tell you next is confidential. It mustn't be spread around."

"You can count on my discretion. What is it?"

"When they took Juraci, her abductors gave her an injection to knock her out."

"And?"

"What they used was Ketamine."

"Ketamine? They used Ketamine on a human being? Are you sure?"

"We found a syringe in her bedroom. It wasn't entirely empty. We had the contents analyzed."

"Jesus. I hope those kidnapperes knew what they were doing. Too much and they could have killed her."

"Do you use it?"

"Every vet does."

"Where do you get it?"

"We order it online."

"Only online?"

"Sometimes we get it from the pharmacy on the corner. They overcharge like hell, but they stock it on the off-chance that one of the neighborhood vets will need the stuff on short notice. Why do you want to speak to Edson? Surely you don't think he had anything to do with the kidnapping?"

"We certainly don't want to jump to any conclusions, but . . ."

"What?"

"He has access to Ketamine, and he has a connection to Juraci Santos, so we have to check it out."

"What kind of connection?"

"Edson's partner is a talent agent."

"Tarso Mello. Their dogs are my patients. So what?"

"Tarso represents Cintia Tadesco."

"And Cintia is the Artist's girlfriend. You call that a connection?"

"A distant one, but . . . yes."

"My father's brother is a *deputado* who knows the President of the Republic. Does that mean I'm connected to the President? I don't think so."

"I see your point. Try to see mine. Ketamine isn't an every-day substance—"

"I beg to differ. It is in my world."

"Which is why we're looking at someone from your world who might have had a connection to Juraci Santos, no matter how remote."

"I understand. But you're wasting your time as far as Edson is concerned."

"Sure of that, are you?"

"Absolutely sure. He's been working here for three years. Everybody likes him. He's kind to people and kind to the animals he treats. He even gets along with my mother. He'd never get involved in anything illegal. Never."

"A sterling reference, nice to hear . . ."

"But you're not convinced. Okay, listen to this: I'm very careful with all of my drugs, but that stuff, Ketamine? I'm even more careful with that. You can use it to get high. Did you know that?"

"I know that. They call it Special K."

"Right. So I keep my Ketamine under lock and key. It's a controlled substance, and I'm obligated to do it, but even if it wasn't, I'd do it anyway. I never give the key to anyone. I have it with me right now." Doctor Polo took a key ring out of his pocket, separated one of the keys and held it up. "This is it. This is the one."

"You'll pardon me, Doctor Polo—"

"Please call me Laerte."

"—Laerte, but keys can be duplicated, locks picked. Mind you, I'm not accusing Edson of any of those things, but . . ."

"It isn't just the lock and key. For controlled substances, I keep a diary of purchase and use. Every time a shipment comes in, I write it down. Personally. Every time I use some of it, I write it down. Personally. I can account for every drop of every controlled substance that's gone through this clinic."

"Can I see the diary?"

"Certainly."

The vet was still holding his keys in his hand. He used one to open a drawer in his desk. Taking out a notebook, he flipped through the pages.

"Here it is," he said. "Ketamine. Have a look."

He put the notebook on the desk between them, turned it so that Gonçalves could read, and pushed it closer.

Unlike many doctors who treat people, Polo had a fine and very legible hand. Gonçalves ran his finger down the column with the dates. The records for the drug went back more than four years.

"How long did you say Edson has been here?"

"Three years."

Gonçalves turned the pages. Each entry was in the same handwriting. Nothing was crossed out or obliterated. Nothing appeared to have been altered. He turned to the last page and checked the final listing.

"It says here," he said, "you have seven vials on hand."

"And I do."

"Would you do me a favor and check?"

The vet stood up, went to a grey cabinet standing in the corner of his office and used his key to open it.

"Here," he said. "Count them yourself."

Gonçalves did. There were seven. He took one out and examined it.

"Would this be enough to put a human being to sleep?"

"I'm a vet, remember? Not an anesthetist. But I can tell you this: there's enough Ketamine in that vial to knock out ten medium-sized dogs. If I used it all in one syringe, it would do for a horse."

"Thank you, Doc—Laerte. I appreciate your cooperation. Could I see Edson now?"

"Certainly. Stay here. I'll send him in. Then I'll go try to satisfy my mother's curiosity."

Chapter Twenty-Nine

GONÇALVES HAD NO PRECONCEIVED notion of what Mello's partner might look like, but he certainly didn't expect what he got.

Edson Campos was a hollow-chested slip of a man with thinning brown hair and a wart on his chin. In a suit and tie, he might have looked at home in a bank; in his light-brown scrubs, he looked like someone trying, unsuccessfully, to look as if he belonged in a veterinary clinic.

Gonçalves introduced himself.

Edson's reaction was immediate.

"Gonçalves? My partner told me about you. You're the one who went to his office and harassed him."

"Harassed him? He told you I harassed him?"

"Didn't you?"

"No, I didn't."

"He said you did."

"And I'm saying I didn't. Could I see your identity card, please?"

"I can't imagine why he'd tell me you did, if you—"

"The card, please."

Edson searched his wallet, located the card and handed it over.

Gonçalves made a note of Edson's RG—his national registration number—and checked his date of birth. The vet tech was thirty-three, but appeared to be older. He also appeared to be nervous.

"I have sixteen cages to clean before I go home," he said.

"This shouldn't take long," Gonçalves said. "Are you familiar with the drug Ketamine?"

"Why are you asking me?"

Gonçalves considered telling him to stop beating around the bush and to answer the question. But then it occurred to him he'd probably get more cooperation if he told him about the syringe. So he did.

Edson folded his arms protectively across his hollow chest.

"It seems to us," Gonçalves went on, "that someone who elected to use Ketamine is likely to be someone familiar with veterinary medicine."

"And you think that might be me?"

"I didn't say that."

"You think I stole Ketamine from Doctor Polo?"

"No, I don't. There's nothing missing from Doctor Polo's stock; I checked that already. But let's not get ahead of ourselves. The source of the drug isn't the key issue here."

"What's the key issue?"

"The *knowledge* of Ketamine: what it is, and how it works."

"I know what it is, and I know how it works. I'm a vet tech, for Christ's sake. But if you think I had anything to do with the abduction of that woman, you're barking up the wrong tree. I'm no kidnapper."

"No?"

"No. First you persecute my partner and now you're persecuting me. What is it with you people?"

"Do you know Juraci Santos?"

"Yeah. I know her. Her poodle, Twiggy, is one of our patients."

"Not any more."

"What?"

"Twiggy is dead. The kidnappers killed her."

Edson looked shocked.

"Killed her? Killed Twiggy? Why? She was the sweetest little thing. And she wouldn't have posed a threat to anyone."

"We don't really know why they killed her. But they did."

"How . . . how did they do it?"

"Broke her back, apparently."

Edson closed his eyes and rubbed the bridge of his nose. For a moment, Gonçalves thought he might cry.

"Jesus," he said. "Poor Twiggy."

Gonçalves paused for a few seconds, then said, "Could we get back to the Ketamine?"

"Oh. Yes. Sure. The Ketamine. Well, what you're suggesting . . ."

"Yes?"

"It's just ridiculous. I'd be scared to use that stuff on a human being."

"You would?"

"Anybody would. Anybody who isn't a doctor. Ketamine is an anesthetic. You give someone too much of an anesthetic, and it'll kill them."

"How much is too much?"

"For a person? I have no idea. Ask me about a dog. Or a cat. You don't believe me, do you?"

"Let's move on."

"Move on to what?"

"The secondary issue: sourcing. Suppose you couldn't steal the stuff from a clinic, and you needed to get your hands on some Ketamine, how would you go about it?"

"I wouldn't. I just wouldn't."

"Not you. Some other guy. A kidnapper."

Edson uncrossed his arms, rubbed his chin, gave some thought to the question. "He might try a disco."

"A disco?"

"Yeah. Drug dealers hang out in discos. So do drug users. Ketamine isn't only used by vets. It's a recreational drug. They call it Special K."

"How come you know that?"

"Everybody knows that."

"No, Senhor Campos, not everyone knows that. As a matter of fact, there are many, many people who *don't* know that. But *you* don't seem to be one of them. So think hard. How did you come to know about a recreational drug called Special K?"

"I don't remember."

"Try hard. It might be important."

After a while, Edson said, "It was at the Maksoud Hotel, just after a presentation put on by one of the pharmaceutical companies. There was this guy I was sitting next to. He struck up a conversation. We went out and had coffee together. He told me."

"How did the subject come up?"

"Look, I never saw this guy before, or since. I don't even remember his name. I didn't like the way he talked about animals. Hell, I didn't even like *him*. I thought he was a slimeball."

"I ask you again: how did the subject come up?"

"He was dealing, okay? He wanted to buy Ketamine. He said he could offload anything I could supply, said he'd pay a good price for it. But I wasn't interested, and I told him so, and that was the end of that."

"Where else might a kidnapper get his hands on some Ketamine?"

"I don't know."

"Come on. Give me some help here. Think!"

"If he was a certain kind of vet tech, he might go to a pharmacy."

"What do you mean by *a certain kind?*"

"Some of the guys, not me, pick up extra money by doing operations."

"What kind of operations?"

"Spaying, neutering, removing growths, stuff like that. After a few years in the business, after seeing those kinds of operations a few hundred times, they get to thinking there's nothing to it."

"So they offer to do it cheaper."

"That's right."

"And they need Ketamine."

"Uh huh. And pharmacists, well, hell, you know how pharmacists are. If they know you, and they think you have a good reason . . ."

Edson left the rest of what he might have said hanging in the air.

But he didn't have to spell it out. Gonçalves knew what he was suggesting. Brazil's National Health Service suffered from a shortage of doctors. It could take weeks to get an appointment. Private doctors were too expensive for many people, so they turned to pharmacists to prescribe. The pharmacist who insisted on being shown a doctor's prescription for every drug he sold was soon a pharmacist without a clientele.

"That pharmacy on the corner," Gonçalves said. "You think they'd sell Ketamine to a vet tech without a prescription?"

"I wouldn't know. I never asked."

"But you *did* buy Ketamine there."

"A couple of times, but only when Doctor Polo told me to and always with a prescription."

"Always?"

"Always. Every single time. I swear."

Gonçalves believed him. But he decided to have a chat with the pharmacist anyway.

* * *

THE CLINIC was closed, and the doctor's mother had left for the day, but the reception area wasn't empty. The vet was there, watering plants with a green plastic pitcher.

"I like to do this myself," he said. "Mom always gives them too little or too much. You like gardening?"

"Not particularly," Gonçalves said. "Who owns the pharmacy on the corner?"

"Why are you asking?"

"Because I want to have a chat with him about their stock of Ketamine."

"Where's Edson?"

"Cleaning cages."

"Good boy. Are you convinced, now, that he didn't have anything to do with kidnapping Senhora Santos?"

"We don't jump to conclusions, Laerte. We leave our options open."

Doctor Polo shook his head. "With all due respect," he said, "I know the man, and you don't. He didn't have anything to do with it. You'll see."

"Okay. Your opinion is duly noted. Now, as to the guy who owns the pharmacy . . ."

"His name is Guido, Guido Brancusi. But it'll be a waste of time talking to him. He's hardly ever there. He's got another job with one of the chains downtown. He only comes in at night, and it isn't always every night. He's got this terrific woman who runs the place for him. She's the one to talk to."

Gonçalves perked up. Women were both his recreation and his passion.

"Pretty?"

"Not particularly."

"So what do you mean by terrific?"

"Efficient. Capable. Smart. Reliable. Nice figure. Just not a pretty face. She does everything for Guido, controls the stock, pours and labels the prescriptions, handles the book-keeping, works behind the counter, hires and fires the other women who work in the shop. If I could get rid of my mother, I'd hire her in a heartbeat."

"What would your friend Guido think of that?"

"He'd be furious. But he's not my friend, so I don't really care."

* * *

THE PHARMACEUTICAL paragon esteemed by Doctor Polo went by the name of Vitória Pitanguy.

"Not here," the girl behind the pharmacy's counter said. She was a teenager with a silver nose stud.

"Day off?" Gonçalves asked.

"Out to lunch."

Gonçalves looked at his watch. "Lunch?" he said. "At this hour."

"That's what she calls it. Actually, she's with her boyfriend."

"Maybe you can help," Gonçalves said and showed her his warrant card.

The studded one studied it. "I'm at your service," she said. "Like completely."

Gonçalves, sensitive to such things, picked up on the innuendo immediately. And, just as quickly, concluded she was too young for him.

"Do you know what Ketamine is?"

"Something vets use."

"Do you know what they use it for?"

"Not the faintest."

"Do you sell much of it?"

"Not so much."

"To whom do you sell it?"

"Well, duh! To vets, of course. It's a controlled substance. All the sales will be in the book."

"Can I see the book?"

She leaned her elbows on the counter, displaying cleavage.

"Mind if I ask you a question?"

"Ask."

"How old are you, anyway?"

"You wouldn't believe me if I told you."

"I'm eighteen; eighteen, as in the age of consent."

"Thank you for sharing. Please get the book."

The book, to Gonçalves's disappointment, was arranged by date and wasn't cross-referenced to specific drugs sold. The pharmacy appeared to be doing a good business. To break out sales of Ketamine could take some time.

"Thanks," he said. "I may have to borrow this."

"I can't give it to you. Not without Vitória's permission. I'll have to check with her first."

"When's she due back?"

"That depends. Was the shop next door still closed?"

"I didn't notice. What's that got to do with it?"

"The guy who owns the shop is her boyfriend. He hangs a sign on the door, and they take off, sometimes for hours. Want to know what I think?"

"What?"

The girl leaned closer, lowered her voice and giggled.

"I think they go to that motel on kilometer 31 for a quickie. I've got a proposal for you, though."

"What?"

"I could talk to her as soon as she gets back. And then, if she agrees, I'll give you a call, and you can come back, and uh oh—"

"Uh oh what?"

"She's back."

Behind him, Gonçalves heard the front door shut. A woman hurried in and set a course for a door marked *office*.

"Vitória," the girl said, her tone of voice changing from playful to serious, "this gentleman is from the Federal Police."

Vitória Pitanguy changed tack and approached them. To Gonçalves, who was somewhat knowledgeable about such things, her spicy perfume smelled expensive.

"Federal Police?" she said.

"It's about this book." Gonçalves tapped it with his finger. "I need to borrow it."

"I can't give it to you," she said.

"Why not?"

"We're required, by law, to maintain it here at all times. We could get a visit from a *fiscal*, or we could be fined."

"It's a federal investigation. We need it. Why don't you just let me give you a receipt?"

"Because we also need it to enter new shipments and purchases. What do you want it for?"

"To track your sales of Ketamine."

"That's not much of an answer, Agent . . ."

"Gonçalves. No, it isn't. But it's the only answer you're going to get."

"I assure you, you're not going to find any irregularities in that book. Every new shipment that comes in I enter myself. I always check the sales in the book against the stock and the prescription records. And we never sell Ketamine without a prescription."

Gonçalves, in spite of his frustration, was impressed. Vitória Pitanguy was every bit the efficient manager Doctor Polo had described.

"If I have to," he said, "I'll get a warrant."

"Why don't I just copy it for you?"

"Can you do that?"

"Sure. There's a copier in the back. And a little espresso machine as well. Would you like one while you wait?"

Chapter Thirty

"IT'S TINY," MARA SAID, "no bigger than a five-year-old's thumbnail."

She'd found a tracking device that fit Silva's specifications, small and powerful, and she'd called a meeting to tell them about it.

Arnaldo raised a hand. "Is that your description or someone else's?"

Mara raised an eyebrow. "Someone else's. What of it?"

"Would I be correct in assuming she's a female?"

"Is that relevant?"

"And that she has a five-year-old daughter?"

"Arnaldo Nunes," she said, "the sexist detective. May I go on?"

"Granddaughter?"

"Mario, please tell Senhor Nunes to shut up."

"Shut up, Arnaldo. Go on, Mara."

"Unfortunately," she said, "the device is a prototype."

"In other words," Silva said, "they only have the one."

"Correct."

"How long would it take to get a second one made?"

"Three weeks."

"Damn. What are the chances of it breaking down on the job? How reliable is it?"

"I'd better let Lefkowitz tell you about that. He called Brasilia and talked to her."

"Did I hear you say *her*?" Arnaldo said.

"Get him in here," Silva said.

Minutes later, Lefkowitz joined them.

"Well?" Silva said. "What do you think?"

"I'm sold on it. Mind you, the lady I spoke with is hardly objective. She talks about it like it's her baby. If she was here with us right now, she'd be opening her purse to show us a picture of the little darling."

"I rest my case," Arnaldo said.

"As I recall, Senhor Nunes," Mara said, frostily, "Mario told you to shut up."

"What's going on?" Lefkowitz said, looking back and forth between Mara and Arnaldo.

"They do it all the time," Gonçalves said.

"And you should ignore them," Silva said. "Keep talking."

"There's a base station that comes with it. The read-out is along the lines of a GPS receiver. As a matter of fact, it *is* a GPS receiver—adapted specifically for the purpose. It's mapped for the entire country and accurate to a radius of two meters. The device itself is shockproof. You can drop it out of an airplane, and it'll keep working. It's waterproof. You can implant it under skin. If Juraci had been wearing one when she was kidnapped, we'd know exactly—"

Lefkowitz stopped short when Germaine, one of Mara's people, opened the door.

"New email from the kidnappers," she said.

"Let's hear it," Silva said.

"The answer to the proof-of-life question is a blue Volkswagen Beetle."

The answer was correct. The question the Artist had asked during the press conference was *What present did I give my mother when I signed my first contract with the Spartans?*

"Continue," Silva said.

"Put the diamonds in a brown leather case. Tie a white string to the handle. There are to be two couriers, not one.

Instruct them to go to the Rodoviaria Tietê, arriving no later than 10:15 tomorrow morning."

Arnaldo snorted in frustration. The Rodoviaria Tietê was the largest bus station in all of Latin America. At 10:15 in the morning it would be a busy place, crowded with pick-pockets and thieves as well as honest citizens.

"Tell them to stand near the public telephones to the right of the ticket windows. At 10:30, precisely, one of them will ring. They are to answer it. The couriers are not to be placed under surveillance. They are not to carry cell phones. Follow these instructions exactly, or Juraci Santos will be killed."

Germaine finished reading and looked up. Mara thanked her, and she left. Silva turned to Lefkowitz.

"Will that tracking device work in the Metro?"

The Metro, São Paulo's underground railway system, ran directly under the bus terminal.

"No," Lefkowitz said, "it won't."

"Why not? Cell phones do."

"Cell phones get their signal from an antenna strung through the tunnels. The device works via satellite."

Silva rubbed his chin. "Not good. They could instruct the couriers to get on a train, leave the diamonds under a seat and get off."

"They could," Hector agreed. "But they'd have to bring them above ground sooner or later. And when they do, we'll be on to them. Why two people?"

"Why indeed?" Silva said.

"The note doesn't specifically exclude the use of cops as couriers," Gonçalves said.

"No, it doesn't," Silva said. "Which is why those two couriers are going to be you and Hector."

* * *

THE FOLLOWING morning, the two federal cops were in
the appointed place at the appointed time. It was Hector who
took the call.

A distorted voice said, "Listen closely. I'm not going to say
it twice. Go to the Metro platform, direction Jabaquara. Wait
there until train number 391 comes along. Go into the third
car, middle door. There'll be a paper stuck behind the first
seat on the left. Repeat your instructions."

"Direction Jabaquara. Train 391. Third car. Middle door.
Paper behind the first seat on the left."

The caller hung up.

"Let's go," Hector said and set off, threading his way
through the crowd.

"Man or woman?" Gonçalves said, hurrying to catch up.

"Could have been either one. You know those devices
they sell in joke shops? Change your voice? Fool your friends?
One of those."

"Where to?"

"The Metro."

"Well, there's a surprise—not. You notice the way people
are looking at me?"

"They're not looking at you. They're looking at the handcuffs and the case."

The attaché case containing the diamonds was shackled
to Gonçalves's wrist.

"Maybe I should open my coat," he said, "and show my
gun."

"You do," Hector said, "and somebody will try to steal it."

                              * * *

THE METRO stank of axle grease, unwashed bodies and
ozone. They had to wait for almost twenty minutes before
Train 391 came along. When it did, it was carrying seven

passengers in the third car. Two of them were tough-looking young men, one black, one white, seated side-by-side.

"Right where the goddamned paper is supposed to be," Gonçalves whispered.

"Don't sit," Hector said. "Brace yourself against the door."

When the train was rolling again, Hector leaned over and addressed the black guy.

"Excuse me," he said, "but my friend and I were seated in those seats a while back. We think we might have lost a paper. Mind if we have a look?"

"What's with the case and the handcuffs?" the man asked.

"They don't concern you"—Gonçalves opened his coat—"but this might."

"Hey, no need to get nasty. I was just asking. You want to have a look, have a look. Me and my friend, we'll go sit over there."

He stuck an elbow into the ribs of the white guy. They both got up, but kept looking back as they moved off.

"So much for trying to be polite," Gonçalves said.

Hector was already looking at the note he'd fished out from behind the seat.

"Exit the train at Praça da Sé station," he read. "Follow the instructions taped under the bench, next to the candy machine, at the right-hand extremity of the platform."

"It's a goddamned scavenger hunt," Gonçalves grumbled.

The next note told them to board a taxi with the license plate TBD32F. It would pick them up in front of the north exit.

And it did.

The driver handed Hector an envelope, and then pulled off into traffic. Hector broke the seal, read the note, and handed it to Gonçalves.

Don't bother to question the driver. He knows nothing. The next cab bears the license plate TVR25J.

They questioned the driver anyway. His story was that a kid had come up to him with five hundred Reais and an envelope. He was told where to wait until two men came looking for him. He'd know they were the right men because one would be carrying a brown leather case with a white string tied to the handle. He was to hand them the envelope and then take them to KM post 28 on the BR116. That's all he knew.

The BR116 was the major artery leading to the neighboring State of Paraná. At KM 28, the second cab was waiting.

It was an unseasonably warm day. Gonçalves took off his jacket, mopped his brow with his handkerchief and approached the driver.

"You have a note for us?"

"No note. You have a case with a white string tied to the handle?"

Gonçalves held it up. "Where are we going?"

The driver eyed the handcuffs. They must have come as a surprise to him. "The *Caverna do Diabo*," he said.

It was a cave complex, locally famous, and a popular destination for school trips.

"That's got to be at least two hours away," Gonçalves said.

"Closer to three. Get in."

Gonçalves turned to Hector. "Can they track us that far?"

"They can track us across the whole country," Hector said. "Do what the man says."

"Not before he gets his air-conditioning working."

The driver shook his head. "Not gonna happen. It's busted."

"What?"

"You deaf? The air-conditioning. It's busted."

"Screw this guy," Gonçalves said. "Let's get another cab."

"Screw you," the driver said. "It's not my fault if I can't afford to fix it."

"We've got no choice," Hector said, "We've got to follow the instructions to the letter."

"So stop wasting my time," the driver said. "and get in the fucking cab."

Chapter Thirty-One

THE ROUTE TO THE Caverna do Diabo passed kilometer after kilometer of banana plantations—and not a single bar, shop, or restaurant where they could buy something to drink. The driver was prepared for that. He'd brought a bottle of mineral water, and from time to time, he'd open the cap and help himself to a swig. He made a great point of smacking his lips when he did it. And he didn't offer the bottle to Hector or Gonçalves. When the two federal cops arrived, they were parched and irritable.

"Wait for us here," Hector told the driver.

"It's gonna cost you," the driver said.

"Cost us? What do you mean *cost us?*"

Hector's throat was so dry it came out as a croak.

"I got paid to bring you here. I didn't get paid to bring you back."

"So how much do you want to bring us back?"

"You aren't gonna find another taxi out here."

"How much?"

"Or public transport either."

"How much, I said."

"Four hundred Reais."

"Four hundred Reais! You're a thief. I'm going to report you."

"Report all you want. Any more than thirty kilometers from the center, and I'm off the meter. I can set my own price. And my price is four hundred, half now and half before we leave."

"What?"

"I'm not going to hang around out here for nothing. And I'm not going to drive you back to town and have you stiff me for the other two hundred."

Hector took out his wallet, threw two hundred Reais onto the front seat and got out.

"Don't slam the fucking door," the driver said.

Hector slammed it anyway.

"Refreshment stand over there," Gonçalves said. "Let's get a drink."

Their feet kicked up little puffs of dust as they crossed the parking lot. Halfway there, a man in a green uniform intercepted them. He pointed at the case Gonçalves was carrying.

"Is that a white string on the handle?"

"It is," Gonçalves said.

"Then follow me. I'll lead you to the birds."

"Birds? What birds?"

The man seemed puzzled. "You don't know about the birds?"

"If I did," Gonçalves said, "I wouldn't be asking. You work around here?"

"Well, duh!" the man said. "If I didn't, why would I be wearing this uniform?"

"Because you drive the local garbage truck?"

"I'm a park ranger, wise ass. So watch your step."

"And I'm a federal cop. So you watch your step."

"A federal cop? At your age? Don't make me laugh."

Gonçalves fished out his ID and held it in front of the ranger's face.

"Well, I'll be damned," the ranger said. "You don't look to be any older than—"

"Answer the question."

"What question?"

"What goddamned birds?"

"The goddamned birds I'm supposed to be taking you to."

"Cool down," Hector said, "both of you."

"He started it," the ranger said, pointing at Gonçalves.

"The hell I did," Gonçalves said.

"Tell us about this place." Hector said. "Let's start there."

The ranger positioned himself so he could turn his back on Gonçalves.

"This place," he said, "is the Jacupiranga State Park. You know what spelunkers are?"

"People who like to explore caves?"

"Right. This is one of the best spots in the whole country to do just that."

"I know. Caverna do Diabo."

"Not just Caverna do Diabo, which, by the way, is so huge there's another entrance called the *Gruta de Tapagem*. For years, people didn't know the two were connected."

"We're not here for tourism," Hector said.

"Well, hell," the ranger said, getting annoyed again. "You're the guy who wanted to know what this place was all about."

"Show us the goddamned birds," Gonçalves said, getting annoyed right back.

"This goddamned way then," the ranger said.

"Hold it," Hector said. "First I want a drink."

They went to the refreshment stand where Gonçalves, who'd offered to pay, discovered that water was eight Reais a bottle. It did nothing to improve his temper.

Each cop drank two bottles. In São Paulo, they could have bought a case of beer for the same money.

"Now," Hector said, "the birds."

It wasn't far, not more than a ten-minute walk. The ranger brushed some vines aside and led them into a small opening in the face of a hill—the entrance to a cave. From somewhere in the darkness they could hear cooing, and the flurry of feathers.

The ranger switched on a flashlight. The beam glittered along limestone and finally came to rest on a stack of cages against the far wall.

"What the hell is this?" Gonçalves said.

"Pigeons," the ranger said. "He told me to make sure none of them got out because, if they did, they'd fly off and never come back."

"Who was the *he?*"

"Some kid. I never saw him before."

"How old?"

"Maybe sixteen."

Hector looked at Gonçalves, "Another damned cut-out," he said.

"A what?" the ranger asked.

"The guy who put these pigeons here didn't want to be identified," Hector explained. "He paid someone else to talk to you, probably brought some street kid from São Paulo."

"That's what you call a cut-out?"

"That's what we call a cut-out. How would they have known about this cave?"

"You can buy a map of all the caves at the refreshment stand. It costs four Reais."

"Half the price of the goddamned water," Gonçalves grumbled.

"Don't blame me," the ranger said. "I don't set the goddamned prices."

"Why do you suppose he chose this particular cave?" Hector asked.

"The caves are rated from one to five stars. Five stars are the best, the ones nobody wants to miss. This is a one-star. One-stars are nothing."

"So this one wouldn't be visited often?"

"If somebody comes in here once a year, it would be a lot. And then it's probably only because they're looking for an out-of-the-way place to take a shit."

Gonçalves wrinkled his nose. "Shit? Is that what stinks in here?"

"That's the birds. They've been here for a week. I've been feeding them. That was part of the deal."

"You're a state employee, right?"

"Right."

"Aren't there regulations about keeping pigeons in caves owned by the State?"

"If you're looking for an excuse to bust my balls, forget it. This *isn't* a cave owned by the state. We're beyond the borders of the park. And what I do with my free time is my business."

"What are we supposed to do with the pigeons?" Hector asked.

"If you hadn't interrupted me, I woulda told you already. Look here."

Perched on top of a large sack of pigeon feed was a cardboard box. From the box, the ranger took a mantle lantern, which he lit, then a smaller box and an envelope.

"You're supposed to read what's in the envelope," he said, extinguishing his flashlight and putting it back in his pocket.

"What's in it?"

"I got no idea. The kid told me not to open it."

Hector took out a pair of latex gloves, pulled them on and broke the seal. Inside, there were two sheets of paper. He positioned himself so light would fall on the first one and read it aloud:

"Follow these instructions exactly:

Divide the diamonds into sixty units of approximately the same weight.

Remove the carrier bags from the box.
Put a unit of diamonds into each bag.
Zip each bag shut.
Fasten each bag to a pigeon (as shown).
Release each pigeon after affixing bag.
Do not delay. We are timing your activities. If the first pigeon is not underway within thirty minutes of your arrival, or if the pigeons do not continue to arrive at their destination at intervals not to exceed one minute, Juraci Santos will be killed. Upon receipt of the diamonds, you will receive an email stating when and where she is to be found."

"Caralho," the ranger said when Hector finished reading. "So you guys are gonna pay the ransom for the Artist's mother? That's what this is all about? Wait until my wife hears about this."

"Shut up," Gonçalves said. "We weren't expecting this. It throws a kink in our plan. We've gotta think."

Hector unfolded the second sheet. It was a sketch by a bad artist: a pair of hands held a pigeon while another pair of hands tied-on a carrier bag. He held it up for Gonçalves to look at.

"*Merda*," Gonçalves said. "So that's why there had to be two of us. What now?"

Hector returned the two sheets to the envelope and put the envelope in his pocket.

"What's your name?" he said to the ranger.

"Norberto Fatio."

"Go outside, Norberto. Make sure we're not disturbed."

"Sure. Sure. Anything I can do to help. Hell, why didn't you tell me in the first place what this was all about? You think I want those fucking Argentineans—"

"Just go, will you?"

Norberto scurried out the door.

"So what now?" Gonçalves repeated.

"You have your pocket knife?"

"I always have my pocketknife."

"Cut the tracking device out of the lining of the case."

"You're going to put it into one of those carrier bags? Send it along with a pigeon?"

"What else can we do?"

"They're gonna find it."

"Of course they are. But, with any luck, they'll still be there, unloading the ransom, when Gloria shows up."

"There must be a telephone around here somewhere. Let's get that park ranger to call your uncle and tell him about the birds. Maybe he can get Gloria into the air ahead of time, put her on a path to intercept them."

"Good idea. I'll go talk to our friend Norberto. You get that case off your wrist and start dividing the diamonds."

Chapter Thirty-Two

"How fast is it going?" Silva said.

Lefkowitz made a quick calculation.

"About forty kilometers an hour," he said. "And it's airborne."

"How can you tell?"

"It's moving out over a lake. No decrease in speed."

"Carrier pigeon," Arnaldo said.

Mara, entering the room, heard him.

"I'm astounded," she said. "For once in your life, you're right."

Lefkowitz swiveled around in this chair and looked at her.

"What do you know that we don't?"

"Some park ranger just called in with a message from Hector."

Mara went on to explain, ending with, "That's what you've been following, Lefkowitz—a carrier pigeon."

"As soon as it lands," Silva said, "the kidnappers will find the device."

"And our teams are going to be far, far away when they do," Lefkowitz said.

"Get them into the air immediately," Silva said.

"It's already happening," Mara said. "I spoke to Gloria. Rotors on the helicopters must be turning as we speak. Now, Nunes, tell me, how did someone with your limited cranial capacity hit on carrier pigeons?"

Arnaldo didn't rise to the bait. "My sister's got a neighbor, a penitentiary guard. He told me a story a while back. Some of the prisoners were raising pigeons in their cells. The warden thought it was a nice, safe hobby, *Birdman of Alcatraz* and all that crap. But no, turns out these birds were homing pigeons. The felons were using them to get cell phones and drugs into the prison."

"Cell phones? Since when can a pigeon carry a cell phone?"

"They were breaking them down into components, then reassembling them within the walls."

"Cute," Lefkowitz said. "They start the birds off with smuggling. Next thing you know they're carrying around tiny brass knuckles and beating up on other birds in the neighborhood. The felon's perfect pet."

"The way it works," Arnaldo said, ignoring the levity, "is this: you get the birds before they learn to fly. You feed them. Bingo, they begin to think of the place as home. When you release them, they come back. They always come back. They come back even if you take them hundreds of kilometers away."

All four of them looked at the screen, where a flashing green dot was showing the pigeon's steady progression.

"Straight as an arrow," Lefkowitz said. "The little dear knows exactly where she's going."

"If she does," Arnaldo said, "it's a he."

"Shut up, Nunes."

Silva tapped the screen with a forefinger. "What town is this?"

"Porangaba. Looks like she, or he, is going to pass right over it."

Porangaba was about a hundred KM northeast of the cave complex.

"Let's get Gloria and her people moving in that direction," Silva said. "Do carrier pigeons fly at night?"

The others looked blank.

"I'll talk to Gloria first," Mara said, "and then I'll find out."

* * *

FIVE MINUTES later she was back.

"They only fly at night," she said, "if they're trained to do so. Otherwise, they roost and start flying again at first light. Let's hope she—"

"He," Arnaldo said.

"—isn't so trained. How long has *she* been in the air?"

"The bird," Lefkowitz said, remaining strictly neutral, "took off just before four. It's flying at about forty kilometers an hour."

"Sundown tonight will be at around eight," Silva said. "Subtract four from eight and that gives us four hours of flying time."

"And four hours at forty an hour," Mara said, "means *she's* likely to roost at about one hundred sixty kilometers from her take-off point."

"Who said that thing about the best laid plans of mice and men?" Lefkowitz asked.

"A poet by the name of Robert Burns," Silva said. "And I don't think I'm going to like what you're about to tell me."

"You're not." Lefkowitz was fiddling with the knobs on the receiver.

"We lost the signal?"

"Just now. It went out like a light."

Chapter Thirty-Three

THE TRACKING DEVICE'S LAST known location turned out to be a cow pasture. Both helicopters were able to land, and a search was initiated. Twenty minutes later, Gloria called in by radio.

"No sign of the pigeon," she said, "just blood and feathers. The bag is here, and so is the device, both of them all chewed up. We figure the pigeon must have been attacked by a bird of prey."

"Of all the goddamned pigeons in the State of São Paulo," Silva said, "some goddamned hawk had to pick that one?"

"Of all the goddamned pigeons," Gloria said, "some goddamned hawk did."

"Okay, Gloria, thanks. Stay where you are. I'll get back to you." Silva hung up and turned to Lefkowitz. "Work out a compass course based on the pigeon's line of flight. We'll give it to Gloria's pilots, tell them to fly further along the line, see if they can spot something."

"Spot what?"

"Hell, I don't know. There was a whole flock of those damned pigeons. Some may still be in the air."

"Not unless they still had a long way to go."

"We'll also have them look for henhouses, for chicken coops, for dovecotes, for any other place they might have gone to roost."

"I've got some topographical maps downstairs. I'll go get them."

Lefkowitz was back in three minutes. Within a few more, he was talking to one of the helicopter pilots.

"Get Silva on the radio," the pilot said as Lefkowitz was wrapping up, "Gloria wants to talk to him."

"How far do you want us to go?" Gloria said when she heard Silva's voice.

"As far as you can before dark. Then we'll talk."

* * *

Cornelio Braga was, by no means, the only chicken farmer to run through a scale of emotions that day. But his reaction was typical.

First, surprise at having an extremely noisy Helibras AS 350 B2 land in his front yard. Then fear, when a black-clad team wearing balaclava helmets and carrying machine pistols leapt out under swirling blades. Finally anger, when the woman in charge of the operation offered him a token apology and was getting ready to depart.

"Sorry? Sorry doesn't cut it, Senhora. Or is it Senhorita?"

"Senhorita," Gloria Sarmento said, struggling to be polite, a quality that didn't come easily to her.

"If figures," Cornelio sputtered. "What kind of a guy would be interested in a woman who jumps out of helicopters and carries a machine gun?"

Raul Franco, her number two, and Gloria's secret heartthrob, was standing next to her at the time. Gloria's oblique overtures in Raul's direction had yet to be reciprocated, so Braga's remark struck closer to home than he could possibly have imagined. It caused her to lose her temper.

"My personal life is none of your goddamned business, Senhor Braga."

"You have any idea how many hens I got in there, *Senhorita?*"

Cornelio managed to make Senhorita sound like an epithet.

"No," Gloria Sarmento said, "and I don't—"

"Five hundred, that's how many." Braga stabbed a finger in the direction of his hen house. "You know what makes a hen stop laying? Stress, that's what. You know what stresses a hen?"

"I don't give a—"

"Too goddamned much noise for one thing. You got any idea what you people just did to my egg production with that machine of yours? Any fucking idea?"

She was opening her mouth to tell him that she didn't fucking know, and that she didn't fucking care, when she glanced to her right. Raul, that bastard, was smiling. He was *enjoying* this.

She turned to him and tapped a forefinger on his finely-sculpted chest.

"From here on in," she said, sweetly, "*you* are the squad's official liaison to chicken farmers."

Raul stopped smiling.

"Hell, Gloria," he said. "Give me a break. You got it wrong. I wasn't . . ."

Gloria didn't wait for the rest. She sneered at Cornelio, shouldered her MP-5 and strode back to her helicopter.

It was nice to be the boss.

* * *

As DARKNESS fell, Lefkowitz pointed to the map and said, "The lead chopper is here, just short of Riberão Preto."

"Tell them to pack it in for the night," Silva said.

"They've got four hundred thousand candlepower search-lights on those things, you know."

"Not good enough. Those lights only illuminate whatever you've got them pointed at. It's too easy to miss something. And the rest of the gear, the heat detection stuff isn't going to do us any good either. Those birds are already under cover, or they're sitting in trees with a hundred million other birds. Tell them to start again at first light."

"Which brings us back to Gloria's question," Lefkowitz said. "How far do you want them to go?"

"Take it out to five hundred kilometers beyond Riberão Preto."

"As far as that?"

"For now. We might have to go even further."

Lefkowitz turned to the radio, and Silva to Mara.

"Let's try shaking something loose on the diamonds. How about we take another shot at jewelers, dealers in gemstones and receivers of stolen goods?"

"Receivers of stolen goods?" Mara said. "Good luck with that one."

"Probably useless to ask, I agree, but maybe not. Even crooks hate the idea of us having our butts kicked by Argentina. They might feed us some anonymous tips."

"You've got a point," she said.

"I'm brimful of ideas," Silva said. "That's why I'm the boss."

"And here I was," Arnaldo said, "thinking you got the job just because you're older than everyone else."

Chapter Thirty-Four

THEY RIPPED OFF THE duct tape that covered Jordan Talafero's mouth, pulled out the handkerchief and stuck a hose down his throat.

Toninho Feioso, the author of the hose idea, had heard, somewhere, that such a procedure, followed by turning on the water full-blast, could be particularly painful to the victim. He, therefore, decided to give it a try, because, in his opinion, Jordan Talafero was a *canalha* who deserved the very worst that he and Gaspar could dish out.

The result of the hose operation was gratifying. So gratifying, in fact, that Toninho was loathe to give it up. It took quite some cajoling on Gaspar's part before he finally agreed to turn off the water and replace the handkerchief and the duct tape.

Toninho meant "little Tony", but this was a misnomer. Little Tony was neither little nor named Tony. Some of his colleagues, Gaspar for one, knew that much, but no one claimed to know what his true name actually was. No one ever had the guts to ask.

Feioso meant "ugly," which was entirely appropriate. Toninho Feioso was the ugliest of men, and he appeared even uglier when he was attacking your kneecaps with a ball peen hammer, as Jordan Talafero, after they'd finished with the hose, had occasion to find out.

"And this, you bastard, is for the guy downstairs," Toninho informed Talafero, the statement eloquently punctuated by the crack of breaking bone and a muffled scream from beyond the duct tape.

Toninho, who wasn't very smart, couldn't remember the name of Miranda's downstairs neighbor, which was Atilio Nabuco, and he didn't care much about Nabuco anyway, but he had previously dedicated bones on other parts of Talafero's anatomy to Miranda, his wife, and each of his kids. He was grasping for names since it appeared he was going to run out of them before he ran out of bones.

Gaspar would have liked a turn with that ball peen hammer, but he knew better than to interrupt Tony when he was exercising his professional skills.

Gaspar, therefore, confined himself to questions of the kind Talafero could respond to with movements of his head.

"I'm gonna ask you one more time," he said, "did you, or did you not, plant that fucking bomb that killed the Captain?"

For the first time, Talafero nodded.

Gaspar took a step backward, looked at Tony and smiled. Then he turned back to Talafero.

"You shoulda come clean in the first place, admitted it right away, saved us all this trouble. Then you coulda been dead by now."

Under normal circumstances, it wouldn't have been much of a reward for honesty. But Talafero, at that moment, wanted nothing more than a quick bullet to his head.

Gaspar, however, wasn't quite ready to give it to him. Some questions remained.

"There was something about diamonds," he said. "The boss was gonna talk to the federal cops. You know anything about that?"

Talafero shook his head.

"And the Artist's mother? You have anything to do with grabbing her?"

Again, Talafero shook his head.

Gaspar turned back to his colleague.

"Well, I guess that's that."

"Yeah," Tony said, "that's that."

He took out his pistol.

"Hang on," Gaspar said.

"What?"

"Lend me that hammer."

Chapter Thirty-Five

TALAFERO'S BODY WAS FOUND on the street in front of what remained of Captain Miranda's building.

Silva was watching the TV coverage and sipping a coffee when Hector joined him in the conference room.

"I just got off the phone with São Paulo homicide," he said.

"And?"

"They fingerprinted Talafero's corpse. We got a match."

"To the fingerprint on that fragment of electrical tape?"

"Exactly."

"That's it then. Talafero killed Miranda."

Hector waved a sheet of paper.

"Additional confirmation," he said.

"What's that?"

"The contents of a note found pinned to Talafero's body."

Silva patted the pockets of his jacket.

"I left my glasses in your office."

"I'll read it. 'This canalha killed the Captain. He didn't have anything to do with the kidnapping of Juraci Santos.'"

"That's it?"

"That's it."

"Must have been meant for us."

"Must have been. But why would they bother?"

"Miranda wanted to help. My guess is they either honored his wishes, or feel the same way he did. For us, it doesn't matter. What matters is we've got another dead end."

"Appropriate choice of words."

"Quite intentional."

"The kidnappers have their diamonds. If they intend to release her, or kill her, wouldn't they have done it by now?"

"Not necessarily. They'll want to be sure about the worth of the stones, evaluate them before they take further action."

"So what now?"

"I'm going to have another talk with our consultant, Professor Rosa. Call Arnaldo and ask him to order up a car."

* * *

ROSA WAS waiting in the interrogation room. No handcuffs this time. He greeted them with a smile and a deep intake of breath, as if he was capturing a scent. "You bring with you the air of freedom."

"All I agreed to do, Professor," Silva said, "is to testify on your behalf. I don't make the final decision, so don't blame me if they don't let you out of here."

"You were the last impediment, Chief Inspector."

"You've bribed all the members of that parole board? Is that what you're implying?"

"Tut, tut, tut, Chief Inspector! You shock me. I'm not implying any such thing. Even if those sterling citizens were to accept bribes, where would I get the money?"

"More than half of the money you took from your victims was never found. You must have squirreled away a bundle."

"Alas, if it were only true. In those, my halcyon days, I lived high off the hog. The best wine, luxury hotels, fine restaurants. I owned a Ferrari, you know, *and* a Porsche."

"I know it very well. We confiscated both of them. But you could have done all you did, and bought all you bought, and still have a bundle left over."

"Goodness, no, Chief Inspector. You have no idea how expensive luxuries are. But then, I wouldn't expect you to, given your well-known incorruptibility. I admire you. I truly do."

"You're convinced you're going to get out of here, aren't you?"

"I am. And I shall go and sin no more. I'm reformed."

"I daresay that, even after you've paid those people off, you'll *still* have enough not to have to work ever again."

With a gesture, Rosa dismissed the thought. "I'd work even if all of my needs were provided for. Most prisoners vegetate. Many retired people do the same. But I abhor idleness. That's why I'd like to work with you."

"Not for the money? You don't need it, is that it?"

"Money is always nice. But it's the intellectual challenge that appeals to me. What brings you back this time?"

"The ransom has been paid."

"Has it now? How did they arrange for delivery?"

"Carrier pigeons," Silva said and went on to explain.

When he was done, Rosa pushed back from the table and applauded slowly. "Bravo," he said. "A *tour de force*. I seem to have seriously underestimated the intelligence of those people."

"Put your thinking cap on, Professor. I really need your help."

"And I really want to give it, believe me I do. Here's one thought: they would have known, even before they started, that this would be the high-profile kidnapping of the year, perhaps of the decade."

"Yes. Go on."

"They would have anticipated that Juraci's face would make the front page of every newspaper in the country; they would have expected her kidnapping to be the lead story in every newscast. She'd be transformed from someone that almost no one recognized into someone that virtually everyone recognized. And it would have occurred within a matter of hours."

"Which leads you to postulate . . . what?"

"It would have been inadvisable to take her far from the scene of her abduction. This neighborhood of Juraci's, Granja Viana?"

"What about it?"

"What's it like?"

"It's not the country, but it's not the city either. Semi-rural, the occasional horse farm, that sort of thing."

"Then that's where she is. They're holding her in Granja Viana, or somewhere close to it. Think about it. Every hour, every minute that she was in transit would have augmented their risk. It wouldn't matter if she was well concealed. It wouldn't matter if she was sedated. Traffic accidents, documentation blitzes from the *Policia Rodoviaria*, things like that, can always interfere with the best laid plans. They would have wanted to get her into a place of security as quickly as possible. That place is unlikely to be one that's recently rented or acquired. That attracts too much attention. People get curious about their new neighbors. It's likely to be a place that the kidnappers have been visiting for some time, a place where they've achieved invisibility through familiarity. It would be best, too, if the place had some land around it, a garden, or a field, where they can bury her once they're finished with her."

"Makes sense. Other thoughts?"

"I assume your estimable Mara Carta is already looking into the bird angle?"

"She is. But she's come up blank. Breeders, she tells us, sell them for between forty and sixty Reais each. Even at the lower price, sixty birds would have cost twenty-four hundred, a major purchase in that business. No breeder she's spoken to, and she's spoken to a lot of them, recalls making a sale of that magnitude. Ever. We're extending our area of inquiry, but our current hypothesis is that the kidnappers have been doing their own breeding."

"I'm not talking about *acquiring* the birds. The kidnappers would have expected you to try to track the birds back to their source. They would have done everything they could to prevent you from doing so."

"What *are* you talking about then?"

"Alternative profiles for the people who came up with the idea of using carrier pigeons."

"Such as?"

"An ex-convict, for example. Such birds are used in places like this, you know."

"We know," Arnaldo said.

"Or someone who might have read about carrier pigeons in a newspaper, or seen a documentary on television."

"Which would lead us nowhere."

"Not necessarily."

"How so?"

"Turn it around. Mara and her people can, quite quickly, do a media search. If they discover that there *hasn't* been a television program or an article in a consumer publication in the course of the last six months, what would that suggest?"

"That the kidnappers didn't get their information from one of those sources."

"Exactly. If the people who used those carrier pigeons didn't get the idea from a prison experience, or by talking to ex-convicts, or from the media, where *did* they get the idea from? That could narrow the search considerably. Maybe, just maybe, this brilliant idea of theirs, the idea to use carrier pigeons, wasn't so brilliant after all."

Silva stroked his chin. "My gut feeling," he said, "is that they wouldn't make a mistake that elementary. It's likely the brilliance remains."

"Perhaps. But my core argument stands. If I were you, I'd be looking for people who keep, or know someone who keeps, carrier pigeons, who had access to a key that would get them into Juraci Santos's house, and who have a hideout in or near Granja Viana."

"You make it sound simple, Professor."

"I'm not saying it's simple. But when you get to the end of it, you'll find someone there who fulfills all three of those characteristics. I guarantee it."

Chapter Thirty-Six

ONE OF THE PRIME requisites in Nelson Sampaio's former profession, corporate law, was obfuscation. Sampaio was an expert at it, and he quickly recognized it in others.

He was recognizing it right now, seventeen minutes into the briefing he'd requested on the Santos case.

"Let's cut right through the crap," he said, looking around the table. "You people don't know where the birds came from, you don't know where they went, the diamonds are gone, and you've got no line on where Juraci Santos might be. You've got zip."

"I think that's a fair summary, Director," Silva said.

The director snorted. "What about that postman? You interrogate him?"

"We did. It led nowhere."

Sampaio referred to his notes, raised his head to lock eyes with Silva.

"You think Jordan Talafero had anything to do with it?"

"We did once. Not anymore."

"That bicheiro? Captain Miranda?"

"No."

"Cintia Tadesco?"

"It's possible."

Sampaio made some check marks on the yellow legal pad in front of him. The tip of his pencil slid further down the page.

"And that ex-agent of hers, whatshisname?"

"Tarso Mello."

"Yeah, him."

"Also a possible suspect."

"You interview Juraci's former servants? The ones she had before the two who got shot?"

"We did," Mara said. "We went back two years. We're satisfied they're all clean."

"How about professional enemies? People like Joãozinho Preto? The Artist broke his leg. That must have pissed him off."

"Joãozinho's mother is Italian. She got him a passport, and he bought himself a villa in Tuscany. He's been living there for six months."

More check marks.

"And that other striker? Whatshisname? The guy who's convinced himself he's as good as the Artist is?"

"Romário de Barros?"

"Yeah, him. If the Artist is out of the picture, he's the logical replacement, right?"

"Right."

Sampaio drew a circle around something. Then he put a big asterisk right next to it.

"Well there you go. That gives him a motive. Without the Artist, *bingo*, Romário is the star of the Cup."

"The Argentineans have got Dieguito Falabella," Arnaldo said. "Dieguito can run circles around Romário de Barros."

Sampaio refused to be sidetracked.

"You didn't talk to him, did you?"

"We didn't think it was necessary," Mara said.

Sampaio turned on her. "Why the hell not?"

Mara stood her ground. "Every year at this time, Romário earns a bundle doing a football clinic for rich kids. He was in Campos do Jordão, doing just that, on the night of the kidnapping. He's got more than a hundred witnesses to prove it."

"He could have hired someone else to do it. Talk to him anyway."

Mara nodded and made a note.

Sampaio turned back to Silva.

"Did you consult with Godofredo?"

"No."

"Why not? As I recall, I instructed you to do so."

"You did, Director, but I haven't had the time."

Sampaio stabbed his pencil in Silva's direction.

"But you had plenty of time to talk to that felon, Rosa, right?"

"We talked to him, yes."

Sampaio dropped his pencil and held out his hands, palms upward.

"And?"

Silva told him about Rosa's conclusions.

Sampaio shook his head. "Rosa's all wet. You're wasting your time with that guy."

"I don't think so, Director."

"But I do. And the last time I heard, I'm running this shop." He picked up his pencil. "Let's go over this again step by step." He reversed the pencil and tapped the eraser three times on the table. "Answer me yes or no. Lefkowitz thinks the kidnappers had a key to Juraci's house, correct?"

"Yes."

"And you're inclined to agree with him?"

"Yes."

"Three sets of keys were found in the house?"

"Yes."

"Both the locksmith and the Artist confirm that Juraci ordered four?"

"Yes."

"The fourth set was with the Artist and his girlfriend."

"Yes."

"But it seems to have gone missing for a while and then mysteriously turned up?"

"Not so mysteriously. The Artist—"

The director waved his pencil. "All right. All right. Strike the word mysteriously. The fourth set went missing and later turned up. Yes or no?"

"Yes."

Sampaio leaned forward, a sign he was coming to the end of his peroration.

"And it's obvious the Artist wouldn't kidnap his own mother."

"Yes."

"And, therefore," Sampaio said, with a smile of triumph, "his girlfriend, Cintia Tadesco must be involved."

"No."

"No?" Sampaio's smiled faded. "What do you mean no? I just took you through it step by step. It's as plain as the nose on your face. She's in it up to her neck."

"Not necessarily. Not if there was a fifth set of keys."

Sampaio tossed down his pencil in a sign of frustration.

"A *fifth* set? Who said anything about a fifth set?"

"I'm introducing a supposition."

"Introducing a supposition, my ass! You're groping. Groping in the dark. How big is Granja Viana?"

"Big. It stretches over two municipalities."

"So there's no way you could search every house, right? I mean, it would take you weeks."

"It would."

"And by that time, Juraci Santos is going to be either free or dead. Same thing applies to investigating carrier pigeons. By the time you finish investigating every enthusiast, every club member, every dealer in birds, she'll be free or dead."

"I'm sorry, Director, but that really is all we have to go on at the moment."

"Meanwhile, the Minister has his teeth in one side of my ass and the President in the other. What are you smiling at?"

"The metaphor, Director. Only the metaphor."

"If Captain Miranda found someone making inquiries about diamonds, how come you can't?"

"We're trying, Director. We have men on the street asking questions; we've been in contact with all of our confidential informants."

"Why don't you talk to your snitches?"

"Confidential informants, Director, are what we call snitches."

"I know that, I know that," Sampaio said, recovering quickly from the *faux pas*. "What I meant was, why don't you talk to them instead of just being in contact with them?"

It made no sense. Nobody bought it, and Sampaio could see nobody bought it. He went on hurriedly.

"So what now?"

"Now," Silva said, "we're hoping for a break."

"A *break*? What kind of break?"

"On the diamonds. We've circulated details of the weights, quality and cuts to law enforcement nationwide. We've asked them to get in touch with dealers and jewelers in their area."

"You think they'll do it?"

"All of them have their own problems to deal with, and most of them are understaffed. But, in this case, I think the response is likely to be better than usual."

"Why?"

"They know the Artist won't be doing his best unless we find his mother. And everyone in this country wants to see the Artist doing his best."

"And you really think people are going to buy into the idea that finding the diamonds will help to find *her*?"

"I do."

"I don't. If this situation wasn't so serious," Sampaio said, "I'd laugh you right out of this conference room."

Chapter Thirty-Seven

IF, IN THE SUMMER of 1939, anyone in Salerno had suggested to Francesco Romanelli that he might emigrate to Brazil, he would have laughed them out of his shop.

Francesco had a prosperous jewelry business. He counted some of the leading families of Sicily among his customers. He had a strapping son of nineteen, Marcello, offspring of his union with Maria of Blessed Memory. He had a handsome new wife, Clara, eighteen years his junior, who tolerated his marital attentions and infidelities with equal stoicism. And for the first time he could remember, maybe for the first time ever, the trains all over Italy were running on time. Six years later, Marcello was dead, killed in that insanity in North Africa. Francesco's business was in ruins. The country was an economic basket case, and *Il Duce*, the man who'd made the trains run on time, had been strung up on a lamppost in Milan.

Before the war, Francesco's youngest cousin, Giuseppe, the one who stood to inherit the least, had picked up his family and moved to someplace in America called Brodowski. Francesco still had Giuseppe's address somewhere. He found it, wrote a letter, and much to his surprise, got a reply within a month.

It turned out that this Brodowski was, indeed, in America, but it was *South* America, Brazil to be precise.

Giuseppe was happy with his life there. There were opportunities for Francesco as well. Giuseppe would be happy to have company from the old country. Francesco could stay with him for as long as he liked.

So Francesco, as soon as he'd saved enough for the fare, sold out, packed up his few remaining goods and took Clara off to Brazil. She was, by then, already pregnant with Luigi.

Francesco and Clara's only son was born on a coffee plantation in the interior of the State of São Paulo. By the time he was eleven, his father had saved enough to set up a modest shop in the neighboring city of Riberão Preto, where he proceeded to teach his son, Luigi, everything he knew about jewelry and gemstones.

By the time Francesco died, in 1991, Luigi had surpassed his father in knowledge of precious stones, but he'd never held in his hand a stone more precious than the one he was holding now.

He looked across the counter of his shop, taking in the fellow who was offering it for sale. There was definitely something shifty about him, which immediately caused Luigi to remember the circular that some *cabo* from the *Polícia Militar* had dropped off on the morning of the previous day.

He'd done no more than scan it, but he remembered where he'd put it: on the right-hand side of his worktable.

"I'll have to take a closer look at this," he said to the man who'd brought the stone. "Have you got a few minutes?"

The man said he did, so Luigi told Priscila, his sole employee, to keep an eye on things while he did an evaluation. He went into the back, switched on the light and read the circular, this time with care.

The police were looking for diamonds *of exceptional quality and cut and weights between three and five carats*. It was just such a stone that he held in his hand.

If he'd had any idea how little the shifty man knew of the gem's true value, and for how little he'd have been willing to sell it, Luigi might not have called the police.

But he didn't know, so he did.

***

THREE DAYS had passed since the disappearance of the birds, and in all that time there hadn't been a single break in the case. True, Juraci Santos still hadn't turned up dead, but that was little solace for Silva. He didn't feel they were any closer to finding her, and he feared she might already have been murdered.

The call, therefore, came like a ray of hope breaking through dark clouds of despair. He and Arnaldo set out immediately for Riberão Preto.

Helio Fortunato, the delegado who'd called, was waiting to receive them.

"Where's our perp?" Arnaldo said when introductions were complete.

"It's not him," Fortunato said. "He's not part of it. But he can give you a description of the woman you're looking for."

"*Woman?*" Silva said. "We're looking for a woman?"

"It seems you are."

"That bitch," Arnaldo said.

"What bitch?" Fortunato said.

"Cintia Tadesco," Arnaldo said, "Tico's girlfriend. It's gotta be her."

"That bombshell?" Fortunato said. "You figure?"

"More like wishful thinking," Silva said. "My colleague here isn't too fond of the lady. How about filling us in?"

"I think it would be better if you heard it from the man himself. Come on. It's this way."

Fortunato took them down a green-painted corridor to a windowless interview room, blue with cigarette smoke. There was a ring welded to the steel table, one to which a prisoner could be shackled, but the man seated there wasn't hand-cuffed. He was smoking a cigarette, one of many by the looks of the overflowing ashtray. He looked nervous.

"I'm out of smokes," he said to Fortunato. "Be a pal, Delegado, and see if you can't get me a few more."

Fortunato took a pack out of his pocket, removed four cigarettes and lined them up on the table. Then he made the introductions.

"Senhores, meet Tancredo Candido. Tancredo, this is Chief Inspector Silva, and this is Agent Nunes. They're from the Federal Police. They want to know how the stone came into your possession."

"Right. Right," Candido said. He used his glowing butt to light one of Fortunato's cigarettes, and took a deep drag. Then he launched into his story. "The woman who rented the place," he said, "she was—"

"Wait. Stop," Fortunato said. "Start by telling the officers about what you do for a living and where you do it."

"Oh. Right. Right," Candido had just taken another puff. He held it in while he said, "Well, it's like this: I'm a *caseiro*. I take care of a *sitio* owned by Senhor Yakamura." Then he exhaled the smoke.

"Who's Yakamura?" Arnaldo asked.

"A rich *Paulista*."

"Not Japanese?"

"That too." Candido waved his cigarette, the ember a glowing jewel in the dimly-lit room. "I mean, that's what he *looks* like, but when he talks, he *sounds* like he comes from São Paulo."

"Go on."

"Right. Right. Where was I?"

"Sitio."

"Right. Right. There's the main house, a swimming pool, a little house for me and about two hectares of land. That's it. Yakamura doesn't live there, hardly ever visits, rents it to people who get it into their heads it'd be nice to have a little place in the country." He took another drag. "City folks, always city folks. First couple of weekends they generally show up with just the family. Then they start inviting friends. They do barbecues. They get drunk. Sometimes they screw each other's wives. I remember one time—"

"What we're really interested in," Silva said, "are the circumstances pertaining to the diamond you tried to sell."

Candido finished the cigarette and ground it out in the ashtray. This time, he didn't light another from the stub.

"Oh. Yeah. Right. Right. So these people who rent the place?"

"Yes?"

"They mostly get tired of it pretty quick. I mean, unless you're eating, or getting drunk, or screwing somebody's wife it's pretty boring, right?"

"The diamond, Tancredo."

"I'm getting there. So one family after another moves along, and Senhor Yakamura rents it to another one. Now, me, I stay on, because I take care of the place. I cut the grass, and clean the pool and fix the little things that go wrong. The water's from a well, for example, and the damned pump—"

"We don't care about the pump," Arnaldo said. "We care about the diamond. Where did you get it?"

"Anybody got a light?"

Fortunato tossed him a pack of wooden matches. He took one out of the box and struck it. Candido used the flame to light his cigarette, shook out the match, exhaled more smoke. "One of the birds brought it."

"Birds?"

"See? You don't know about the birds. And now you're gonna want me to tell you about the birds, which I already would have if you'd let me tell it my way in the first place."

"Then tell it your way," Silva said.

Tancredo tossed the match in the ashtray, picked up the box. "Can I keep these?"

"Sure," Fortunato said. "Keep talking."

"Right, right. Well, it was like this: about four months ago Senhor Yakamura rented the place to this woman. She shows up with five crates of birds and a couple of sacks of the shit they eat."

"These birds," Silva said. "Were they carrier pigeons?"

"Yeah, but I didn't know that until later."

"This woman. Describe her."

"A lot younger than you guys."

"How much younger?"

"I dunno."

Silva closed his eyes and rubbed the bridge of his nose. Getting information out of this guy was like pulling teeth. "Thirty-five?" he said. "Forty?"

"Yeah, like that."

"Like what?"

"Thirty-five."

"What else?"

Tancredo took another puff. "What else do you want to know?"

"Hair? Was she pretty?"

"Brown hair. Kinda curly. Not bad looking."

"How tall?"

Candido held up a hand, palm down, to indicate her height.

"Average," Silva said. "Her eyes? What color?"

"Brown . . . I think."

"How was she dressed?"

"Tight pants. Nice ass."

"What else do you remember?"

"About how she looked?"

"Yes."

"What's to remember? She was normal. She had a nice ass, that's all. And, oh yeah, she smelled good."

"What do you mean she smelled good?"

"What I said. She smelled good."

"Her soap? Her deodorant?"

"Yeah, her soap maybe. What's deodorant?"

"Never mind. What happened next?"

"She tells me it's a hobby of hers, raising these birds. She says she's busy in town all week, and she'll only visit on the weekends, and maybe not every weekend, so she wants my help."

"What kind of help?"

"Feeding them, cleaning the cages, that kind of stuff. I tell her okay, I'll do it. She asks me how much I want to earn. I tell her four hundred a month. She says she'll pay two."

"But you accepted?"

"Yeah. I never figured she'd pay four. I was just trying it on. A week later, she's back with a van—"

"What kind of a van?"

Tancredo ground out his butt, getting ash on his fingers in the process. He wiped it off on his pants.

"One of those Volkswagen things," he said. "White, like most of them are. In the van, she's got all the stuff to hammer together a house for the birds. She stands around being bossy while I do it, and then she has me move the pigeons from the cages into their new house, which isn't very difficult because they're little, and they're not flying yet."

"And then?"

"And then she tells me to keep feeding them and to let them out when it looks like they're about ready to fly. I ask her if she isn't worried about losing them, and that's when she tells me they're homing pigeons, which means they'll always come back as long as I keep feeding them. So I keep feeding them. Pretty soon they're taking off, and flying around and coming back to their house to sleep."

"And the woman?"

"I don't see her for a while."

"How long?"

Tancredo thought about it while he lit another cigarette. "More than a month. When she finally shows up, she stays just long enough to make sure the birds are doing their thing, coming back to their house at night. Some hobby, huh? You know what I thought?"

"What?"

"I thought she didn't give a shit about those birds; she only cared about what they could do, which, as it turned out later, was absolutely right."

"What happened next?"

"Four weeks or so later she's back again. Just to have a look, make sure I'm feeding the birds. She does the same thing, maybe four or five weeks after that."

"And then?"

"And then, on her next visit, she has me put all the birds in the cages she brought them in, but she leaves their little house right where it was. 'They'll be flying back,' she says, 'and, when they do, they're going to have little bags tied on them.' She tells me not to mess with those bags and, she says, if I do, she'll have her husband cut my balls off. How about that, huh? Is that any way for a woman to talk? Cut my balls off!"

He took a puff and shook his head at the sad decline in the vocabulary of women.

"You believed her?"

He pointed at Silva with his cigarette. "You bet I did. You should see the bitch. She's mean."

"But, despite her warning, you messed with those bags anyway, didn't you?"

He looked pained that Silva would ask. "One of them. Just one. I was curious. I mean, wouldn't you be? Her making such a big deal of it and all?"

"Just curious?"

"Honest to God. Just curious. It wasn't like I was planning anything ahead of time. I wasn't. But, when I saw what was inside . . ."

"You started thinking how you could keep some of those diamonds for yourself."

He sighed and extinguished the third cigarette. "Yeah. And I counted the birds, and I noticed one of them hadn't made it back."

"So you decided to make it two?"

"I did. I figured she'd have no way of knowing. And she didn't. She showed up, took the birds, had me break down the little house I'd set up and took that too. I haven't seen her since. That's the end of the story. I got nothing else to tell you."

"Listen to me, Tancredo," Silva said, "I really don't care about you trying to nick those diamonds."

Tancredo raised his eyebrows. "You don't?"

"No, I don't. We've got bigger fish to fry. So here's what we're going to do: if you cooperate, I'm not going to charge you."

"You're not?"

"No."

Tancredo smiled, showing tobacco-stained teeth. "Right. Right. I'm your man. How do I cooperate?"

"First off, I'm going to send an artist from São Paulo. He'll sit down with you and, based on your description, try to work up a sketch of what the woman looked like."

Tancredo looked dubious. "I'll try. But I got a lousy memory for faces."

"Just try your best."

"Sure. What else?"

"You'll return the diamonds to us, you'll stay here in safety for a few days, and then we'll let you go back to that sitio of yours. That's it. You're off the hook."

"If I'm gonna be off the hook, why do I have to stay here at all? And what's with the *in safety* bit?"

"You know the Artist's mother has been kidnapped?"

"Doesn't everybody?"

"The diamonds were the ransom."

"No!"

"Yes."

"So that sweet-smelling bitch with the nice—"

"—was involved in the kidnapping. Did you hear about what happened to Juraci Santos's maids?"

"I saw it on TV. The kidnappers killed them, right?"

"Yes, the kidnappers killed them. They killed them because the maids could identify them. And they'll do the same to you if they get the chance."

"Jesus Christ."

Tancredo Candido burst into a fit of coughing—and reached for the last of Fortunato's cigarettes.

Chapter Thirty-Eight

"CINTIA?" GONÇALVES SAID. "Disguised? Wearing a wig?"

"Not Cintia," Silva said.

"Why not? She's in show business. She must know all about makeup and that sort of thing. She's—"

"—almost as tall as you are. Read what's up there on the board." Silva looked around the table. "Any other suggestions?"

The task force was assembled, once again, in a conference room at the São Paulo field office. Silva had chalked the salient points of the caseiro's description onto the blackboard. They team went back to staring at them.

Female.
Brown, curly hair.
Average height.
Age +/- 35.
Good figure.
Unremarkable eye color.
Smells good. (Perfume?)
Abrasive attitude.

"There's something . . ." Gonçalves scratched his head. ". . . something that rings a bell . . ."

The others looked at him expectantly.

"But it just won't come to me," he said.

After a while, Mara said, "I must have talked to two dozen pigeon fanciers. Up to now, I haven't come across a single female."

"Good point," Silva said. "Call them back. Ask them if they know any women who share their passion."

"Not passion," Arnaldo said. "She didn't show any interest in the birds. She was just using them."

"Arnaldo's right," Silva said. "Call them anyway, but mention that."

Mara started to get up. Silva raised a hand.

"Something else," he said. "This might be a long shot, but ask them if they've ever heard of a fellow by the name of Edson Campos."

* * *

"Women who fancy carrier pigeons," Mara said, when she returned to the room, "are like women attracted to Arnaldo Nunes."

"What's that supposed to mean?" Arnaldo said.

"Rare," she said. "Very rare. But I got solid hits on Edson Campos. In the pigeon world, Senhor Mello's partner is very well known indeed."

Silva leaned forward in his chair.

"Familiar with Ketamine," he said, "lives in Granja Viana and keeps pigeons. Maybe we're finally getting somewhere."

"And maybe not," Gonçalves said. "I talked to Campos. He's a wimp. I don't think he has it in him to get involved in something like this unless . . ."

"Unless what?"

"Unless Mello talked him into it. *That* guy's a slimeball. I wouldn't put anything past him."

"If Mello and Campos are in on it," Silva said, "that would probably exclude Cintia Tadesco."

"Don't tell me that," Arnaldo said. "I don't want to hear it."

"Think about it, Arnaldo. She had a falling out with Mello, told us she was going to fire him."

"So what?"

"If they were partners in crime, I doubt she'd run the risk of alienating him. Not now. Not until things have cooled off."

"Yeah, I suppose you're right," Arnaldo said, grudgingly.

"The world is full of disappointments," Mara said.

"What was the falling out about?" Gonçalves asked.

"Cintia wouldn't tell us."

"When we were talking to her," Arnaldo said, "she got this far-away look in her eyes, as if she'd just put two and two together. Then, a little later, she said she was going to fire him."

Silva turned to Mara. "Have you got a home address for Campos and Mello?"

"I do."

"Get a search warrant," he said.

* * *

"REMEMBER ME?" Gonçalves said.

"Of course I remember you," Tarso Mello said, blinking out of bloodshot eyes. "What do you want?"

Mello was unshaven and uncombed, dressed in a faded T-shirt and jeans, barefoot and reeking of whiskey. To Silva, he didn't look in the least like the dapper talent agent Gonçalves had described.

"These are colleagues of mine," Gonçalves said, making the introductions, "Chief Inspector Silva, Delegado Costa and Agent Nunes. And *this* is a search warrant for the premises."

He held it out.

Mello made no attempt to take it.

"What do you need a search warrant for?"

"You can read it if you like."

Mello brushed it aside.

"I'm shitfaced. I don't want to read anything, and I don't care if you search my place or not."

Up to that point, Silva had been harboring suspicions about the man's involvement. Now, he relaxed the hand that had been hovering over his pistol. His gut was telling him that Mello wasn't one of the people they were after.

Mello followed the cops into his living room.

"You people want a drink?"

"No," Silva said, answering for all.

"But you won't mind if I have one, will you?"

Mello's speech was slurred. He picked up a bottle and emptied it into a glass, spilling some of the whiskey onto his hand and even more onto the floor.

"I suggest you go easy on that stuff," Silva said.

Mello licked his hand, and then rubbed it on his pants.

"Am I under arrest?"

"Not yet."

"Not yet, huh? Sounds ominous. But since I'm not under arrest, *not yet*, I figure I can drink as much as I want in my own house." He took a gulp of the Scotch. "What are you looking for?"

"Not what, who. Juraci Santos."

"And you think you're going to find her here? Ha!"

"Where's Edson?"

Mello, for the first time, showed a degree of concern.

"What do you want Edson for? Edson didn't do anything. You leave Edson alone."

"No need to get upset, Senhor Mello."

"People in authority make him nervous. He had a difficult childhood, spent some time in an orphanage."

"I'm sorry to hear that," Silva said, "but we have to talk to him. Where is he?"

"He's out in back, messing around with his pigeons."

"I'll go get him," Gonçalves said.

"No. No, you won't," Mello said, protectively. "If anybody has to get him, I will."

"Then I'll go with you," Silva said.

* * *

UNDER ARNALDO'S watchful eye, the two suspects were left to cool their heels in the living room. The other three cops busied themselves with a thorough search of the premises. Silva didn't really expect to find anything, but decided to be thorough since they were there anyway.

The contents of a chest of drawers in the master bedroom gave Hector pause. He summoned his uncle to have a look.

"Have Babyface keep an eye on Campos," Silva said. "Tell Arnaldo to bring Mello in here."

* * *

MELLO HAD dispensed with the glass and taken to drinking directly from a bottle. It was a new bottle, and the level was already down by a quarter. He brought it with him into the bedroom.

"Nice house you've got, Senhor Mello," Silva said. "Been here long?"

Mello stifled a hiccup. "I bought it when Cintia became my client, mortgaged myself right up to my ass. Now"—he stifled another hiccup—"I'll have to sell it."

"Yes. She told us you two had a tiff."

"A *tiff?* Is that what she called it, a tiff?"

"I'm paraphrasing."

Mello's anger seemed to have suppressed his hiccups. "It wasn't a tiff. It was an all-out argument, and it wouldn't have happened if it hadn't have been for you people. You don't care how many lives you fuck up, do you? As long as you nail the guilty, whatever you do to innocent people like me doesn't matter a damn."

"That's not true, Senhor Mello. If we've caused you a problem, and you had nothing to do with the crime we're investigating, I'm truly sorry."

Mello took another swig from his bottle. "It's too goddamned late for sorry."

"Your argument with Cintia had something to do with your collection over there, didn't it?"

"My collection is none of your business."

"I didn't say it was. Nevertheless . . ."

Mello sighed.

"If I tell you, will you get the hell out of here?"

"We'll get out of here after we've had a chat with Senhor Campos," Silva said, "but you can speed our departure by cooperating."

Mello, still clutching the bottle, went over to the chest of drawers, opened one of them and removed a flimsy pair of lace panties.

"La Perla," he said with a catch in his voice. "I bought them on the Corso Monte Napoleone in Milan."

Tears spilled out of both eyes and started to roll down his cheeks.

"Senhor Mello—"

"Shut up for a moment, won't you? Can't you see I'm drunk? I'm trying to tell you. Just be patient." He sank down on the bed. "Where was I?"

"The Corso Monte Napoleone in Milan."

"No. Cintia. I was talking about Cintia. She's a collector herself, shares my passion."

"She knows you collect women's lingerie?"

"Of course she damned well knows it! Why do you think she reacted the way she did? But she's got it wrong! All wrong!"

"None of that stuff is Cintia's?"

"Not a stitch of it. Not a goddamned stitch! I'd never steal a piece from someone else. It would be dirty. Even if you washed it over and over, it would be dirty. I only wear new things, things I buy myself."

"Some of that lingerie looks pretty small," Hector said. "It might fit Edson, but not you."

"You leave Edson out of this! He had nothing to do with anything. It must have been one of Cintia's goddamned maids that stole that piece."

"But she blamed you."

"She blamed me because you"—he shot an accusing finger at Silva—"went up there and started asking her about where she found the set of keys to Juraci's house, and she told you they were in a drawer with her lingerie."

"I don't see how that could possibly—"

"She's missing a Chantelle Chantilly Culotte Thong. They only make it in fuchsia. But I don't have it. I don't own a damned thing in fuchsia. I hate fuchsia! Go ahead. Look through all the drawers. See if you can find anything in fuchsia."

"I don't think that will be necessary, Senhor Mello. Just finish the story."

"She saw me coming out of her bedroom during the party. A day later, she discovered the thong was missing. Your questions caused her to connect the two events and come to an absolutely erroneous conclusion."

"And that conclusion was that you stole a pair of her panties."

"What have I been telling you? And, as God is my witness, it's not true! I went in there to use the bathroom. I went there because the guest bathroom was occupied. I never went anywhere near her drawers. I never opened one. I never took the piece. I told her that. But did she believe me? No, she didn't believe me; she fired me, that's what she did. And it's your fault."

Mello took another hefty swig of his whiskey. Silva signaled to Arnaldo and Hector. They left Mello where he was and went into the living room to question Campos.

"How is he?" Campos said.

"Drunk," Silva said.

"He hasn't slept since yesterday. It's just so . . . *unfair*. Cintia Tadesco is a perfect bitch."

"Tell us about your pigeons," Silva said.

"My pigeons? Why?"

"Carrier pigeons were used to deliver the ransom for the Artist's mother."

"And you think I had something to do with it?"

"Did you?"

"Of course not."

"Then you'll have no objection to answering my questions. Why don't you sit down."

Campos shook his head. "I'd prefer to stay on my feet. What, exactly, do you want to know?"

"How many pigeons have you got? Do you keep them anywhere other than here? How long have you been doing it? Who else do you know who keeps carrier pigeons?"

Four questions. Campos counted off the replies by extending the fingers on his right hand.. "Nineteen. Only here. Ever since I was thirteen years old. Lots of people." He dropped the hand to his side. "What else?"

"Senhor Campos, you're obviously an intelligent man, and you don't strike me as the criminal type. You know our objective here. Why don't you make an effort to be more cooperative?"

"Why should I? You—"

"You should," Silva said evenly, "because you'll have us out of your hair a lot faster if you do."

"Nothing would please me more."

"So think. How can you help us?"

Campos reflected.

"The best way," he said, "would be if you let me ask you some questions. Then something might occur to me."

"Go ahead."

"How many birds were involved?"

Silva turned to Hector. "Remind me. How many?"

"Sixty," Hector said.

Campos didn't bother to conceal his surprise. "*Sixty?* Sixty birds?"

"That's what I said."

"That's a lot. Nobody I know has sixty birds. It's complete overkill."

"They had a lot of diamonds to transport."

"Diamonds?"

"Juraci Santos's ransom was in diamonds. Five million American dollars worth."

Campos whistled. "Five million dollars. That's more than ten million Reais."

"Considerably more."

"Where were the birds released?"

"About two hundred and eighty kilometers from São Paulo, a spot near Caverna do Diabo."

"Who did the releasing?"

"We did," Silva said.

"You did? You? The Federal Police?"

"The Artist decided to pay. We assisted him. We didn't know they'd be using pigeons until we got there. We had to follow their instructions and dispatch the diamonds. If we hadn't, they would have killed Juraci Santos."

"How were the diamonds attached to the birds?"

"Little carrier bags made especially for the purpose. Instructions were waiting on how to affix them."

Campos stroked his chin. "And once it was done . . ."

"The birds flew away, and we lost them."

"You simply let them fly away? You didn't try to follow them?"

"We managed to plant a tracking device, but we only had one, and a bird of prey brought down the pigeon carrying it."

"So you have no idea where the diamonds wound up?"

"In fact, Senhor Campos, we do."

"Where?"

"At a sitio near Riberão Preto. The owner rents the place, but hardly ever visits. A caseiro works there. He was paid to feed and care for the birds, but he knows nothing. He wasn't involved in the plot."

"Chief Inspector, are you aware of the fact that those birds have to be conditioned from the time they start moving around on their own?"

"We know that, yes."

"That's why nobody buys or sells fully-grown carrier pigeons. It would make no sense. Once they were released, they'd just fly home to wherever they were raised."

"So we've been told."

Campos started pacing back and forth. "The birds would have to be at least three months old before they could fly the distance you're describing. It would be nothing for a fully-grown bird, but it's a long way for a young one."

"Conclusion?"

Campos ran a hand through his hair. "This thing must have been planned months in advance." He stopped pacing and turned and looked at Silva. "You mean to tell me that the people who supplied the birds didn't go back, at least once, to make sure they were being properly conditioned by this caseiro? And, if the caseiro wasn't involved in the plot, some-one else would have had to have made the pickup, right?"

"Someone did. She's—"

"She?"

"It was a woman."

"You're sure of that?"

"We're sure."

Silva took him through it, step by step. He told him about the jeweler, told him about Tancredo Candido, told him how the woman had threatened Tancredo with grave bodily harm if he didn't follow instructions. By the time he'd finished, Edson Campos had come over to their side and entered into the spirit of the chase.

"So you've got a description of this woman?" he said. "You know what she looks like?"

"We have a description, but it's a sketchy one."

"Don't you people normally do an artist's rendition in a case like this?"

"We're trying. We're not being very successful. The wit-ness doesn't have a good memory for faces."

"Tell me your sketchy description."

"About thirty-five years of age, of average height, with curly, brown hair, a somewhat abrasive attitude, a foul mouth and what the cut-out described as a nice ass."

"Brown eyes?"

"Why? Does the description suggest someone to you?"

"You may think this is a weird question, but was she wear-ing Promesse?"

"What?"

"Promesse, from Cacharel. It's a perfume, a springtime scent, more for teenagers than for a woman of her age. But that's beside the point. The question is was she wearing perfume?"

"As a matter of fact," Silva said, "she was."

"Holy Crap."

"Holy Crap what?"

"Holy Crap," Edson Campos said, "I know who you're looking for."

Chapter Thirty-Nine

THE KIDNAPPER WAS TOO anxious to eat, too excited to watch television, too agitated, even, to sit down. He put all of his nervous energy into digging the grave. From the time his partner left until he heard the sound of her car crunching gravel in the driveway, all he'd done was dig.

But here she was, back at last. He threw the shovel aside, climbed out of the hole and circled the house at a run. She saw him coming, grinned, and held up her leather bag like it was the World Cup and she'd just brought it home.

He reached her, wrapped his arms around her, held her close.

She dropped the bag and pushed him away with the heels of her hands.

"You're filthy," she said.

"I can get dirtier than this," he said, nuzzling her ear. "Want a demonstration?"

"Mmmm," she said. "Let's go inside. But not without this." She picked up the bag.

He took her hand and led her to the house. She'd shed her blouse before he'd locked the front door, was out of her panties before he'd removed his shirt.

They made frenzied love on the couch. But she didn't linger when it was done. Still wearing her socks, and nothing else, she grabbed the bag, opened it, and turned it upside down over his naked belly.

The banknotes tumbled out, six bundles, bound together by rubber bands.

"How much?" he said.

"Thirty thousand."

"Thirty thousand? That's all? Thirty thousand for all six rings? The bastards cheated you."

"Sure they did. Every one of them. And I don't care."

"Because that makes it all the more likely they'll keep their mouths shut?"

"Exactly. Did you finish?"

"It's not deep enough. I want to go down another thirty centimeters or so. When are you going to do it?"

"As soon as you're done. I'll need your help to carry her. That bitch is fat. I won't be able to get her up the stairs on my own."

"Why don't we just walk her to the hole? You could pop her there. Then all we'd have to do is pitch her in."

"Noise," she said. "Suppose she starts screaming?"

"Nobody's gonna hear her. Not out there."

"Never can tell."

"There you go again," he said. "The Queen of Caution."

"That's me. Did you pack?"

He stepped into his pants, then shook his head. "I've been digging."

"Ever since I left?"

"Ground is hard as a rock."

"I'll pack for both of us then."

He shook his head. "No," he said, "you won't. We don't have to leave for the airport until seven. I'll finish digging, you pop her, and *then* we'll pack."

"How come?"

"Because, I'm not going to take hardly anything, and you aren't either. The days of me being your pack animal, lugging stuff you're never gonna wear, are over. From here on in, every place we go, you can afford to buy new clothes."

"Goody," she said. "Paris, here we come."

Chapter Forty

"HER NAME," EDSON CAMPOS said, "is Vitória Pitanguy."

"Vítória Pitanguy?" Gonçalves said. "The pharmacist?"

"She's not a pharmacist. Her boss is the pharmacist. She just manages the place. Doctor Polo thinks the world of her. I've always thought she was a bitch."

Gonçalves smacked his forehead.

"What?" Silva said.

"When we were looking at that list you put up on the wall, studying the description? And it wouldn't come to me? Well, it just did! *She's* the one I was trying to remember. I met her in the pharmacy. She came in using this perfume that smelled like berries, berries and . . . something else."

"Bergamot," Campos said.

Silva looked at him. "What?"

"Bergamot. That perfume I was talking about. Promesse. It smells like bergamot and berries. Vitória drenches herself in it, calls it her signature scent."

"She's got a boyfriend," Gonçalves said. "The girl in her shop said she has a boyfriend."

Edson nodded. "Samuel Arns, the locksmith. His shop is next door."

"Damn," Hector said.

Silva turned to his nephew. "I don't believe this. You met her too? When you were talking to Arns?"

"She dropped by his shop when I was interviewing him. We weren't introduced. But the perfume? I remember that."

"How come you didn't mention it before?" Arnaldo said.

"Why should I? Lots of women wear perfume. It wasn't until Campos here mentioned bergamot that—"

"Wait a minute. You know what bergamot is?"

"Sure. It's a citrus fruit, like an orange."

"And you happen to know that because?"

"They use it to flavor tea. Earl Grey tea. Gilda drinks the stuff."

Arnaldo might have said more, but Silva put a hand on his arm. "It's all coming together," he said. "Vitória is Arns's girlfriend, and Arns makes the keys for Juraci." He turned to Hector. "Have you got the telephone number of his shop?"

Hector nodded and tapped the pocket over his notebook.

"And you, Haraldo," Silva said. "Have you got one for the pharmacy where Vitória works?"

"Sí, Senhor."

"Call both places, make sure both of them are on the job."

"And if they are?" Hector said.

Silva waved his hand vaguely. "Think of something that doesn't make you sound like cops and hang up."

Gonçalves and Hector went out to where they could get better signals for their cell phones.

"She used me," Edson said. "She used me to get information about carrier pigeons."

"How long ago was this?"

Edson thought for a moment.

"Six months ago, maybe seven."

"Tell me about it."

"I was talking to one of her girls about my pigeons. She butted in. Next thing I know she's asking me all sorts of questions. She even asked if she could come over and look at my birds."

"And you agreed?"

"Sure."

"You didn't find this sudden interest of hers a bit strange?"

"Carrier pigeons are my hobby. I'm crazy about them. So, no, I didn't find it strange at all. Not then."

"But you did later?"

"Yeah, I did."

"Why?"

"Because, after her visit, and after all our talk, and after lending her three books on the subject, she just dropped it."

"Dropped it?"

"One week she couldn't talk to me enough about carrier pigeons. The next week, when I went into the pharmacy and asked her if she'd bought any birds, she told me she'd gone cold on the idea, that she was no longer interested."

"All this was six months ago?"

"At least."

"And four or five months would be sufficient to train pigeons?"

"Hatch them and train them," Edson said. "No doubt."

Hector walked in, shaking his head. "The telephone at Arns's shop has been disconnected."

Gonçalves was next. He still had his phone in his hand. "Vitória Pitanguy resigned," he said. "As of yesterday, she no longer works at the pharmacy."

"Uh oh," Arnaldo said.

"Tell me, Senhor Campos," Silva said, "do Arns and Pitanguy live together?"

"Yes."

"Here in Granja Viana?"

"Yes."

"Where?"

"Just up the street."

Chapter Forty-One

VITÓRIA PITANGUY WAS SORTING shoes. As he entered the bedroom, wiping dirt from his hands, Samuel Arns frowned at the open suitcase on the bed.

"We agreed you were going to buy new stuff."

"That was your idea," she said, "not mine. I'm fond of my shoes. Did you finish?"

"I finished."

"Then let's go finish *her*."

She tossed a pair of patent-leather pumps into the suitcase, opened a drawer and took out a pistol.

"That's the same gun," he said.

"What makes you think so?"

"Pink grips."

"It's not the only Taurus with pink grips."

"Is it the same gun, or isn't it?"

"It's the same."

"Goddamn it, Vitória! You promised to get rid of it."

"And I will. Just as soon as I use it."

"You're always going on about how we have to be cautious, and then you go and do something like this. If the cops catch us with that pistol, it'll be all over."

"They're not gonna catch us. And in less than five minutes it *is* going to be over. I'll wipe it clean, throw it in the hole along with Juraci, and that will be the end of it. All *you* have to do is shovel in the dirt and plant the rose bushes. Get off my back. It's a great day. Don't ruin it."

"I don't like it when you lie to me."

"Let's not fight. Let's just bury her and tidy up around here. Come on."

"Wait."

"Wait for what?"

"Get your hood."

"My *hood?*" She laughed. "Why bother? Dead people don't talk."

Chapter Forty-Two

JURACI HEARD FOOTSTEPS, TWO sets, hurrying down the stairs. It was the hurrying that frightened her. They'd never done that before.

The hair rose on the back of her neck. She stretched her chain to the limit and wedged herself into one corner of her cell.

But when the door swung open, a wave of relief swept over her. The people standing there weren't wearing hoods, or blue overalls, or gloves. And she *knew* them: Samuel Arns, the locksmith, and Vitória Pitanguy, the woman who managed the pharmacy next door to his shop.

"Thank God," she said.

But then she saw the pistol in Vitória's hand and the expression in Vitória's eyes.

"You're the ones?" she said

She couldn't believe it.

Vitória tossed a key onto the floor at her feet.

"Open the padlock," she said. "And take off the chain."

"You're the ones who kidnapped me?"

"We're the ones. Shut up and open the lock."

"You're going to release me?"

"Do it."

"I won't. I won't do it."

"You will, or Samuel here will kick you in the face. Isn't that right, Samuel?"

"That's right," he said.

Juraci looked from one to the other—and picked up the key.

"Where are you taking me?" she said as the chain slipped from her ankle.

"I told you to shut up. Kneel and face the wall."

Juraci remembered the moments before they'd rendered her unconscious, remembered the gunshots. *Kneel*. The significance of the word came to her in a rush. A hand reached into her chest and squeezed her heart.

"Why?" she said. "Why are you doing this? My son—"

"Get on your knees. Now."

"No. Don't do this."

"Then stand there and watch it coming." Vitória lifted the pistol and aimed it at her forehead. "Look right here, right in the fucking muzzle."

The doorbell rang.

Juraci opened her mouth to scream, but then, suddenly, the muzzle of the pistol was in her mouth, the metal rattling against her teeth.

"Don't," Samuel said, lowering his voice. "Whoever it is will hear the shot."

"Duh," she said. And then, to Juraci: "Not a sound out of you, bitch. You hear me? Not a goddamned sound."

"Are we going to answer the door?"

"Answer the door? Are you crazy? Just be quiet. They'll go away."

* * *

AND THEY might have, if there hadn't been two vehicles in the driveway, one of which fit the description of the vehicle used to transport the pigeons—a white Volkswagen van.

Silva hit the bell button for a second time, and sent Gonçalves to check out the back yard. Less than a minute later, he was back.

"You'd better have a look," he said.

"Stay here," Silva said to the other two. "Keep ringing."

He took off in the wake of the younger cop.

"Over there," Gonçalves said as they entered the back yard. "Beyond the roses."

The trench, two meters long and about half a meter wide, was freshly dug, the pile of soil still damp. Next to it were a dozen rose bushes, their roots wrapped in burlap.

"Damn!" Silva said. "Let's get inside that house."

* * *

THE DOORBELL rang for a fourth time. Then a fifth. Vitória, always high strung, was like a steel wire ready to snap.

"Go up there," she said, "and look through the peephole. Find out who the insistent bastard is."

"What if it's the cops?"

"The cops? Are you insane? Why should the cops suspect us?"

"I just—"

"It's probably some goddamned salesman, or somebody collecting for some charity."

"Yeah. Yeah, that's right. That's what it must be. A salesman." Arns sounded like he was trying to convince himself.

"Stop talking and get up there."

* * *

"THEY DUG a grave," Silva said, rejoining his companions. "It's still empty. We have to get inside. There are French doors around back. They look pretty flimsy."

"Let's hope so," Arnaldo said, "because we're not gonna get in this way. Look at that door. Solid *peroba*. We'd need a ram."

Gonçalves, whose ear had been pressed to the wood, held up a hand. Someone was coming. Silently, the other cops moved into positions where they couldn't be seen through the peephole.

The door was opened by a big man in a dirty T-shirt.

"Samuel Arns?" Gonçalves asked.

"Who are you?"

"Are you Samuel Arns?"

"Yeah. I'm Samuel Arns. Who are you?"

Gonçalves put a hand inside his coat as if he was groping for his ID. What he brought out was his Glock.

"Step back, Senhor," he said. "And keep quiet."

Arns opened his mouth as if to shout. Gonçalves raised the pistol and brought it to within ten centimeters of his face.

"Quiet, I said."

Arns closed his mouth.

Silva and Arnaldo stepped into his field of vision. Arns's eyes darted from one to the other. His Adam's apple bobbed up and down. "What is this?" he said.

"I think you know what this is, Senhor Arns," Silva said. "But just in case you don't . . ."

He took out his warrant card and held it in front of Arns's face.

Arns tried to bluff it out.

"I didn't do anything," he said. "What do you want?"

"What's the hole for?"

"What hole?"

"In the back yard."

"I'm planting roses."

"More than a meter deep? Step aside. We're coming in."

"You got a search warrant?"

"No. But we're coming in anyway."

Arnaldo insinuated himself into the doorway. Arns was big, but Arnaldo was bigger, and Arns stepped aside. All four cops entered the house.

Hector was the last man through the door. "Hey," Arns said, when he saw him. "I know you."

Hector didn't respond.

"Where's Juraci Santos?" Silva said.

"I don't—"

"If she's here, dead or alive, we're going to find her. Why don't you save us both some trouble and just tell me?"

Arns crumbled.

"It wasn't me. I didn't kill those maids. Vitória did. Vitória Pitanguy. She's the one. The whole thing was her idea. I never—"

"Shut up. You'll have time later to tell us your side of the story. For now, you just answer questions. Where's Senhora Santos?"

"Downstairs. In the cellar."

"Alive?"

"She was when I came upstairs, I swear to God she was. But she's with Vitória, and Vitória has a gun."

* * *

THEY TOOK Samuel to the top of the stairs and told him what to say:

"Vitória, they're federal cops, four of them. They're in the house."

"We're covering Senhor Arns with guns," Silva said, "and we won't hesitate to use them on you. Drop your weapon and come out. Now."

They heard Vitória emit a string of curses, heard the clatter of something hitting the floor.

Arnaldo and Silva peeked around either side of the doorway. A moment later, Vitória came into view, her hands in the air.

"You stupid bastard," she screamed. "You stupid, stupid bastard."

Arns knew it was meant for him.

"They found the grave you made me dig," he shouted. "They were going to come in anyway."

"*I* made you dig? So now it's *my* fault? You lying bastard! You're as guilty as I am."

"That's enough," Silva said. "Shut up, both of you. Arnaldo, cuff Samuel. Vitória, keep your hands in the air and don't move. Senhora Santos?"

"I'm here."

"I'm Chief Inspector Silva of the Federal Police. You're safe now. You can come out."

"I can?"

"Yes."

"Got both of the bastards, did you?"

Silva had expected tears of relief, maybe hysteria, but Juraci didn't sound that way at all. She sounded angry.

"Both," Silva said.

"Good."

Juraci stepped out of her cell and into Silva's line-of-sight. She was holding a little pink-gripped Taurus.

And, without uttering another word, she extended her arm and fired two shots into Vitória Pitanguy's back.

Chapter Forty-Three

ON THE DAY FOLLOWING the rescue of Juraci Santos, the *Cidade de São Paulo* published a feature article entitled *The Man Who Solved the Case*.

The content was drawn, almost exclusively, from a press release issued by the Federal Police's publicity office. Two phrases of that release were even used verbatim: *deft and in-depth management of the case* and *intuitive crime-solving skills*. The press office also provided a professionally executed photographic portrait of the hero in question—Nelson Sampaio.

The circulation of the newspaper, that day, reached an all-time high. Pundits accredited the spectacular newsstand sales to the high degree of interest in the case.

Arnaldo Nunes accredited them to purchases made by Sampaio himself.

Silva wasn't surprised that the Director had snatched the credit; he *was* surprised when Sampaio summoned him to demand a detailed accounting of every aspect of the case. Sampaio loathed detail.

"I've been invited," the Director said, "to dine with the Minister of Justice. Telling him stuff he can read in a newspaper isn't going to cut it. I need some tidbits to go with the coffee and dessert." He picked up his Mont Blanc ballpoint. "Start talking."

"Samuel Arns signed a full confession," Silva said.

Sampaio started scratching away, taking notes.

"He did, did he?" he said, without looking up. "When?"

"Less than an hour ago."

"Good. That's good. Hold it back from the press until tomorrow morning. What about his accomplice, that Pitanguy woman? Is she talking?"

"No, but it doesn't matter. We recovered the weapon she used to kill the maids. Her fingerprints are all over it. Arns's prints aren't—and he says Vitória did it. We don't need any more than that."

"What if she says *he* did it?"

"Before Juraci used the pistol, there were two bullets missing from the magazine. In her home, on the day of the kidnapping, she heard two shots just before Arns injected her with the Ketamine. She'll testify to that."

"Good. Too bad there's no death penalty in this country."

"True."

"But let's look at the bright side. That Pitanguy bitch will get thirty years at least."

"Not that long, I'm afraid."

"No? Why not?"

"Her lawyer is Dudu Fonseca."

Sampaio tossed down his pen in disgust.

"Fonseca? That shyster? What's with that? Pitanguy worked in a pharmacy. She's nothing more than a glorified shop girl. Where does she get the money to hire a heavy-weight like Fonseca?"

"Juraci shot her twice in the spine. She's paralyzed from the waist down; she'll never walk again."

"So?"

"So Vitória's bringing a civil suit against Juraci. She and Fonseca are discussing how they're going to split the pro-ceeds. He wants half; she's offering him a third."

"How do you know that?"

Silva didn't reply.

"Are you listening in on conversations between Vitória Pitanguy and her lawyer?"

"That would be illegal, Director, a violation of attorney/client privilege."

"It sure as hell would. But it's a juicy story. I'm gonna use it."

"If you go public with that information—"

Sampaio picked up his pen. "I'm not going public with it. I'm going to talk about it at a dinner, that's all."

"Still, if it gets out—"

Sampaio waved a dismissive hand. "It's not going to get out. And, even if it does, can they prove you're bugging them? No, they can't."

"I'm not concerned about—"

"Am I not making myself clear, Chief Inspector? I'm going to use it, and that's it. *Fim do papo.* You think she'll win?"

Silva gave up trying to talk his boss out of divulging the information. "Win her civil suit? Yes, I think it's likely."

"And that prick Fonseca thinks so too, otherwise he wouldn't be wasting his time talking to her. So the money to pay for Vitória's defense is ultimately going to come from the Artist?"

"Ultimately, it is."

Sampaio snorted in disgust. "It's not right."

"No. Not right."

"Couldn't you just . . ."

"What?"

"You know."

"Claim Vitória got shot while resisting arrest?"

"You said it. I didn't."

Silva shook his head.

"It wouldn't wash. Vitória was shot with her own pistol, which proves she was unarmed at the time. Also, she was shot in the back. If we made a claim like that, Fonseca would make mincemeat out of us. No, Director, I'm afraid it's Juraci, or us."

"Too bad for her then, because it certainly isn't going to be us. Take me through Arns's story. Start right at the beginning. Maybe there's something else I can use."

Silva took a moment to gather his thoughts, then began.

"One morning, about eight months ago, things were slow at the pharmacy, and Vitória dropped by Arns's shop to have a chat. Somehow, they got on the subject of Juraci. Arns told Vitória how she was always firing her servants, changing her locks. From there, they started gossiping about her son, how there was a rumor he was going to be sold to Real Madrid, how much money he'd earned over the last few years."

"So that's when they started thinking about how they could get their hooks into some of it?"

"Not right then. But Vitória kept thinking about it, and a few days later, she hit Samuel with a 'what if.'"

"What if we kidnap the Artist's mother and hold her for ransom?"

"Exactly. At first, he said, he thought she was joking."

"But, when he found out she wasn't, he bought into it."

"According to him, he didn't. According to him, he put up objections."

"Like?"

"What if someone got hurt? What if he and Vitória were recognized? What if Juraci fought back and needed to be subdued? How would they go about collecting the ransom?"

"And she kept coming up with answers?"

"He said they made a game of it. But every time they played it, the game became more serious. Eventually, he said, a plan emerged: on one of the occasions when she changed her locks, he'd make up an extra set. That would give them access to her house. No one was supposed to get hurt. They'd use hoods so they wouldn't be recognized. They'd subdue her with a sedative. Vitória said she'd have no trouble getting her hands on a drug made to order for the job: Ketamine. Where they got hung up, and hung up for quite a while, was how they could collect the money without getting caught."

"Until?"

"Until one day Edson Campos came into Vitória's pharmacy and started singing the praises of carrier pigeons. She recognized the potential immediately, but she also recognized that the pigeons wouldn't be able to carry cash. It would be too heavy."

"So she hit on the idea of diamonds?"

"She did."

"And Samuel ran out of objections."

"Actually, he didn't. His biggest objection remained. He was petrified by the idea of getting caught. But she kept wearing him down. She wrote away for travel folders, showed him ads for gold watches and sports cars, painted a life of luxury and eternal bliss. And, finally, his greed got the better of him."

"So they started trying to find someone to buy the stones, and that bicheiro, Captain Miranda, heard about it, and he got in touch with you."

"No."

"No?"

"Samuel said they never consulted anyone."

"So what did Miranda intend to tell you?"

"We'll never know. Whatever it was, it would have been a false lead, a dead end."

"So no one else was involved in the kidnapping? Just those two?"

"Just those two."

"Who evaluated the stones?"

"Samuel."

"He's a locksmith. What does he know about diamonds?"

"He studied up on diamonds, learned enough to make sure they weren't grossly cheated and bought the equipment he'd need to do it: a jeweler's loupe, reference books, a set of scales, a hardness kit, a light box for grading, and God knows what else. We found it all when we searched his house."

"And to convert the diamonds to cash? How were they going to do that?"

"Samuel's parents are German. He's got dual nationality. He and Vitória planned to marry. As husband and wife, they could live anywhere in the European Economic Community."

"And sell a few stones at a time?"

"A few in London, a few in Paris, a few in Rome. They thought they could go on forever. When we caught them, they'd already sewn most of the stones into clothing they'd be taking with them."

"Most?"

"Some were lost in transit. A bird of prey attacked one of the pigeons. Some were stolen by the caseiro of the sitio where they kept the birds. Those we recovered. A few Vitória sold for seed money."

"Seed money?"

"The cash they'd need to set them up in their new life."

"Who did she sell them to?"

"Samuel doesn't know, and she won't tell us. She's not talking to us about anything."

"The jeweler in Riberão Preto tipped us off. How come the same didn't happen in São Paulo?"

"Samuel's a handy fellow. He bought gold, made rings, mounted the diamonds before she sold them. He says she planned to offer only one ring to each jeweler, and to claim it was a present from her ex-husband."

"Why don't we just canvas all the shops?"

"We're working on it, but we haven't got our hopes up. Samuel says they realized very little from the sales. That's probably an indication the jewelers thought the rings were stolen. I don't expect them to come clean."

"So how much is the Artist out of pocket? How much did it cost him?"

"In Reais, about two hundred and fifty thousand."

"That's small change for him. He probably thinks he got off cheap."

"In fact, he does. His girlfriend, Cintia, is more concerned about the money than he is."

"Because she's already looking at what's his as hers?"

"Probably."

"Tell me about the day it happened. How did it go down?"

"Pretty much as Lefkowitz hypothesized it did. They got to Juraci's at four-thirty in the morning, cut the telephone wires and went to the kitchen door. Samuel had the flashlight. Vitória had to put her reading glasses on to get the key into the lock, so she took off her hood. She planned to put it on again as soon as they were inside, but—"

"—but there was one of the maids, standing at the sink, getting a glass of water."

"Correct. It was Clara, the younger sister. She dropped the glass and started screaming. Vitória pulled out a pistol. Samuel says it came as a surprise. He didn't know she'd brought it."

"You think he's lying?"

"No, I don't. He doesn't seem like the bloodthirsty type."

"But she is?"

"Oh, yes, Director, she's definitely the bloodthirsty type."

"What happened next?"

"Juraci's dog came running in and sunk her teeth into Samuel's ankle. Vitória stamped on it and killed it. Then she sent Samuel to find Clara's sister."

"Which he did?"

Silva nodded. "Hiding in a wardrobe cupboard. He pulled her out, and forced her into the kitchen. Vitória made her kneel on the floor and sent Samuel upstairs to subdue Juraci."

"She must have been awake by then, what with all the racket they were making downstairs."

"She was. She locked the bedroom door, but it was flimsy. Samuel had no problem breaking in. He was going for her with the syringe when he heard the shots. Up until that moment, he said, the thought that the sisters might be in danger never entered his head."

"You believe that?"

"Actually, I do."

"I don't. I don't think a jury will either. And then?"

"He threw Juraci on the bed and injected the Ketamine. She fought back. He tossed the syringe aside so he could use both hands to immobilize her. Vitória told him she'd be unconscious in thirty seconds, but it took longer. So long, he began to believe the drug wasn't working. It made him nervous. So nervous, he forgot to pick up the syringe when she finally passed out."

"So now the maids are dead and Juraci's unconscious. And then?"

"They bundled Juraci into their car. Vitória waited behind the wheel while Samuel locked the door and smashed it with a sledgehammer."

"To make it appear as if that was the way they got in."

"Exactly. The noise woke the neighbor, Rodolfo Sá. Samuel had just remembered that he'd left the syringe in Juraci's bedroom when he saw Sá's light go on. He assumed Sá was going to call the security people."

"Did he?"

"No. But Samuel didn't know that, so instead of going back for the syringe, he made a dash for the car. Less than ten minutes later they had Juraci under lock and key."

"Where she stayed until we broke in and rescued her?"

We. Sampaio believed in his own press releases.

"And that's it," Silva said. "That's the whole story. It was, as we suspected in the very beginning, all about money. No other motive."

"When did they decide to murder her?"

"I think Vitória had it in mind since the beginning."

"Arns tell you that?"

"No. And I don't think she told him, either. She would have known it would make him squeamish. But she kept working on him. Ultimately, he agreed. But I don't think his heart was ever in it."

"Juraci never realized that one of her captors was a woman?"

"She had her suspicions, but she was never really sure. Not until the very end."

"How were they able to get their hands on the Ketamine?"

"Nothing easier. Vitória simply failed to enter the arrival of a shipment into the ledger. She paid for it with a personal check and fudged the bookkeeping."

"Okay, let's leave it at that. I figure I've got enough to talk my way through the whole damned dinner, if I have to. And all's well that ends well."

"Senhor?"

"Vitória and Samuel are going to get what's coming to them. A bicheiro is dead. The filho da puta who sold the Artist to Real Madrid is dead. The Artist's mother came out of it without a scratch. Her son is itching to kick Argentinean ass, which I have little doubt he will. The President of the Republic is happy. And I get to have dinner with the Minister of Justice. Don't you think that, all in all, it worked out well for everyone concerned?"

Except, Silva thought, *for two young women, shot to death as they kneeled in terror on a kitchen floor.*

The Director was looking at him, waiting for a response to his question. Silva groped for something to say.

And then didn't need one, because Sampaio's telephone rang.

Author's Notes

FOOTBALL (CALLED SOCCER IN the USA) is played by
more people, in more places, than any other game in the
world. The FIFA (Fédération Internationale de Football
Association) the body that governs the sport internationally,
is composed of 208 national associations, 16 more than there
are countries represented in the United Nations, three more
than in the International Olympic Committee.

The World Cup, a battle for the most-prized trophy in the
history of sport, is played out every four years and always in a
different country. In 2010, when the Cup was held in South
Africa, 204 countries competed to fill 32 slots. Close to one
billion people watched the final game live on television.

In 2014, for the first time in sixty years, the Cup will be
held in Brazil, the only country to have participated in every
Cup since its inception, and the only country to have won
the trophy five times.

In Brazil, the kidnapping of a football star's mother is, by
no means, a rare occurrence. Three members of the Brazilian
National Team who participated in the 2010 World Cup
were so victimized (Robinho, Luis Fabiano and Grafite). All
the players expressed their willingness to pay ransom, and all
the victims were returned unharmed.

"The Artist", Tico Santos, is a fictional character and
should in no way be confused with "The Phenomenon",
Ronaldo Luís Nazário de Lima, one of the greatest players
the sport has ever produced. It's true that Ronaldo, like Tico,
has had a number of problems with women, and that he once

married a top-model, who took him for a bundle and initiated divorce proceedings within a week—but that's purely coincidental.

Some readers might find it difficult to accept that a judge might be forced to take refuge in his own courthouse. It is, nevertheless, true. My character, Pedro Cataldo, is based on Odilon de Oliveira, a Brazilian federal judge. Oliveira, who, in a given year, brought more organized crime figures to justice than any other judge in the country, was condemned to death by the criminal elements he was sentencing and, at the time of this writing, has spent fifteen months living in a court house in the town of Ponta Porã, close to the frontier between Brazil and Paraguay. Oliveria, 56 years old, sleeps on the floor of his office and is under constant guard by the Federal Police. The price on his head has risen to half a million dollars.

The *jogo do bicho* also exists. It's an enormously popular illegal lottery, a feature of Brazilian life for over 100 years.

Here's how the game works: the numbers between 0 and 100 are divided into 25 ascending number groups, each corresponding to a different animal. (In Portuguese, *Jogo do bicho* means "animal game".)

Numbering begins begin with the ostrich (01, 02, 03 and 04) and ends with the cow (97, 98, 99 and 00).

Let's suppose you bet on the ostrich. The following day, to discover if you've won or lost, you open a newspaper and check some previously stipulated (and totally unpredictable) number. It might be, for example, the last two numbers of the total volume of the previous day's trading on Rio de Janeiro's stock exchange.

If those numbers are 01, 02, 03 or 04, you've won—as has everyone else who played the ostrich.

You can buy your tickets at news vendors, in stores that sell cigarettes, from thousands of different locations—and also from people who sell them on the street.

You cash-in the same way.

People trust the game because, when it comes to payouts at least, the mobsters who run it are scrupulously honest. They have to be. The continued success of their business depends on it.

And they are, indeed, the major patrons of Brazil's great samba schools, something they have long regarded as a social obligation.

The game's closest equivalent, in the United States, is the "numbers racket", also referred to as the "policy racket".

I have treated the two felons in Chapter Fifteen (the scene where Silva and his men raid the warehouse and liberate a Lear's Macaw) rather lightheartedly, but the crime of animal smuggling is far from a joke. It is, in fact, one of the earth's more serious environmental problems.

After habitat loss, animal smuggling is the biggest reason why one-third of the world's wildlife is in danger of extinction. According to the World Wildlife Fund, the illicit trade in animals ranks just behind the illicit trade in drugs and firearms. No one knows how many animals are stolen from Brazil's forests each year, but it is thought to be in the tens of millions.

Finally, the Lear's Macaw is as rare as I have described it. They are to be found in captivity in various places around the world, but the Brazilian government has never issued an export license for a single one.